CHASING A HIGHLAND DREAM

LISA HOBMAN

Boldwood

First published in Great Britain in 2024 by Boldwood Books Ltd.

Copyright © Lisa Hobman, 2024

Cover Design by Alexandra Allden

Cover Photography: Shutterstock

Every effort has been made to obtain the necessary permissions with reference to copyright material, both illustrative and quoted. We apologise for any omissions in this respect and will be pleased to make the appropriate acknowledgements in any future edition.

A CIP catalogue record for this book is available from the British Library.

Paperback ISBN 978-1-80483-670-5

Large Print ISBN 978-1-80483-671-2

Hardback ISBN 978-1-80483-672-9

Ebook ISBN 978-1-80483-669-9

Kindle ISBN 978-1-80483-668-2

Audio CD ISBN 978-1-80483-677-4

MP3 CD ISBN 978-1-80483-676-7

Digital audio download ISBN 978-1-80483-675-0

Boldwood Books Ltd
23 Bowerdean Street
London SW6 3TN
www.boldwoodbooks.com

For my beautiful friend Mel.
I can't believe you're gone and that I will never hear your laugh
or feel your hugs again. But you will always be in my heart.

PROLOGUE
LATE MARCH

Bella Douglas sat at the antique desk in the grand library of Drumblair Castle; the room that had become the office and hub of the future plans for the place. As she glanced around at the vast space, with its floor-to-ceiling bookshelves and rich-coloured leather-bound tomes, she smiled. It had always held a special place in her heart.

These days the castle belonged to her best friend, Olivia MacBain, whom Bella and their other best friend Skye, had met at high school when Olivia won the argument to attend a 'normal' local school, instead of being sent away. On the sudden passing of her mother, and in a rather unexpected turn of events, Olivia had inherited Drumblair Castle instead of her older brother Kerr, who was known for his gambling addiction. Their mother had evidently decided that he would be incapable of protecting the family's legacy. So that task had now fallen on Olivia's shoulders. Of course, Kerr hadn't taken the news well and had threatened to contest the will. Thankfully Olivia's Uncle Innes had stepped in and made sure Kerr realised this would be a waste of time.

As teenagers, Bella and Skye had been regular visitors to

Drumblair Castle, near Inverness, and Bella's passion for interior design had started in this very library. From the imported mahogany and the Adam style plaster mouldings and cornice to the grand carved plant stands and Henry Raeburn ancestral portraits, it was a stunning update that had taken place in the eighteenth century when the laird of the time, and his lady, had decided to *modernise*. It had created an intrigue in all things Georgian for Bella.

Bella had fantasised about living at Drumblair and her first teenage crush had meant she had dreamed of one day marrying Kerr MacBain and living happily ever after within the ancient walls but, of course, things rarely work out how you hope.

These days, Skye was engaged to her childhood sweetheart, Ben, and worked at a city-centre bank, and Bella was PA to her best friend – the newly appointed Lady MacBain – and whilst it wasn't the career in interior design she had dreamed of, it was much better than some of the mundane roles she'd endured since taking the difficult decision to drop out of university when her own mother had become ill. At least her role here was fun and varied.

Following Olivia's unexpected inheritance, her plans to open the castle to the public had been on schedule until a series of disasters had befallen the place over the winter, a stark reminder that the fifteenth-century castle was in a poor state of repair. Then recently a severe storm had damaged the roof further and taken down the scaffolding on the exterior, meaning more repairs were needed. It was late March now and the original opening date had passed. Due to delays in funding, it had now been put back to July.

The door to the library burst open. 'Well, that's it. It's officially *all* ruined,' Olivia said with a deep sigh as she slumped down onto the chair opposite Bella, her shoulders hunched. After such a positive start to the renovations and plans, so much had gone wrong for poor Olivia, but at least, she had the support of Bella and Skye, her mum's step-brother Uncle Innes and, of course, her *almost* fiancé, Brodie.

Bella's heart sank for her friend. 'Oh no, what is it now, Liv?'

'The interior design company for the stable block apartments has given backword just as they were about to start work. The contact I spoke to was very apologetic but vague. What the hell am I going to do now?' It was evident from Olivia's trembling chin she was on the verge of tears, *and* of giving up.

'I'll do it!' Bella blurted without really thinking.

Olivia lifted her chin and, with watery eyes, she frowned. 'But...'

Bella stood and walked around the old desk to perch on it before Olivia. 'I know I'm not qualified. And I know this is a bit crazy, but you know how much I love that kind of thing. You saw what I did with my little flat. You've seen what I've done at my mum and dad's house too.'

Olivia shook her head. 'I know, Bella, but this is a massive undertaking. They've withdrawn *all* their plans, so you'd be starting from scratch without a scheme. It's a crazy amount of work for you to take on and I really don't want to put that much pressure on you, especially seeing as you're employed as my PA, not my designer.'

Bella's heart skipped with giddy excitement. 'I know I could do it, though, Liv. And I'd absolutely love the process, I'm sure.' Olivia fell silent and Bella realised she had put pressure on her friend to accept a ridiculously left-field idea. She scoffed then continued. 'Sorry, I've just replayed what I said in my head and I can see how mad it sounds. This is a business and, of course, you want it doing professionally. I have zero qualifications and no real portfolio to speak of.' She waved her hands as if doing so would erase the previous few moments. 'Forget it. Rewind.' She stood and did a comic backwards walk while pretending to speak in reverse. Doing so caused her stomach to knot with embarrassment and she cleared her throat excessively before saying, 'Sorry... that was... weird... Do you want me to start a search to look for another designer?'

Olivia chewed on her lip and stared silently at the wall for what felt like ages until she stood up abruptly. 'Okay, put together a mood board. How *you* see the apartments looking. Forget what the other company came up with. Show me *your* vision. If I like it, I'll give you a go. But if I don't, I'll have to be completely honest with you. Although please know it won't mean I love you any less. I just have to get this right because the funding allocation was quite strict about the apartments being sustainable.' Olivia bit her lip again and cringed. 'It's terrifying, though, because you're my best friend and I don't want to hurt your feelings but I might have to.' Bella sensed she was already talking herself out of it.

She needed to intervene.

Bella twisted her fingers in front of her and mirrored Olivia's lip chewing. 'You may think this is absolutely nuts and totally bizarre, but I already have a mood board prepared.'

Olivia narrowed her eyes. 'Sorry, *what*?'

Bella felt her cheeks warming almost to the point of spontaneous combustion and she sighed deeply. 'When I realised you were turning the stables into apartments, I had all these ideas, they just kept springing into my mind, so I created a series of Pinterest boards.'

Olivia gave a light, incredulous laugh. 'You've never mentioned this before.'

'No, because you'd got everything sorted. And I only did them for me. I had absolutely no intention of anyone ever seeing them.'

'Are they on your laptop?' Olivia asked, wide eyed, pointing to the desk.

Bella paused and then with hesitance said, 'They... are?'

Olivia held her hands out. 'Well, come on then, Douglas, no time like the present!'

Olivia had put on hold her own career as a fashion designer in New York for the House of Nina Picarro, designer to the stars, when she had inherited the castle, and hoped the apartments could be rented out to artists and creators like herself as an inspirational retreat; plus they would create another income stream to add to the many Olivia had planned for the upkeep of her ancestral home, so they had to be done right.

After a few minutes of scrolling through Bella's designs, Olivia turned her attention back to Bella. 'Seriously, Bells, why didn't you show me these? They're far better than the ones from the company I'd hired.'

Bella's heart skipped again as the possibility of living her actual dream was almost a tangible thing. 'I'm so glad you like them. I... I tried to keep the castle in the forefront of the design without being twee and Disney-ish. After all, it's not a theme park so it's important the apartments stay true to their origins in some way. That's why the stonework is left exposed in some rooms and why I haven't blocked up all the alcoves. I also thought it'd be great to use some of the old furniture pieces from the attic. I remember there being all sorts of wonderful things up there when we used to go sneaking around.'

Olivia's eyes lit up. 'You see, the designers we had were keen to completely modernise the interior of the stables and create a total contrast to the rest of the castle. I went along with it because they had great reviews. But what you've done is mix the old with the new and I love that. It's incredible, Bella. I love how you've turned this old tack recess into wine storage,' Olivia said, pointing to the screen.

Bella shrugged. 'I figured the stone would keep the wine cool like in wine cellars.'

'You're hired,' Olivia stated matter-of-factly.

Bella gasped. 'Seriously? Are you sure you don't want me to maybe do one room and see what you think?'

Olivia shook her head. 'We don't have time for that and, to be honest, I absolutely love everything you've designed. From the rich colours to the lighting. I'd never have thought to use jewel colours on the walls. But I absolutely love the whole look you've compiled. When can you start? You'll need to speak to the builders and decorating team as soon as possible. In fact, they're in finishing off the ceilings today and are due to start plastering the walls tomorrow, so we need to stop that from happening.'

Bella couldn't hide her excitement and grappled Olivia into a hug. 'There's no time like the present!'

1

As Bella stood in one of the newly converted stone stables under a freshly plastered ceiling, clutching her iPad and making notes, she couldn't quite believe this was happening. The structural changes to the exterior of the stables had been done already, in addition to the ceilings, first fix electrics had been installed, woodwork had been sanded and stained, and floors had been levelled. They were now at the point where she could instruct the decorators to carry out the designs she never imagined would see the light of day. And even if it was only temporary, she was about to embark upon her absolute dream job, and at Drumblair Castle of all places. She tried to stifle a squeal of excitement bubbling up from within her but it was suddenly replaced by a squeal of fear when someone slipped their hands over her eyes, making her almost jump out of her skin.

'It's only me,' a male voice said as he snaked his arms around her waist and turned her to face him.

'Kerr! You scared me half to death,' she said with a slap to his chest.

Olivia's irreverent brother stuck out his bottom lip and pouted. 'I'm sowwy. Pwease forgive me.'

Bella sighed but stepped back. 'Forgiven, I suppose. But what are you doing here? You seem to be here more these days than at your own house in the city.'

Bella had adored Kerr since she was a teenage girl and he was her best friend's older brother; all handsome, mysterious and aloof. She had discovered, however, that in reality he was nothing like she had imagined back then. After a very brief relationship in which she had encountered many 'red flags' – one of which being the fact he was accepting money from a female family 'friend', fifty-nine-year-old Adaira Wallace, who was clearly besotted with him, and who she was pretty sure had no clue about *their* relationship – she had ended things, hating herself for lying to Olivia by omission. Kerr, unfortunately, couldn't seem to let go.

During their short dalliance, Kerr had continuously tried to get her into bed but Bella had remained true to herself in her determination not to sleep with him until things felt right. A decision she was very happy about now she had ended things.

Their relationship had remained a guilt-inducing secret from everyone except Granny Isla, as Bella figured Olivia had enough going on with her relatively new role as Lady of Drumblair. Things between the siblings had deteriorated further since Kerr discovered Olivia had been chosen to inherit the castle instead of him, so telling her about them would definitely not have helped.

Until quite recently, Kerr had been doing his best to sabotage Olivia's plans for the castle but with the tiny amount of new-found influence she'd had over him, Bella had managed to convince Kerr he'd been horrible and had helped him to see the error of his ways. He had seemed to make his peace with everything and had agreed to do better. So if anything good was to come of their clandestine connection, that was it.

'I heard that you were taking over the design work here so I wanted to come and say congratulations.'

She smiled, surprised he had no other agenda. 'Thanks, I'm very excited about it.'

Kerr reached out to her again but she moved further away and he sighed deeply. 'Won't you give me another chance? I've told you we can tell Olivia *very* soon,' he said. 'It has to be the right time, that's all.'

Bella shook her head and sighed out her exasperation. 'Not this again, Kerr. I've told you, I'm not prepared to lie to Olivia again, or to be someone's bit on the side, so drop it, will you?'

He held his arms out to his sides. 'Bit on the side? But there's no one else.'

Bella scoffed. 'Tell that to Adaira.'

He ignored her. 'I have to say you look super-sexy in this tight skirt.'

Smoothing down her clothing, Bella replied, 'I didn't wear it to appeal to you. Now I'm busy, so you should go.'

He stepped closer. 'Oh, come on, Bells, you know you still want me. You fancied me for years. That doesn't change overnight.'

She pushed him back firmly and with conviction. 'It *has* changed, Kerr. I'm not going through this again with you. You only want me because I turned you down.'

He stepped back and sulkily stuffed his hands into his trouser pockets. 'You'll regret it.'

Bella rolled her eyes, wondering why she allowed herself to be sucked in by his handsome exterior. 'It's a chance I'm willing to take.'

His expression brightened. 'I'll tell Olivia about us. We'll get it all out in the open. That's what you want, isn't it? To make us official? So let's be official.' He was verging on begging now and Bella was becoming increasingly frustrated.

She gritted her teeth. 'Not any more, Kerr. That ship sailed so long ago it's almost circumnavigated the globe. We're too different. And I want to be with someone who wants to be seen in public with me. And who doesn't take me out using money he took from another woman.' She shuddered at that particular memory.

Kerr stepped closer once again and cupped her cheek, running his thumb gently over her skin. 'I've told you I'll do whatever you want. Name it. My life's complicated, I get it. And yes, Adaira helps me, but it's only financial. She's my friend, that's all.'

'A friend who makes puppy-dog eyes at you constantly, and who moved in with you after your mum died. That's a little more than friendship, Kerr. And if it's one-sided, you're taking advantage of the poor woman.' She pushed his hand away and stepped back again, at which point his nostrils flared.

'Since Olivia inherited Drumblair, I've been left with *nothing*. How do you think that makes me feel when it was all rightfully mine? Emasculated, that's how. And now you're doing the same thing.'

Bella scoffed and turned her back on him for a moment. 'I'm sorry, Kerr, but any such feelings are of your own doing, not mine.' She turned to face him again and noted his furrowed brow. It wasn't like him to appear so dejected. 'Adaira's in love with you and you're using her... Hmm, I wonder why my feelings changed.' Her words dripped with sarcasm. 'And you know very well Olivia inherited this place because you would've gambled it away. I'm happy to be friends with you but that's all I can offer.'

'I'm stubborn, you know. I'll keep trying. I won't give up. I'll win you back one way or another.'

Bella huffed air through puffed cheeks but tried to remain calm as she shook her head. 'No, you won't. My mind's been made up for a while now. And I can be stubborn too.' She smiled to soften the blow.

Kerr's expression filled with sadness. 'I don't want to lose you, Bells.'

'You won't lose me, as a friend.'

His lips formed a straight line and he nodded. 'I should go then. But I'll meet someone eventually, and then you'll definitely regret it when I've got my life back on track.'

'I'm sure I'll be fine. And I really do hope you meet someone; someone who you love enough to change for because Olivia really worries about you, Kerr.'

He harrumphed. 'She's no need to. I'm a grown-arsed adult.' And with that, he walked out of the unfinished apartment, letting the front door close with a bang behind him.

'Aye, a grown-arsed adult who relies on a sugar momma to pay his way,' Bella mumbled into the empty room.

* * *

May

Bella watched from the kitchen as the painters gathered the last of their equipment. In one hand she clutched her iPad, showing its long to-do list, and tucked her short blonde hair behind her ear with the other as she smiled at her surroundings. A sense of pride settled over her. This kitchen was the final room to be completed in the last of the four apartments. The walls were a fresh cream shade that complemented the deep teal-coloured Shaker-style cupboard doors perfectly. The solid wood countertops had been crafted from fallen trees in the grounds of the castle and Bella was thrilled with the overall look she had created.

It was approaching the end of May now and since being given the chance to create and implement the designs for the old stable block, Bella had grown in confidence thanks to the praise of Olivia and the other staff members at the castle. Each of the four apartments had its own colour scheme and each had its own little quirks that made the most of the beautiful old stonework. The structural additions to each apartment had been turned into features too with some exposed copper piping and chandeliers hanging from black cables in the centre of the larger rooms.

Along with the buzz Bella felt when she viewed the rooms she had created came a niggling sadness it was coming to an end and soon the apartments would be rented out to the creative types Olivia had envisaged utilising the spaces. She couldn't help wondering what they would make of it all. She hoped they would love it and be inspired.

'Right, well, that's us done!' Davey Howe, one of the painters, informed her as he pulled on his jacket. 'Steve's putting the rest of our gear in the van and then we'll be off. You know where to find us for your next reno' project.' He held out his hand.

Bella shook it and told him, 'Honestly, the apartments look incredible. I wish I was moving in.'

Davey beamed at her. 'Grand, grand. I hope Lady Olivia is as happy as you are. I *wasnae* sure about the navy-blue walls in the living and dining room in this flat, and the fake panelling in number three had me beat too till I saw it all done. I reckon you were right. It's kind of regal. Fitting for a castle, I suppose.'

'See! I knew you'd end up liking it, Davey,' Bella said proudly and with a little flush to her cheeks.

'Aye, well, we'll be going the now. Pass on our regards to the lady of the house.' He doffed an invisible cap on his head and left.

* * *

Once the decorators had gone, Bella focused her attention on her list. She ticked off the apartments and had one last walk around them to assess the work.

The old furniture that she had selected from the attics had been repaired and cleaned up and would be arriving imminently and then, not too long after, the first paying guests would no doubt arrive.

Bella stood in the centre of the living room in apartment number two and smiled contentedly. The artwork she had purchased would really brighten up the space and she couldn't wait to get the paintings on the walls. She was excited about the great reveal at the corporate event Olivia was holding for the local businesspeople. The original idea for a Nina Picarro fashion show had been shelved on account of the delays, something Bella knew Olivia was heartbroken about.

But then she would go back to being Olivia's PA. Her days would no longer be filled with colour charts, fabric samples and shopping trips for decorative items. She was going to miss that so much. Being able to use her creative flair made her feel so alive. She noticed things so much more when she was being creative, like the pattern of tree bark, the randomness of cloud formations, the fluidity of birds in a murmuration. She found she became aware of all patterns created by nature – something she always tried to incorporate into her designs, even if they were for her eyes only.

Her mum's words rattled around her mind. 'Don't you be putting your life on hold for me, Arabella. If I don't make it through this illness, I want to know you're going to be happy and doing something you love.'

Of course she had assured her mum at the time she wouldn't ditch her future, but how could she have concentrated on studies when her mum was so ill and in so much pain? Not to mention how her dad and brother had been coping too back then. She dropped out of university to make sure she was at home in case she was needed.

These days and especially recently, her mum and dad, and Granny Isla, had all been pushing her to return to studying, but she was almost twenty-nine. It was far too late... wasn't it?

2

Bella arrived home after work, her mind whirring with a confusing mixture of sadness and pride.

She was happy; and at least Kerr had finally taken her at her word that they were over. He had been cordial for the most part, even though she had caught him gazing longingly in her direction on more than one occasion. She wished she had never entered into anything with him in the first place. She had witnessed him being arrogant, surly, stubborn and selfish. So why, oh why, had she been attracted to him? She couldn't quite believe she allowed the short affair to go on as long as it had. What had she been thinking? He had been horrible to Olivia after the will reading, and still had a lot of making up to do.

'Arabella, is that you, hen?' Granny Isla called from the living room as Bella walked along the hallway into the kitchen at the back of the house.

'Aye, Granny,' Bella replied. 'I'm home and I have news!' She dropped her handbag on the kitchen table, then made her way back through the living room and was greeted by Beau, her granny's excitable two-year-old beagle.

As Bella scratched the dog behind his ears, she glanced up at her granny, who was sitting in front of the TV in her purple paisley kaftan, watching a quiz show. 'Have you had a good day?' Her long violet hair was tied in a neat chignon and she had on a full face of make-up; she really was the epitome of the glamorous granny in a cool, eccentric kind of way.

Isla rolled her eyes. 'If you mean have I enjoyed spending my day with a load of gyratics moaning about their ailments and trying to one-up each other on how many pills they take every day, then yes, it's been thrilling.' She pursed her lips.

Bella couldn't help smirking at her granny's incorrect use of geriatrics. 'Granny, you're older than most of the people at the day centre, you know.'

Isla waved a dismissive hand. 'Aye, well, you're only as old as you behave. So I'm practically a twenty-something compared to that lot of whinge bags! Don't get me wrong, they're not all like that, mainly the curly perm brigade.' She scoffed. 'You won't catch me wearing a twinset and pearls and carrying five packets of Werther's Originals and a pot of smelling salts in my handbag. No, thanks. And I don't understand the need to compete for whose aches and pains are the worst either. We're British, we should suffer in silence.'

'If it's that bad, why do you go?' Bella asked as she flopped onto the sofa.

Isla huffed. 'I go to keep them company. To try and show them there's a different way of life than greetin' on all the while. But anyway, there's those have *naeone* to visit them, you know. I like to do my bit for the old folks. And, of course, Maeve Donaldson likes me to do her hair, bless her heart. Her son's a policeman, you know? Very handsome too.' She gave a knowing look.

'So you've said about a million times, Granny. And I've seen him at the day centre, he's not my type. How many more times do I need to say it?'

Isla ignored her and continued. 'Aye, he plays the fiddle and the guitar, you know. He's in a ceilidh band with other police folks. And she's a lovely old dear is his mother, Maeve. My best friend after you and Beau. She's seventy-eight, you know?'

Bella giggled. 'Aye, and you're eighty-five.'

Isla made another scoffing noise. 'Anyway, what's your news?' she asked.

'The apartments are finished!'

Isla widened her eyes. 'Already? That's wonderful, hen. What has Olivia said?'

'She's banned from seeing them until the furniture arrives and the paintings are up.'

Isla beamed at her granddaughter. 'I'm so proud of you and I can't wait to see them.' She sighed and shook her head. 'I've told you I don't know how many times your talent's being wasted. Maybe now you'll listen to me and pursue the career you actually want.'

Bella stood and walked over to kiss her granny on the head. Ignoring her comments, she simply said, 'I'll take you to see them once they're furnished.' She sat on the arm of her granny's chair.

'Speaking of the castle, have you had any more issues with that brother of Olivia's?'

Bella regretted confiding in her granny; the note of disdain in her tone was evident. 'Not really. I think he's finally getting the message.'

'About bloomin' time if you ask me. He may be a posh nob but he's no good for my Arabella.'

Bella had lost count of the number of times her granny had expressed her opinion on the matter. 'Aye, I know how you feel about him, Granny. You've made that crystal clear.'

Isla shook her head and pursed her lips. 'I really don't get what you saw in him. I know he's good-looking but he's ugly on the inside.'

Bella scrunched her brow. 'I don't think you know him well enough to say that, Granny.'

'It's the truth, hen. I've heard stories about him and his antics; his drinking and his gambling. Not to mention his womanising. I worry about you. What you need is to meet a handsome young man who's available and not a shit.'

Bella tried not to laugh. 'Granny! I hope you mind your language at the day centre.'

'Och, I *do* not. I'm *frae Glesga*, don't forget, and we tell it how it is,' she said, allowing her softened accent to give way to its origins for a moment. 'And anyway, they've all been around the block a few times so they've heard much worse. And stop changing the subject. Kermit MacBain is a ratbag and you know he is. What kind of man has two women on the go?' Bella opened her mouth to speak but Isla interrupted, 'A ratbag, that's what!'

Bella stood. 'His name is Kerr.'

'Aye, well, what else could it be short for?'

'It's not short for anything, Granny. It's just Kerr. Mirren's sent me home with some shortbread and some more of her wedding cake from the freezer so we can have that after dinner.' Mirren, the housekeeper at Drumblair, had married Dougie, Brodie's dad and the groundsman for the castle. Their wedding had taken place at New Year and the cake had been huge. Months on and every so often she would defrost a batch to share around. 'Shall I put the kettle on?'

'Aye, I'd love a cup of tea. The stuff they use at the day centre tastes like floor scrapings. In fact, I'm not even sure it's ever seen a tea plant. Probably some random dried leaves *oot* the gardens.' She chuckled.

Bella laughed to herself as she wandered into the kitchen to put the kettle on. Beau followed her, his tail wagging in the hope there may be treats for him too. 'You can't have fruit cake, wee man. It's poisonous to dogs.'

'Your mum called earlier, she wants to borrow a dress of yours for the cruise. I told her you'd call her back later,' Isla called after her.

'Okay. I wish I was going with them.'

'You could've gone. They did invite you. Your dad would love you to be there to celebrate his sixtieth.'

'Hmm, I don't want to leave Olivia in the lurch, especially when the booking system for the apartments is about to go live. I'm in charge of overseeing that.'

Bella had been reticent about moving into her granny's three-bedroom house on Innes Street in Inverness, but at the time it had been necessary when she'd had to move out of her flat after losing her job. She had, for a short time, moved back home into her brother's bedroom while he was at uni – her own bedroom had been turned into a gym/office – but when Callum returned from uni, she had been faced with the prospect of sleeping on the sofa. Living with Granny Isla had always been intended as a temporary situation until she could afford her own place, but now she didn't really want to leave. Isla was such fun for an octogenarian. With her varying hair colours, her boho chic clothes, and her inane ability for malapropisms, there was never a lull in entertainment.

'I've made stovies for tea, by the way. It's ready when you are,' Isla called again. Bella knew she had, thanks to the familiar, mouth-watering aroma of cooked meat and vegetables. 'I got some oatcakes from the wee deli by the day centre. I *wasnae* sure if you were off *oot*, though.'

'No, Granny, I'm looking forward to the stovies! I'll set the table, eh?' She grabbed the mats and plates from the old dresser and laid the table. 'Come on, I'm serving up.'

Isla came through. 'I'm starving. We only had roast pork, veg and sponge with custard for lunch.'

Bella began to plate up the stew and placed a portion in front of her granny. 'Only? It beats the salad sandwich I had.'

'Aye, but they think gyratics eat like sparrows at that place, all fancy pants but no substance.'

Bella smiled and shook her head. 'Anyway, do you fancy coming to visit the castle with me at the weekend? Olivia would love to see you.'

'Count me in. Will that handsome chap of hers be there?'

'Brodie? I would think so. Don't you go flirting with him, Gran,' Bella said with a wink.

'I *wouldnae* dream of it. Can't stop him flirting wi' me, though, eh?' Isla smiled with a mischievous glint in her eyes. Brodie had a definite soft spot for Granny Isla and the feeling was clearly mutual. 'Do you think he'll ever propose properly to Olivia?'

Bella chewed a mouthful of melt-in-the-mouth beef, onions and soft potato before replying, 'Absolutely. He's just waiting for his divorce from that evil, violent woman to be finalised, then I bet there will be an official lavish proposal.'

Isla smiled dreamily. 'Don't you think he's got a look of that actor?' she asked. 'The one named after that fancy rice stuff that's all the rage these days? Although I don't see what's wrong with plain ol' boil in the bag mysel'.'

Bella scrunched her brow and shrugged. 'I have no clue who you mean.'

Isla waved her fork in frustration. 'Och, you do.' She placed her fork down and clicked her fingers. 'Not couscous... the other one...' There was a light bulb moment and Isla's face lit up. 'Quinoa! Aye, that's it, Quinoa something or other. Reeves! Aye, that's him. Quinoa Reeves.'

Bella almost choked on her food as she laughed. 'Quinoa Reeves! Aye, I suppose Brodie does look a little like him.'

Isla scowled. 'Aye, although who names their child after a rice substitute? But then again, Gwyneth Paltrow named her daughter Apple, I suppose.' She rolled her eyes and shrugged.

Bella was a little bewildered by her granny's knowledge of the American actress and her offspring. She briefly considered arguing and explaining the actor to whom she was referring was *Keanu*, but decided not to bother. Her version was cute and funny and would be added to the list of other *Isla-isms* uttered by the Douglas matriarch, which would go down in history.

'Right. It's a date then,' Bella said. 'We'll go and visit Saturday morning. The weather's supposed to be dry and I can't wait for you to see everything in real life rather than photos on my phone.' They chatted about nothing much until they finished their meal. 'Right, I'll go call my mum and then I'll sort the dishes.'

3

Saturday was a dry and bright day, if a little chilly for May, and as Bella drove Fifi, her 'vintage' (some would say ancient) red Citroen 2CV, to the castle with her granny in the passenger seat, her heart skipped with excitement. She couldn't wait to show her granny the newly decorated apartments.

As they travelled up the long tree-lined driveway, Isla sang along with Lewis Capaldi's 'Pointless' playing on the radio in her almost operatic voice.

'I didn't know you were a fan, Granny,' Bella said with a smile. 'In fact, I didn't even know you were aware of Lewis Capaldi.'

'I do like to keep up with the modern tunes, you know. I listen to Radio Highland when I'm baking or cleaning. Beau likes him too. He's from *Glesga*, you know. And he's a handsome young man. Not quite as handsome as his father, though.' Bella was a little confused as to how Isla might know Lewis Capaldi's dad. She needn't have wondered because Isla added, 'Aye, I remember him in that lovely film *Local Hero*. His father, I mean.'

Bella remembered watching *Local Hero* with her granny when she was younger; it was one of Isla's favourite movies because it was filmed on location in Arisaig on the west coast of Scotland, a place she had visited as a young girl.

'Hang on, Granny, Lewis Capaldi's dad isn't an actor. In fact, I'm sure I saw an interview with him once where he said his dad was a fishmonger.'

Isla pondered this for a moment. 'No, Peter Capaldi is definitely an actor, I should know, he's in my favourite film!'

Although Bella could understand the mistake – it wasn't a particularly common name – she informed her granny, 'Peter Capaldi and Lewis Capaldi aren't actually related, I'm afraid.' She tried not to giggle at the mix-up.

'So did he adopt him then? Aw, it's nice Lewis took his name.'

'No, Granny, I mean they may share the *name* but they don't know each other, not really.'

'Well, he must have known him well enough to adopt the poor wee lad.'

'No, Granny, I mean they aren't connected *at all*. Well, apart from the fact Peter Capaldi appeared in one of Lewis's music videos. Anyway, I can understand why you'd think they were.'

'Oh... That's made me a little bit sad.'

Bella felt guilty at bursting her granny's invented bubble. But within moments she pulled the car to a stop in front of the stunning, vast stone structure of Drumblair Castle. The sun glinted off the small panes of glass in the windows and the cerulean-blue sky gave a contrasting backdrop to the picture-perfect image. Arriving at the castle never ceased to excite Bella. In fact, she couldn't remember ever enjoying so-called *work* as much as she had when working on the apartments.

She gave a sigh but smiled. 'Never mind, Granny, we're here now. Come on.'

As Bella helped her granny and Beau out of the old car, she glanced up at the large double oak doors and saw Kerr walking towards them, as handsome as ever, in dark jeans and a chunky pale green Aran jumper. His hair looked damp as if he had recently showered and he was smiling and walking with purpose. Olivia had mentioned he'd been staying in his old bedroom for a few days; helping with sorting through some old belongings of his father's to clear out some space for storage. Things seemed good between them and that made Bella happy.

Beau gave a low, rumbled growl and Isla scoffed. 'Ugh, did you know Kermit was going to be here? He gives me the Bee Gees.'

Bella tried not to smirk as she pictured the dazzling-toothed trio. 'I think you mean the *heebie-jeebies*. And yes, I had an inkling *Kerr* would be here and please don't call him Kermit, especially not to his face.'

Isla shrugged like a sulking teenager. 'It suits him, and he's wearing green.'

'Behave yourself,' Bella insisted. 'And remember what I said,' she hissed as Kerr arrived beside the car.

He smiled at Bella, his eyes lingering a little long on her body. 'Bella, you look lovely as ever,' he said in a deep husky voice. 'And Mrs Douglas, how lovely to see you.' He bent in a condescending manner to address the elderly woman. 'I understand you've come for a tour of the new apartments,' he said in a loud, exaggerated voice.

Isla's face crumpled in disgust. 'I'm no' deaf, you *glaiket bampot*.' She shook her head rapidly, her nose turned up as if he was a bad smell she couldn't get rid of.

Kerr raised his eyebrows but forced a smile and ignored her insult. 'You must be so proud of what Bella has achieved. I'm sure you'll love the décor,' he said without lowering the volume of his voice. 'And you'd better behave yourself, little dog,' he said to the canine, who was still giving *off come closer and I'll bite your shins* vibes.

'Aye, well, I'm sure you've plenty to do so don't let us hold you up,' Isla said with a stony expression.

'Granny, be nice,' Bella whispered through a strained smile.

Isla didn't let up. 'I'm sure Gonzo and Fozzy are waiting for you,' she chuntered, almost inaudibly.

'Granny,' Bella hissed, this time through clenched teeth.

Kerr stepped a little closer. 'I'm sorry, Mrs Douglas,' he said with a hand to his ear to exaggerate his point, 'I didn't quite hear you.' His voice was still annoyingly loud as he tilted his head so his ear was closer to her.

Bella laughed nervously. 'Oh, she said her ears have *gone so fuzzy*. I think I was playing Lewis Capaldi a bit too loud in the car. Come on, Granny.' Bella took Isla's arm and gave an apologetic smile to Kerr.

'Oh, yes, I like Lewis Capaldi too,' Kerr said.

'We'd better get on. See you later,' Bella told him with yet another apologetic smile. 'Come on, Granny.' She made no effort to hide her irritation at the badly behaved matriarch.

* * *

As they entered the first apartment, they were greeted by the pungent, yet not entirely unpleasant, smell of newly applied paint, and the rubber-like odour of freshly laid carpets. The furniture was all in place and the classic shapes and styles of the old renovated pieces Bella had selected from the attics complemented the colour scheme so well. In addition to the strange combination of smells, a vase of fragrant roses from the walled garden adorned the solid oak countertop in the kitchen; the first room on the right. Bella released Beau from his lead and he ran off to sniff and investigate.

They walked on through to the living room and Bella couldn't help the flip of excitement in her stomach on seeing the beige fabric couches scattered with Drumblair Tartan cushions matching the sumptuous thick pile of the rug that covered the oak floor. The addition of new lighting created a bright and welcoming atmosphere.

Artwork from an Isle of Skye-based artist called Reid Mackinnon graced the walls and added a splash of contrasting colour to the room. Bella had ordered the paintings from a little gallery in a village called Glentorrin after seeing them in a TikTok video the artist had made. Some of the stone had been left exposed, harking to the heritage and origins of the stables. An old recess now served as a bookshelf, illuminated by downlights and embellished with tasteful pottery and old leather-bound books.

Isla gasped as she glanced around the rooms. 'Arabella dearie, you've done a bonnie job, hen. I *wouldnae* mind living here mysel'. It all looks so expensive and very classy.'

Bella's eyes welled as she hugged her granny. 'Thanks, Granny. I'm so glad you like it. The others are similar but they all have their own individual touches, giving them their own personality.'

'Well, I think you could give that flamboyant interior design chappy Lulu Lemon off the telly a run for his money, don't you think so, Beau?' Isla chuckled and the dog appeared from the direction of the bedrooms, wagging his tail, clearly in agreement. 'All you need is a twiddly moustache and gaudy suit.'

Bella presumed she was referring to Laurence Llewelyn-Bowen as they had watched his makeover shows together many times. 'Aww, thank you. But I think I'll give the moustache a miss if you don't mind.'

'Hello, hello! Anyone home?' Olivia's voice called from the front door and as she walked into the living room, she enveloped them each in turn in a warm hug. 'Isla, wow, you're looking very glam. I'm loving the purple hair.' She bent to give Beau a scratch behind the ears.

'Och, thank you. You're no' looking so bad yoursel', hen. I think you're wearing castle life *verra* well.' Bella noted the way her granny feigned *poshness* in front of the new Lady MacBain and tried not to giggle.

'Thank you. I must admit I'm loving it now I'm getting the hang of everything. But I wouldn't be where I was now if it wasn't for your granddaughter. Bella has been a huge help to me.'

Isla smiled up at Bella. 'Aye, she's a good lass. We need to find her a man as good as yours now. I was trying to tell her earlier about a nice, handsome policeman I know but she won't hear of it.'

Bella felt her cheeks heating. 'I'm capable of finding my own man, Granny.'

Olivia gave a wink. 'As far as I'm aware, you already have, haven't you? Although you haven't mentioned him in a while.' Bella's stomach lurched at the mention of her secret relationship and she felt her face flush. 'Isla, you and I will have to meet up to have a chat so you can fill me in on the gossip,' Olivia teased.

Isla opened her mouth to speak but Bella quickly interrupted, 'Oh, no, actually that's all over now. But enough about my love life. Yours is far nicer to talk about.'

'It's all over between you and the mystery man? Aww, I'm sorry,' Olivia said with a pout.

'Aye, it has been for a while. But I'm fine. Anyway, is Brodie around? I wanted to ask him how his book is going.'

Childhood friends Brodie and Olivia had connected again after a long time apart. He had been Olivia's first love but she'd had no idea back then that he'd held the same feelings for her, mainly on account of the fact he had been rather mean to her before he moved away with his mother. An abusive relationship had left Brodie somewhat bruised both physically and emotionally, but thanks to Olivia he had found love again. Since their reconnection, Brodie had embarked upon a passion project and had been gathering information about Drumblair Castle, a place he had been familiar with and had loved since childhood, in order to write a book. The plan was to sell it in the castle gift shop when the place finally opened to the public in July. While she was working on the apartments, Bella had been reading pages of the book as it was being written and had learned all sorts of fascinating stuff about the castle and its legendary connections to Bonnie Prince Charlie.

'He finished editing it!' Olivia informed her excitedly. 'It's gone off to the printers.'

Bella was truly delighted. 'That's incredible. What an achievement. Let him know I want a signed copy.'

Olivia beamed with pride. 'I think that can be arranged, seeing as you were his first reader.'

'He should try to get it published instead of just printing it for the castle shop.'

Olivia nodded and held her hands out at her sides. 'Yup. I've told him the same, but he insists no publisher would take it. Ooh, speaking of writers. I have news!'

Bella could see the excitement glinting in Olivia's eyes and her interest was piqued. 'Spill it, MacBain.'

'Okay, so, we had an email yesterday from the agent of a writer who is looking for somewhere to stay while he completes his next crime thriller. A sort of writing retreat, if you will. I wasn't expecting news to get around so fast, but she knows someone who lives in the area who told her about the castle and the renovations and she has asked if he can come and stay for a while. I'm not entirely sure how long, but isn't it exciting?'

Bella widened her eyes. 'Your first paying customer, that is exciting. And I love a crime thriller!'

Olivia grinned. 'I know, I immediately thought of you when she told me what he was working on.'

'Is it anyone I've heard of? Maybe I've read something of his.'

Olivia pursed her lips for a moment. 'Sadly, no. Well, not that I've seen when I've Googled his name.'

Bella's stomach set about fluttering with butterflies. 'Which is?'

'Aiden O'Dowd,' Olivia said with a smile. 'I've searched and searched but can't find anything about him.'

Bella racked her brains but couldn't place the name. She'd read hundreds of thrillers, and crime fiction stories, and felt sure she would know if she had read anything by him. 'No, that doesn't ring a bell with me. Maybe he's quite new.'

Olivia shrugged. 'I don't think so. She said he's been writing a while. It's apparently set in a castle, so she thought it would be the perfect place for inspiration.'

Bella grinned. 'Oh, well, another author for me to discover. When is he coming to stay?'

'He's moving in sometime around 23 July, I believe.'

Bella widened her eyes. 'But that's opening day for the castle! Talk about adding to the stress pile.'

Olivia shook her head. 'It'll be fine. We'll have plenty of time to get everything put back to normal after the event. It'll be easier now the fashion show will be my designs and I'm using local models.'

Bella noted a hint of sadness in Olivia's eyes. She'd known how much the original fashion show idea had meant to her. 'It'll be amazing, you know,' she said, hoping to reassure her.

Bella was already trying to picture the author from his name. 'Aiden' felt quite young, perhaps like the man who played Poldark in the remake. Although the photos of crime writers she'd actually seen didn't fit that mould.

Olivia interrupted her thoughts. 'Speaking of the corporate

event, I'm afraid I'm going to need you to take on an extra task. Brodie wants to whisk me away for a few days and I tried to decline but... I can't say no to him,' she said dreamily. 'Then when I get back I'll need to knuckle down with my designs for the fashion show part of the event.'

Bella nodded. 'Sure, boss. Let me know what you need me to do.'

Olivia beamed. 'Thanks, honey. I'll need you to handle the e-invites for local businesses and people who we think might benefit from knowing about the castle as a venue; local press, national press, magazines, etc. I really appreciate your help. I know you've had a lot on with the apartments and you could probably do with a rest. But they need to go out as soon as possible, really.'

Bella shook her head. 'No, I'm all good. And I'm happy to help.'

'Fantastic. Well, I'll get the list over to you on Monday. In the meantime, I'll leave you to show your lovely glamorous granny around the apartments. Enjoy, Isla! And pop up to the kitchen for a cuppa when you're done. I'm sure Mirren will want to see you and wee Beau.' She kissed Isla on both cheeks and left them to look around.

Once Olivia had left the room, Isla nudged Bella. 'See, that's what you need. Someone who won't take no for an answer when he wants to sweep you off your feet. Not someone who wants you to be at his beck and call behind his other woman's back when it suits him.'

Bella sighed as sadness washed over her. 'I know, Granny. I'd love a relationship like theirs.'

As if feeling bad for ribbing her, Isla linked arms with her and tiptoed up to kiss her cheek. 'Aye, well, you never know, hen, this fancy crime author chappy might be the one.'

Bella snorted. 'Not likely. Most crime and thriller writers are older married men or middle-aged women. And I'm not into either.'

Isla raised her eyebrows. 'You know that's called stereotyping, don't you? I didn't think that was the kind of thing you young folks did. And anyway, you never know. There's always an exception to the rule.'

Bella smiled. 'We can all dream, I suppose. Now come on and let me show you the rest of the apartments.'

* * *

Once they were finished, they made their way up to the main floor of the castle to see Mirren, the housekeeper, and Marley the Labrador–German Shepherd cross. The huge fluffy cream dog stood and wandered over to greet Beau when they walked through the door, his tail wagging and his eyes bright.

'Isla, how lovely to see you,' Mirren said as she hugged the elderly lady.

'Hello, Mirren, and hello, Marley. I'm sure you get bigger every time I see you, fella,' Isla said as she scratched the friendly animal behind his ears.

'Do you fancy a cuppa and a slice of wedding cake?' Mirren asked, pointing to the teapot.

Isla chuckled. 'Was your wedding cake the size of a *heilan coo*? It seems never-ending.'

Mirren laughed. 'Aye, it turns out people prefer red velvet cake these days to the traditional fruit cake. Me and Dougie will be eating it into next year, I think!'

Isla smiled. 'Well, I'm happy to help you get rid of it, it's delicious.'

Mirren poured tea for the three of them and cut some hefty chunks of the moist fruitcake, placing it onto china plates. 'So what do you think of the apartments? Your girl has done well, hasn't she?'

Isla took a big bite and chewed while nodding in agreement. Eventually she replied, 'Oh, they're beautiful. I was saying she's better than those fancy pants designers on the telly. They're fit for kings and queens. Too posh to let out to just anyone, though. I'd hate to see them get the treatment you see on the Tick Tack Toe videos.'

Mirren scrunched her brow. 'The what?'

Isla gestured as if typing on a phone. 'You know, the Tick Tack Toe app. One of the staff at the day centre loaded it down onto my telephone. You watch videos on it; mostly of dogs doing silly things and people getting planked. Anyway, I saw some films of people who own those rental holiday places. Left in a right state they were. Trashed was the word they used.'

'I think you mean TikTok, Granny, and people get pranked, not planked,' Bella said with a giggle.

Isla turned to her. 'Aye, that's what a said.'

'Oh, I don't think we need worry about that,' Mirren told her. 'I think Lady Olivia has a mind to let them to people such as business folks and writers and the like.'

Isla crossed her arms under her bosom. 'Aye, well, they can be as bad. And she won't want to end up with squatters. Folks today think they can take whatever they like and hang the consequences. Do you know, I watched one of those Tick Tack videos and there were people in America running out of shops with arms full of stuff and not paying for a single thing? Because they know they can get away with it. It's dreadful. They *wouldnae* have got away with it in my day. People respected the *polis* then.'

'Och, I know, Isla,' Mirren agreed. 'Some folks these days think they're above the law.'

Bella sat silently watching the two women putting the world to rights while stroking Marley's back. 'I'll be back in a minute,' she told them and stood to leave the room.

As she left the bathroom a few moments later, Kerr approached her in the hallway. 'Hey, have you got a minute?' he asked as he twisted his hands in front of him.

Bella scrunched her face and glanced in the direction of the kitchen, worried about who would see them talking. Seeing the coast was clear, she returned her attention to him. 'Sure, what's up?'

'I've been thinking about my relationship with Olivia and... I think you may be able to help me get to a better place with my sister.'

She narrowed her eyes. 'How so?'

He inhaled deeply and blew the air back out. 'Okay, so I know Olivia has asked you to deal with the event invites. And I was thinking I could help.'

'Oh...' She shook her head and tried to find a way to let him down gently. 'I don't think Liv would go for it, Kerr, she asked me to do it as part of my role as her PA.'

He ran his hands through his hair and hung his head. 'I know you think I'm a joke, Bella. Most people do. But I want to help. In spite of what people think, I'm great at organising and I know all the right people to invite. I really think I could be useful.'

Bella widened her eyes. 'But... the thing is it's such an important task and she's trusted me with it all... I couldn't simply tell her I'd handed it over to you—'

He held out his hands. 'Don't tell her until the job's done. Then you can admit I helped and she can see how useful I've been. It might help my case as a born-again big brother. You can trust me, Bella.' His expression was filled with sincerity and she thought perhaps it would help the siblings get back on the right track.

'*Can* I trust you? You wouldn't do anything crazy, would you?'

His brow crumpled again and his expression filled with hurt. 'I can understand why you'd think that way. I... I wanted a chance to do something good for Olivia. To show her I've changed. But I get it. I really do.' He turned to walk away.

Regret ate away at Bella's resolve. The genuine pain in his eyes had tugged at her heart. 'Okay. You can help. But you need to know how much this event means to your sister so bear that in mind, okay?'

He turned to face her, his expression filled with hope. 'I promise,' he assured her with a smile. 'And thanks for the chance.'

4

Thanks to winter storm damage to the castle, poor Olivia hadn't felt like celebrating her birthday back in April. Even though Brodie had tried to cajole her into it, she'd had too much on her mind. So, at the end of the second week in June, Brodie and Olivia returned from their few days away – a belated twenty-ninth birthday treat for Olivia – just in time for the *Birthday Bash* Brodie had insisted he was throwing for her.

Brodie had made all the arrangements prior to whisking Olivia away and he had asked for the long gallery to be set out with tables and chairs in readiness for their return. He had even hired in a catering team so Mirren could have the night to enjoy herself and had sent out invites to as many of Olivia's friends as he could.

He had organised live music in the shape of a local band who were, to use his words, *stonking*. And he had organised her favourite traditional Scottish food – haggis, neeps and tatties but with a twist – plus plenty of single malt.

* * *

The long gallery was decked out like a high-end party venue and Bella was excited to see it looking so incredible; a glimpse of what the future held for the beloved castle. Fairy lights were strung around the potted trees edging the room and each table was lit with candles and had a MacBain Tartan table runner. Bella was impressed with Brodie's organisational skills to say the least and only a tiny bit envious of her best friend.

After she had eaten more than her fair share of haggis bon bons, Bella let her gaze scan the room. Mirren and Dougie were chatting with Olivia's Uncle Innes by the buffet table and the rest of the grounds team were already sitting around a table together. Kerr was standing, whisky glass in hand, with Adaira as she appeared to be telling him an intriguing story by the look of concentration on his face. Things were clearly still 'on' between them.

Bella stood with her friends, Skye and Ben, as they sipped their drinks and enjoyed the atmosphere bringing the gallery to life. Olivia joined them and linked arms with Bella as Brodie took to the stage.

'Ladies and gents, can I have your attention, please!' Brodie called out over the PA system. 'I want to thank yous all for coming tonight. As you all know, things were a bit fraught around Olivia's birthday in April, so we had a very quiet celebration. But I want my girl to have the party she deserves! So happy belated birthday, Liv!' Everyone lifted their glasses and toasted Olivia. 'Annnnd, it's also selfish because I've been looking forward to a really good knees-up. So, I'd like to introduce you to this evening's entertainment. But you'd better be on your best behaviour because they're all officers of the law! Please give a warm Drumblair welcome to Copper-caillie!'

The gathered crowd of friends and family whooped and cheered as four men and one woman took to the stage. 'Cheers,

Brodie, evening, everyone,' a bearded man holding a violin and bow said at the mic. 'I'm Harris and I'll be your MC tonight. We've got Melanie on keyboards, Bruce on the bodhran, Craig on the guitar, Gordy on the accordion and whistle, and yours truly on the fiddle.' Everyone applauded and Bella's eyes widened in shock. It was the policeman her gran had tried to set her up with. He looked completely different up there. He continued, 'Now, we'd usually be doing a ceilidh but instead, tonight we're sticking to rock and pop tunes for a change, as per Brodie's request. So, while yous all chat and drink, we're going to kick things off with a wee gentle one. It'll sound a bit different to the original but hopefully you'll enjoy it. Taking the lead on vocals for this one is our keyboard player Mel, AKA PC Sherburn.' Everyone applauded and Mel took a bow. 'This one is Fleetwood Mac's "Gypsy".' Another round of applause ensued.

Bella tugged on Olivia's sleeve. 'That's the policeman my granny keeps trying to set me up with!'

Olivia squinted. 'Which one?'

'The beardy one at the microphone!'

Olivia grinned. 'Ooh, he's handsome, why *won't* you go on a date with him?'

Bella scoffed. 'I'm not being set up by my eighty-five-year-old granny.'

Skye leaned in. 'Why not if he's a catch?'

Bella scrunched her nose. 'He's not my type. I'm not into beards.'

Olivia rolled her eyes. 'You're being picky. I think he's got kind eyes.'

Skye fluttered her eyelids. 'Yes, he has. Like Ben.'

'Ugh, you two,' Bella said with a shake of her head and a roll of her eyes. 'You're as bad as my granny. It's a good thing she's not here tonight or I can imagine the three of you sitting in a corner planning my wedding to a man I don't even want to date. You'd be like the three witches from that bloody Shakespeare play. Anyway, I'll leave you to swoon over PC Plod; I'm off for some more wine.' She huffed, turned and left them.

As she stood watching the band from a safe distance, Kerr appeared beside her. The band was playing a Proclaimers number now, and the audience were, of course, singing along. Mirren and Dougie were on the dancefloor along with Innes and one of the gardeners who had been there as long as Bella had been coming to the castle. It was turning into a fun night and a great belated birthday party for Olivia.

'They're great, aren't they?' Kerr said, nodding towards the stage.

'I suppose they are, yes,' Bella replied as she watched Harris, the sergeant, grinning and stamping his foot as his fingertips deftly danced along the neck of the instrument resting on his shoulder. There was something innately fascinating about a man who had musical talent. She watched his hands moving with intrigue and was surprised to hear his singing voice was as good as his fiddle playing. She had only seen Harris from a distance at the day centre when he had been there to visit his mother, but he was certainly gifted, although she wouldn't be voicing her thoughts to her granny; that fire needed no more fuel.

'Brodie's good for Olivia, isn't he?' Kerr asked out of the blue; the question felt somewhat rhetorical.

Bella glanced at Kerr. 'He is. You should be happy she's found someone who loves her like he does.'

Kerr nodded and clenched his jaw. Without looking at her, he said, 'It's all most of us ever want.' And with those uncharacteristically philosophical words, he pushed off the wall where he was leaning and walked away.

5

Summer at Drumblair Castle was a sight to behold. The trees were filled with lush green leaves and the grounds were awash with a sea of colour. The gardeners did an incredible job at planting and maintaining the gardens, the beds were bursting with blooms, and even when it rained, the droplets of water simply added to the beauty, appearing like tiny diamonds on the petals.

After thinking things through over and over about Kerr, Olivia and the invitation list, Bella decided it would probably be a good thing for him to be seen doing something supportive without being cajoled into it. Hopefully when Olivia found out how helpful he had been, things between her and her brother would take one more step towards healing, and if Bella could be instrumental in that, she felt it had to be the right decision.

The siblings had never been close and it had always saddened Olivia. She had tried so hard to have a relationship with Kerr, but he'd harboured jealousy for such a long time and her inheritance hadn't helped matters, but now Kerr was trying to make amends, Bella wanted to help – for Olivia's sake.

Kerr had already started on his journey to be better; he had assisted Olivia in sorting through their parents' belongings and paperwork, he had met the new staff and chatted to them about the history of the castle. He'd been friendlier towards Bella too when he'd been around, making cups of coffee when she was working, holding doors open when he saw her with arms full of paperwork. It appeared he had finally got the message and a weight had been lifted from her shoulders.

Bella had – still with a little trepidation – handed the guest list over to Kerr while she dealt with other pressing matters around the castle from enquiries about the open day, to acquiring raffle prizes for the event, to staff training. She checked in regularly to ensure everything was on track and was told the same thing repeatedly: 'You can trust me, Bella. Everything is going exactly as it should be. I'm doing this for my sister, and for you... my friend.' She couldn't help noticing the sadness in his expression when he called her that.

* * *

With so much going on at the castle, Bella was frazzled, arriving home tired out and ready for sleep by seven in the evening. Her granny was understandably worried about her burning the candle at both ends but Bella did her best to assure her it was temporary and she really was fine.

Olivia had spent less time doing 'castle stuff' and had spent more time with the seamstresses and models when she wasn't with Brodie, preparing her segment of the corporate launch event. She was even more in love with Brodie than she had been they'd gone away and had reported on her return that his divorce was on track. Bella guessed it was only a matter of time before there would be another castle wedding. But in the meantime, they had an event to organise. An event that would showcase the castle and its potential as a venue for meetings, training days and team building as well as a wonderful place for a day out with the family. And even though there would no doubt be a substantial financial outlay, Olivia had insisted you had to speculate to accumulate. And the expense had been drastically reduced now Nina Picarro and her team from New York were not attending.

The stage crew would be here early on 26 June to set up. Brodie had arranged a local band to perform to show the versatility of the castle and an outside catering crew had been arranged by Mirren, who would be overseeing the food service. There would also be a castle tour given by Olivia herself, where she would tell the attendees all about the gift shop, café and children's play area that would be in place for visitors to the castle when it opened to the public. There were lots of pieces to this puzzle and they all needed to fit together perfectly for the whole evening to be a success.

The week of the corporate event arrived all too quickly, and in a blink of an eye the castle was bustling with people setting things up. A team of people arrived to construct Olivia's runway in the castle's beautiful long gallery and one end had been separated off with curtains to act as a dressing room. Rows of chairs had been brought in especially and placed facing the runway, which would also double as a stage for the local band Brodie had booked; sadly Coppercaillie weren't available due to their day jobs. A crew of electricians worked on installing temporary lighting to spotlight the models in Olivia's fashion show, where she would be showcasing her Drumblair Tartan designs. It looked totally different to the night of Olivia's birthday party, proving how versatile it would be as a venue.

* * *

On the morning of the fashion show, Bella was up, showered and
dressed early. Isla was sitting in her chair by the window watching
people going about their daily routines, with Beau at her feet. The
dog jumped up to greet her, tail wagging and eyes bright.

'Morning, Beau,' Bella said as she scratched the dog behind his
ears. 'And morning, Granny.'

'I've made a pot of tea and a pan of porridge, hen. You should
eat before you leave. You need to keep your energy up.'

'Tea is fine, Granny, but I'll take it to go in my travel mug if you
don't mind, I don't have time to sit and eat now. I'll grab something
at the castle, I promise.' She kissed her granny's cheek and dashed
out of the door.

Bella arrived at the castle earlier than usual. She had insisted
to Olivia she would be there to help with the last-minute preparations, even though Olivia had tried to encourage her to sleep in
and rest.

Olivia was definitely stressed but it was a happy kind of
stressed, Bella decided; her best friend was in her element. Olivia's
own Drumblair Tartan designs were absolutely stunning and Bella
watched with a proud smile as Olivia buzzed around models at the
final fitting, ensuring every sliver of fabric hung right. It had to be
perfect, Bella was very much aware of this fact. It would mark the
beginning of Drumblair Castle coming into its own as a venue, a
tourist attraction and a retreat destination. Olivia's legacy and
future hung on this and Bella was determined to help it be everything Olivia wanted.

The atmosphere was electric and even though Bella was
exhausted, she was the happiest she had ever been. Not only was
she working at a stunning, dream location for her best friend but
she'd had a hand in creating the wonderful setting people would

enjoy for years to come. It was now simply a matter of everything falling into place.

As Bella walked through the long gallery, sidestepping people with clipboards, walkie talkies and mobile phones, she glanced up at the portraits that seemed to be watching everything unfolding with guarded interest and she wondered what they would say if they could speak.

* * *

The guests would begin arriving at five in the afternoon and would be served with canapés and Champagne. This would be followed by a tour of the castle at 5.30 p.m. to show off all the work that had been carried out to prepare for the public opening and finally the fashion show would take place at 6.30, followed by live music by the local band who, as it turned out, Brodie had convinced to play for free seeing as the local and national press were to be attending.

Bella had never realised how much work went into to putting on a corporate publicity event and was relieved the majority of her tasks were already complete. She was excited and looking forward to watching the models parading down the runway in Olivia's wonderful designs, and to breathing a sigh of relief when it was all a massive success. Because, again, *it had to be.*

At four o'clock, Bella closed the door on the library and changed into a black slim-fitting dress that hugged her curves. She applied make-up and tidied up her blonde waves. A glance in the large over-mantel mirror showed her neatly presented and fresh-looking in spite of the sleepless nights she'd had in the run-up to the event. She took a deep, calming breath before leaving and making her way to the long gallery for one last check.

The long gallery had been completely transformed. Pedestals topped with vases of fresh flowers sat around the room, their gentle fragrances floating through the air and their bursts of colour complementing the old artwork adorning the walls. The shimmering white fabric backdrop of the stage was seamless and looked like it had always been there.

Welcome to Drumblair Castle

was being projected from a booth at the opposite end of the gallery and calming classical music played from well-hidden speakers. A buzz of excitement vibrated through the air and Bella could feel her nerves jangling.

'Doesn't this look incredible?' Olivia said as she arrived beside her.

'It's stunning, Olivia. You must be over the moon,' Bella said as she hugged her best friend.

'I'm just sad that Nina and her crew couldn't be here,' Olivia said, her eyes momentarily filled with sadness. 'Especially Harper.' Harper was Olivia's New York bestie and flat mate when she'd lived in the Big Apple and Bella knew how much she missed her.

Bella squeezed Olivia's hand. 'I'm sure she'll come over as soon as she can.'

Olivia inhaled deeply and smiled. 'I'm sure she will too.' She turned to Bella. 'This evening is so important, and you've worked so hard. I'm guessing everyone RSVP'd to the invites? I'm sorry I dumped that on you and just left you to get on with it, but I knew you'd do an amazing job. I bet we're going to have a full house.'

Bella forced a smile but didn't admit she hadn't been able to check the RSVPs because Kerr had handled it all, and every time she had tried to check in with him, he had sulked and given her puppy-dog eyes while commenting she didn't trust him. 'Yes, I bet,' was all she managed to say.

Mirren appeared in the doorway. 'Lady Olivia, I think some of the guests have arrived early. Would you like me to show them through to the dining room?'

Relief flooded Bella's body like a wave of hot water. People were early! Kerr had done his job well. She made a mental note to thank him for his help and, of course, apologise for doubting him.

'Oh gosh, that's eager! I'll be right there,' Olivia said, beaming. She turned back to Bella and grappled her into a hug. 'I honestly don't know what I would do without you.' And with that she kissed Bella on both cheeks and left the long gallery. Bella allowed a flutter of excitement to replace the worry.

6

Bella arrived outside the dining room doors at 5.20 and was about to enter when Mirren opened the door from inside. A distinct crease of worry furrowed her brow and her face was pale.

'Mirren? Is everything okay?' she asked, glancing past the housekeeper and into the dining room. 'You look like you've seen a ghost.'

Mirren shook her head. 'Lady Olivia is getting really worried. No one has arrived yet. She asked me to come and find you to check over the RSVP list. She's worrying she made some ridiculous mistake on the date.'

Confusion washed over Bella. 'But... you said guests had arrived early.'

'Aye, but only the staff, Skye and her fiancé Ben, Innes and your granny. No one else is here yet, none of the businesses or press and it's gone five. She's thinking people aren't coming. She's beside herself, the poor wee lamb. I was coming to look for you so you could reassure her about the RSVPs.'

Bella's stomach plummeted to the floor and she felt the colour drain from her own face. She steadied herself on the door jamb. 'But... I don't understand.'

'No, neither does Olivia. She knows you'll have done everything right but she's worried people aren't interested and she's thinking maybe she invited the wrong folks.'

Bella forced a smile. 'No, that can't be the case. Leave it with me.' She turned and dashed off to the library, where she took her phone from her handbag and dialled Kerr's number. There was no reply.

Shit, shit, shitty shit. As she paced the room, anger bubbled up inside her, all aimed directly at herself, for having the stupidity to hand over such an important task to someone with a less than perfect reputation. Why had she insisted on seeing the best in him? She tried Kerr's number again but once again there was no reply. She rifled through her emails to locate the list she had forwarded to him and decided she would begin calling around to each and every number. It was the least she could do, seeing as this was entirely her fault.

* * *

The door opened and Kerr wandered in like he hadn't just ruined Olivia's event. He nonchalantly sauntered over to her and gave a long whistle. 'Well, look at you, I could eat you right up in that dress,' he said before flicking his tongue out to skim his lips lasciviously.

'Kerr, what the hell have you done?' Bella blurted.

He shrugged but his face remained expressionless. 'I'm not sure I know what you mean.'

Bella took a deep breath as she tried to compose herself. 'Of course you do! You promised me you'd help. You assured me I could trust you. What did you do about the invites? Did you even send them?'

He smirked. 'Whoops, there may have been a glitch in the space-time continuum, and they got lost in the black hole of the internet.'

Her skin prickled and her eyes welled with angry tears. 'You did this on purpose,' she whispered, half in disbelief and half with the sad and disturbing realisation he hadn't changed at all. 'This was sabotage, wasn't it?'

He stared at her with one eyebrow raised. 'Maybe you'll think twice about messing me around in future,' he replied with a curl of his lip. 'And maybe my darling sister will realise she can't just invite strangers into our family home! *My* home. It's all rightfully mine!'

Bella's stomach knotted with guilt and shame at what she had allowed to happen to her best friend. 'How could you *do* this? You said you were fine with being friends. You said you wanted to help, to make amends with your sister.'

He snickered. 'You believe people too easily; always giving them the benefit of the doubt, even after you've unceremoniously dumped them for no reason.'

Before he could continue, Olivia cleared her throat, making her presence known from the doorway. Bella glanced over with a gasp to find her surrounded by the only guests to have arrived. Among them, the ground staff, Granny Isla, Uncle Innes and Bella's parents.

Olivia's face was ashen and her eyes glassy. She stared at Bella. 'You and Kerr? *He* was your secret relationship?' Her lower lip trembled. 'That's why you wouldn't tell me?'

Realising how this must now look, Bella lurched forward, pleading with her best friend, 'Oh god, Olivia, please let me explain!'

Olivia took a step back and held up her hand. 'No! Were you in on this together? Did you both plan this?' Olivia asked in a small, quivering voice. 'Did you both want to see me fail so badly?'

Kerr grimaced. 'This is not your castle! It's mine. Mum can't have been in her right mind leaving it all to you! It should be me deciding the future, not you!' he bellowed at Olivia. 'And she was just collateral damage. She shouldn't have messed me around,' he said with a derisory nod towards Bella; his callous manner caused her to flinch. He turned his attention on Bella again. 'I warned you I didn't like being told no.'

Bella slowly shook her head as tears spilled over from her eyes. 'How could you do this to your own sister? You could've left her out of this.'

He glanced around at the silent group of spectators, his chest puffed up with pride at his own apparent cleverness and he shrugged as his focus landed once again on Bella. 'I could've left *her* out of this? She stole my inheritance! And you dumped me. No one dumps me. Especially not some jumped-up secretary who just happens to be good at decorating.'

Bella covered her heart with her hand and gasped as if he had slapped her. But before she could retaliate, there was a loud growl and Isla stormed forward, swung her handbag which connected with Kerr's cheek with a sonorous thwack, before she proceeded to yell, 'Don't you dare speak to my Bella like that, you *lavvy-heided* walloper!'

There was a split second of astonished silence before Bella's dad shouted, 'Yes! Well bloody said, Mum!' and began to bang his hands together. 'It's a good thing she got to you first, you spoilt brat.' The other staff and Bella's friends joined in with the applause as several of the models and members of the band turned up to see what the commotion was.

Kerr stood rubbing the fuchsia-coloured patch on his cheek, his eyes widely, psychotically glaring in disbelief at Isla; a silent, raging stunned stupor. 'I'll sue! You stupid old hag!' he shouted, which didn't seem to help his case.

When the applause had died down, Bella walked towards Olivia and took both of her hands. More tears spilled onto her cheeks, blurring her vision. 'I'm so, so sorry, Olivia. I know you won't be able to forgive me, and I can't say I blame you. But please know I didn't do any of this intentionally. I was stupid enough to believe him when he said he wanted to help. That he wanted to prove to you he'd changed and wanted to see you succeed. I can't believe I was ever sucked in by him. And I'll never forgive myself. He's a bitter, jealous, twisted man and I honestly don't know what I ever saw in him.'

Kerr scoffed. 'What? Because I didn't send a load of invites to dumb people inviting them to a stupid fashion show in my own home? A home that's about to be turned into a bloody circus? I've been forced to fund myself when I'm the true heir and everyone knows it!'

Bella's nostrils flared and her eyes widened. 'Shut up, you pathetic excuse for a man,' she said through gritted teeth. '*You* have funded jack all! You've manipulated me *and* Adaira and it's gone on long enough. I think I'll be setting her straight on a few things after what you've done and the hurt and pain you've caused. I'm angry I ever saw good in you, and I feel so badly for that poor woman, funding your gambling habit while you treated her like a cash cow. I'm done with you. Don't you ever so much as speak to, look at, or come near me again, do you hear?'

Kerr turned his head slowly, studying every expression staring at him. 'Don't worry, I deserve so much better than you. I'm supposed to be laird of this damned castle. Me! And in spite of what you think your stories will do to Adaira, she'll still love me. She'll still be loyal. Unlike you.'

'Oh no, she won't,' came a voice from the back of the crowd of people and a composed Adaira, dressed in a classic black Chanel dress, pushed through the bodies to stand before him. Her face crumpled with disgust, and she slapped his other cheek, the smack echoing around the now silent library. She inhaled a deep breath and shut her eyes for a split second before she smoothed down her dress and informed him calmly, 'I think deep down I've known for a very long time you're a lying, cheating bastard. And the sooner you're out of my life, the better. You had better tell your tenants at Drumblair Villa they need to leave so you can move back in, because you're no longer welcome in my home.' And with that, she turned on her heels and stormed out.

7

Bella couldn't believe what was happening. Her heart thumped so hard in her chest it was almost painful. After all the – now known to be fake – attempts to make amends, Kerr had actually set out to ruin Olivia once again and had dragged Bella down in the process. How could she have been so utterly stupid? Especially when she knew he'd done his best to cause trouble for Olivia since the will reading. At that precise moment, she hated herself.

'What does Adaira mean by *the tenants at the villa*, Kerr?' Olivia asked.

He swung around and glared at her. Through gritted teeth, he growled, '*You* stopped giving me money, so I had to sublet it to pay my damned way! I had to move in with Adaira when you were back in New York.'

Bella gasped. 'Well, you kept that from me!'

Olivia shook her head and, as tears of anger and betrayal welled in her eyes, she told him, 'I suggest you do what Adaira says. Because you're no longer welcome in this castle either. Get out.'

Kerr's face contorted with rage. 'You can't throw me out of my family home! You have no right!' he screamed, stamping his foot like a petulant toddler.

Brodie and Dougie stepped forward and Brodie told him, 'Olivia won't be the one doing the throwing. You've sunk to an all-time low, Kerr. I suggest you leave, right now, pal.'

Kerr gave a low chuckle. 'Says the man who was beaten up by his own wife.'

Bella watched as Brodie's jaw clenched and unclenched. Innes placed a hand on his arm to get his attention and shook his head. 'He's not worth it.'

Kerr turned to Olivia. 'You should keep your guard dogs under control, sis.' He stuck out his bottom lip and feigned sadness as he addressed the crowd of people surrounding him. 'Such a shame this evening is all completely and utterly ruined, though. I was looking forward to seeing all the confused faces, watching as your skeletons walked up and down in their ridiculous shreds of tartan and lace, wondering what the hell you'd dragged them to.' He grinned and gave a humourless chuckle before he too walked out of the library, shoulder checking several people as he did so. Brodie, Dougie and Ben followed him, Bella presumed this was to make sure he actually left and did no further damage.

Once Kerr was gone, Olivia crumpled to the floor, sobbing. 'He's right, it's all ruined.'

Mirren rushed to her side and enveloped her in her arms as her body shuddered.

Bella lurched forward. 'No. It's not ruined. I have the list of guests. Is anyone willing to help me phone around and see who we can gather together?'

Olivia looked up at her. 'It's too late, Bella. Forget it.'

Innes walked across the room and stood by Bella. 'It's not ruined. We can still make this happen. It's 5.55 now, let's say it will take half an hour to call people if we all take a portion of the list.

We can do the house tour at 8 and the fashion show at 8.45 with the canapés and Champagne as people watch, then the buffet while the band plays their set. If we explain the situation, say a glitch in the new internet connection perhaps, I'm sure people will understand. We can say it's a casual affair, no need to dress up especially, less pressure that way.'

Olivia straightened up a little. 'You really think we can do this, Uncle Innes?'

He nodded. 'Absolutely!'

Bella nodded. 'And I think Innes is right; if a few of us chip in with the calls, we can do it. We have nothing to lose. We can at least try.'

Olivia's face brightened and she smiled. 'Okay, let's give it a go.'

Bella printed out the list and handed sections to Skye, Ben, Brodie, Mirren, and Innes, keeping the last section for herself. Olivia went to revisit the running order of the show and see if anything would need to be changed. Everyone with a list went off to find a quiet corner in which to make their calls, but before Olivia left the library, Bella stood before her again.

A multitude of emotions vied for dominance within her as Olivia narrowed her eyes. 'Honestly, Bella, what were you thinking? You know what Kerr's like. You've witnessed what a shit he can be and you still fell for him?'

Bella shook her head. 'I promise I didn't fall for him. It wasn't anything as deep as that and I knew you'd hate it, that's why I ended things.'

Olivia sighed and closed her eyes briefly. 'But you could have fallen for him, then what? I genuinely can't believe you even contemplated a relationship with that cruel, heartless narcissist.'

'I know, and I'm so sorry.' Bella swiped away tears as they fell at pace down her cheeks.

Olivia shook her head. 'I'm not upset with you for dating him, however briefly it may have been, I'm upset you kept it from me but more than that, I'm upset you didn't think of yourself and what he would do to you. He isn't worthy of you, Bells. You deserve better and he's my brother so I know what I'm talking about.'

Bella simply nodded.

'But then again, I allowed him to be here too. I believed his lies so I'm just as much at fault.'

Bella sniffed. 'I'm 100 per cent sure he was only using me when I look back. I feel so stupid.' Her chin trembled. 'Everyone must think I'm an idiot.'

Olivia softened. 'No one thinks that. They all care for you and know he's a manipulative swine.'

With regret knotting her insides, Bella said, 'I'm so sorry, Olivia. Everything you've said is true and I'm sure you want to fire me after all this, but instead, I'd like to offer you my resignation, effective after the fashion show.' Her lip quivered. 'I'm ashamed at how stupid I've been. And I'm so very sorry for betraying you. I promise it wasn't deliberate. I convinced myself Kerr was actually a decent human being. I couldn't have been more wrong, and I hope you can somehow find it in your heart to forgive me someday, even though I don't deserve it. You're one of the best people I know, and I've been so lucky to have you in my life.'

Olivia gave a small smile. 'I've dealt with my brother my whole life, Bells. I know how convincing he can be, he was the same when we were kids, sadly. But after how he's been behaving lately and the fact that we've been getting on so well, even *I* hoped he'd changed. I clung to that hope and waited for him to prove me right. Sadly, he couldn't do that. He fooled me too. And he didn't deserve you, Bella. You've adored him since you were a teenager and I've watched you pine over him for so long I dreaded this day happening. But I honestly hoped you'd see him for what he is before he got his claws into you.'

Bella gulped and her stomach lurched. 'You knew?'

Olivia nodded and a smile crept onto her face. 'You didn't hide it as well as you thought. The fact you used to blush profusely every time he walked into the room was a bit of a giveaway.' Her smile faded. 'But I really hoped he'd leave you alone. I could tell he was aware of your feelings, too, but I knew he'd hurt you. It's as if he waited until he could make the worst impact. I suppose he's not capable of being decent after all. He has to twist and spoil everything; he always has. Let's not allow him to do that to our friendship, though, okay?'

Bella shook her head as more tears cascaded down her face. 'Of course not. And I'll stay until you find someone to replace me if that helps.'

Olivia squeezed her hands. 'Do you really want to leave? Is that what'll make this whole debacle easier for you? I mean, I can understand you wanting to stay away from Kerr, but as far as I'm concerned, he isn't welcome here any more. So, is it what you really want?'

'No!' Bella sobbed.

Olivia smiled. 'Then I don't accept your resignation. You made a mistake. But so did I. And you've done so many amazing things here. I meant what I said when I told your granny I don't know what I would've done without you. But I also agree with her you deserve someone decent. And I'm afraid that's not my brother.'

Bella flung her arms around Olivia. 'Thank you! I love working here and I'd be devastated to leave. And I can assure you I'm off relationships for a very long bloody time.'

Olivia hugged her tightly. 'Don't say that. But maybe let me vet the next guy.' They both giggled and Bella's shoulders relaxed.

8

At 7.50 p.m., Bella stood at the entrance to the castle and watched as the last few guests arrived. Not everyone could make it at such short notice on a Monday evening, but Bella was pleasantly surprised and relieved so many had. The last few hours had been draining to say the least, both physically and emotionally.

As they arrived, the guests were ushered into the long gallery, ready for Olivia to give a welcome speech. Bella stood at the back of the room with her granny holding her hand and smiling up at her reassuringly. There were local press officers, business owners, bloggers and local social media influencers in the audience; slightly fewer than had been originally planned but more than Bella could've hoped for under the circumstances.

All eyes turned to Olivia. 'It's so wonderful to see so many of you here and I can't thank you enough for taking time out of your evenings at such short notice. I know my team explained the situation and I can assure you all this kind of thing will not happen again.' She glanced around the height of the room and held her hands out at her sides. 'With that said, I would like to welcome you all to Drumblair Castle.'

Applause ensued and Bella watched as Olivia's shoulders visibly relaxed. She continued, 'You are here to witness a new phase in the life of this historic building. First, you'll be taken on a tour of the castle, followed by a fashion show of my own Drumblair Tartan designs and finishing off with the amazing local band Fire in the Middle!' Cheers and whoops followed.

'This evening will showcase the very best Drumblair has to offer as an event destination, a retreat and a visitor attraction. But first, a wee bit of history. The MacBain clan came from Lochaber and settled here hundreds of years ago in the fourteenth century and Drumblair Castle has had a MacBain at the helm ever since. It's said the Bonnie Prince himself was holed up here before the Jacobite uprising, making plans for taking back the throne he saw as rightfully his. It's also said that Drumblair remained a stronghold for supporters of the Stuart line even long after Culloden. The honour of being warden to this stunning piece of architecture now lands with me. My mother and father loved this place so much and they knew it needed to move with the times for its legacy to remain intact. Opening the place to the public was a difficult and scary decision, one that wasn't met with positivity from everyone, sadly, but it was necessary. Without such steps, the place would have eventually crumbled, and I know for a fact my parents would've been heartbroken if that had happened. So this is my phase... *our* phase of Drumblair. And I very much hope you can see the potential as I can. Please enjoy.'

Applause rang out around the long gallery louder than before, and Bella released her hand from her granny's as they both joined in with the standing ovation. The gathered people were split into groups and each group followed its guide for a tour of the MacBain family home. Mirren, Dougie, Brodie and Olivia all led off in different directions and Bella felt her knees weaken as relief flooded her once more.

'Are you all right, hen?' Isla asked, cupping her cheek. 'You've gone *awfy* pale.'

Bella nodded, covering her granny's hand with her own. 'I think so. I'm angry with myself for letting my heart rule my head. It won't happen again. That's it now.' She meant it with every fibre of her being.

Isla gave a sad smile. 'Arabella Douglas, you absolutely don't *need* a man in your life, that much is so true. You're a modern lassie, for sure; independent and all that and you don't ever have to lose yourself. But don't close your heart off to the possibility of genuine love, dearie. Kermit wasn't genuine. I don't think he's an ounce of decency in his whole body.'

Bella widened her eyes. 'I should have listened to you.'

Isla nodded. 'Aye, well, I suppose there comes a time when you have to learn from your own mistakes. It's what makes you a better person, so they say. I tend to trust my gut feelings; they don't usually steer me wrong.' There was a thoughtful pause when Isla seemed to drift off a little. But within seconds, she was back on her train of thought. 'Now, speaking of love, I met your grandpa Caelan when I least expected it. I'd had my heart broken by a scoundrel who had messed me around and I was like you, I'd had enough. But your grandad was the perfect gentleman. Didn't play games. Treated me with respect. And I fell head over heels in love in spite of myself. That's what I wish for you. Your grandad was no looker like Tom Jones, or poet like Lewis Capaldi with his words, but he always put me first. That's what I want for you, someone to share your beautiful life and heart with. And I'm sure it'll happen someday, if you let it.'

Bella chewed her lip. 'But with that kind of love comes the possibility of getting hurt again, Granny. And if not that, the pain of loss, eventually. I'm not sure I can cope with that. I'm not as strong as you.'

Isla's eyes brightened. 'I miss your grandad more than words can express but I wouldn't change a thing, not even now he's gone. We had fifty-five years of happy marriage and I laughed so much and loved so deeply in those years. The pain of losing him is nothing compared to the joy of loving him.'

Bella realised her chin was wobbling on hearing her granny's heartfelt words and she reached out to hug her tightly. She missed Grandpa Caelan desperately too but couldn't imagine the pain of loving someone for so long and then losing them like Isla had. But hearing her granny speak of joy in that way sparked a little flame of hope inside Bella that she knew she would have to remember and cling to if she was to dare to give her heart away again.

9

The tours had been a huge success and the atmosphere in the place was electric with excited chatter. Once the fashion show was in full swing, and Bon Jovi's 'You Give Love a Bad Name' reverberated through the hidden speakers and around the room, both male and female models paraded down the runway dressed in Olivia's stunning designs. Next Simple Minds' 'Don't You (Forget About Me)' played over the sound system, in keeping with the eighties-inspired creations which were sometimes outlandish but completely unique; Olivia's style and creativity there for all to see. While the local TV station hadn't been able to attend, there were press photographers and social media influencers snapping away on both sides of the runway.

Bella could see Olivia's face was flushed as she stood with her hands clasped nervously in front of her, whereas Brodie beamed with pride from the opposite side of the room as he whistled and banged his hands together to show his appreciation for her work.

Bella was delighted, not only for the success of the show but for knowing they had proved Kerr completely wrong and had scuppered his latest attempt at ruining things for Olivia. One thing was certain in Bella's mind: now Olivia had very little related family left, the one she had chosen for herself was as solid a foundation as the stone that formed the heart of Drumblair.

* * *

At the end of the evening, as people filed out, Bella watched from a distance as Olivia was congratulated over and over and told multiple times by various people they'd be in touch about hosting events at the castle. A local journalist interviewed her briefly, holding up an old-fashioned tape recorder to catch Olivia's enthusiasm for a piece in the *Inverness Courier*.

When the last guest had gone, Bella hung back and watched as Brodie wrapped Olivia in his arms. 'How are you doing?' she heard him ask.

Olivia shook her head and burst into tears. Seeing that brought a lump to Bella's throat and she walked away. The reality of the whole evening was finally sinking in and while Bella was grateful that Brodie instinctively knew Olivia needed him, she couldn't help feeling utterly responsible for her best friend's tears.

* * *

Even though the evening had ultimately been a success, Bella couldn't help berating herself. At the end of the night, she chatted briefly with Adaira and apologised for the situation with Kerr.

'Don't worry, Arabella, dear. I was a fool to think he was actually interested in me. I shudder when I think of the nights we spent together. What must have been going through his mind?'

Bella gulped at hearing their relationship was deeper than he had admitted. 'I'm so sorry. He... he told me you weren't really together in that way.'

Adaira gave a small, crestfallen smile. 'Of course he did,' she replied before walking to her waiting taxi.

Bella was riddled with so much guilt for so many reasons. A knot had formed in her stomach and wouldn't loosen.

Her granny arrived by her side. 'Come on, the taxi's here, hen, you can leave Fifi here for the night,' she said, patting her arm. 'And stop it.'

Bella scowled at her perceptive granny. 'Stop what?'

Isla wagged a finger. 'I can see the cogs whirring in that *heid* of yours. It's done and finished. You didn't spoil everything, even though that's what you're telling yoursel'. I chatted to Olivia earlier and she's worried about you. She doesn't want you to feel bad. She knows none of this was deliberate on your part.'

Bella smiled in spite of the stinging sensation behind her eyes. 'Thanks, Granny.' She followed Isla to the exit. 'Actually, I'm going to say goodbye to Liv. See if she needs me to stay and help tidy up.' Isla nodded.

Bella found Olivia and Brodie were still in the long gallery, sitting on the chairs that faced the runway. Olivia was still crying and that hard ball of emotion knotted Bella's stomach even tighter.

Brodie released Olivia and whispered something before gesturing at the exit. He smiled at Bella and gave a small wink and a nod, as if to say everything was okay, before he stood and left the room.

Olivia turned and quickly wiped at her eyes. 'Hey, you. I'm glad I've seen you before you leave for the night.'

Bella approached her slowly, warily. 'Olivia, I just wanted to tell you again how sorry I am.' She began to sob, all the guilt she was feeling that had eaten her up for so long poured out all over again.

Olivia pulled her into an embrace. 'Hey, shhh, it's okay, Bells. Honestly. I'm not crying because of you. I'm exhausted, that's all, and emotional over Mum and Dad,' she said. 'And the fact that even though Kerr's my only remaining family apart from Uncle Innes, he is nothing like how a brother should be. My mum and dad would be heartbroken if they could see what was going on with us. That's what hurts the most. He and I should be comforting each other, supporting each other.' She shook her head. 'It's like having no brother at all but a mortal enemy. I have no clue how we got here.' She held Bella at arm's length. 'We're absolutely fine, you and me, okay? I'm being totally honest with you. So let's forget all about it and get back to being us, okay? You're the family I choose.'

Bella nodded and smiled before hugging Olivia tightly. 'What about tidying up?'

Olivia glanced at the room. 'That's waiting until everyone's had a long sleep in and a good breakfast. Now go home and get some rest. I need you beside me at this place.'

Hearing Olivia say those words caused more tears to spill over at the same time as a wide smile spread across her face.

* * *

Bella re-joined her granny in front of the waiting taxi. 'I feel bad leaving Fifi here,' she informed her.

Isla rolled her eyes. 'It's a car, a tin can on wheels; it doesn't experience feelings of abandonment. Unlike my Beau, who'll be needing a pee. Danny next door has been to let him out but still...' She glanced at her watch.

Bella gasped. 'Tin can? Granny, I'll have you know Fifi's my pride and joy.' She sighed, drained from the events of the evening and the thought of sleep definitely appealed. 'But okay, you win. I'm too tired to argue.'

As the stonework of the castle, illuminated by floodlights, faded into the distance, Bella smiled, grateful for the second chance she had been given with Olivia.

10

Following the corporate launch event, bookings began to flood in for the use of the castle from businesses who had attended and from word of mouth; a mixture of awards ceremonies, weddings and other functions. A travelling theatre group even got in touch about hosting an open-air performance of *Romeo and Juliet* in early autumn.

Bella was in charge of the diary and was excited, and once again relieved, it was filling up fast. The pre-bookings for castle tours were already mounting up too and it was now only a matter of two weeks or so before the doors would be open to the public. It was such a relief to Bella to know she hadn't ruined the whole thing.

Kerr hadn't been seen since the night of the event; evidently, he had decided to do the right thing, for once, and keep a low profile. Or maybe there was some other reason for his silence; that was the scary thing with Kerr, you never could tell. Bella hadn't wanted to ask Olivia if she'd heard from him for fear of her getting the wrong idea about her enquiry.

Now the apartments were finished and the corporate launch

was done, Bella was making the most of her spare time, spending it with her granny. They had taken Beau on a few walks around the city and had even visited the castle grounds so Beau could play and roll around with Marley, and Brodie's younger dog, Wilf. It was such a joy to see them playing, their excited yips of delight echoing through the trees like the happy cries of children.

By 1 July, the opening day was creating a real buzz of excitement in Drumblair village according to the ground staff, most of whom were residents. Summer was in full swing and Bella was enjoying taking her lunch breaks down by the loch, where a cool breeze floated in off the surface of the water. And even though she was enjoying her involvement in the opening day preparations, her heart was still hankering after the excitement of being creative. She had hoped perhaps she would be called upon to carry out more interior design work when Olivia decided the cottages on the edge of the estate would make good holiday lets, but she wasn't asked, seeing as Olivia was up to her ears in interviewing and training new staff.

* * *

One morning, at the end of the second week in July, Bella was startled awake when she heard, 'No! No! Oh no!'

The panicked and distressed shouting coming from downstairs caused Bella's eyes to spring open and for her to jolt upright, her heart hammering at her ribs. The sun was beginning to peep through the crack in the curtains and a quick glance at her phone told her it was just after 5.30 in the morning, her granny's usual getting-up time. She dashed from her bed and grabbed her dressing gown, tugging it on as she hurried to the top of the stairs.

With a knot of dread churning in her stomach, she called out, 'Granny! What's wrong? Are you okay? Is Beau okay?' As she reached the bottom of the stairs, she came to a halt, immediately seeing the issue. The ground floor of the house was inches deep in ice-cold water.

Bella gasped and covered her mouth with one hand. 'Oh no! What the hell?'

Her granny appeared, her full-length nightgown tucked up into her knickers forming a kind of balloon around her crinkly knees, and her little canine friend was beside her, almost paddling, chest deep in the water. 'Aye, that's what I said too. I think it's a burst pipe or something, but I thought they only happened in winter. July is meant to be summer!'

Bella rolled up her pyjama bottoms and trudged through the icy water that took her breath away. She stood in the doorway to the lounge and assessed the devastation. The carpet was under water, as were the lower part of the sofa, the curtains and the boxes of photographs that were under the coffee table and that was just the lounge.

'My lovely things,' Isla said with a sob. 'All ruined.' She covered her mouth with her hand and leaned on the doorframe.

Bella walked over and picked up the photo boxes. 'Don't worry, Granny, we'll dry them out. I'm sure we can save some. It's amazing what can be done these days.' Seeing the pain in Granny Isla's eyes caused her throat to constrict. 'We'll save as much as we can, I promise.' Thoughts scrambled around her head, whirring at a hundred miles an hour. 'Okay, we need to call Dad.'

Granny Isla shook her head. 'We certainly don't need to do that. They're on their way to the cruise ship for their 1830 holiday.'

Bella shook her head. 'Eighteen-thirty? They're not going on an 1830 holiday. Those are for single people who are... well, between eighteen and thirty and want to get drunk and have se... and party.'

Isla's eyes widened. 'Oh! That's what it means? I thought that was just when the boats were built. That's a relief, I'm not sure I'd want to go on a boat that old.'

'No, they're going on a regular sightseeing cruise on a normal, relatively new boat, Granny.'

'Aye, well, whatever, you're not ringing your dad. Let him enjoy his holiday.'

Realising the responsibility was now on her, Bella thought aloud, 'Okay, so I need to contact the water board... and a plumber... and the insurance company. Come on back upstairs where it's warm and get dried off. Poor Beau must be freezing!' She tucked the photo boxes under one arm and held out her hand. Isla took it. 'Come on, Beau, you too, come on, lad,' she called to the bemused beagle. He didn't need much encouragement and skipped up the stairs but stopped to make sure Isla was following. Then he attempted a full body shake whilst precariously perched with his front paws on one step and his back ones on the step beneath. His long ears flapped all around his face as he shook, causing quite a draught.

Bella rubbed her hand up and down her granny's back. 'You go on upstairs, and I'll go and find the stop cock to turn off the water. I'll turn off the electric too to be safe. Then I'll call the water board emergency line.'

Once Isla was halfway up the stairs, she paused and glanced down at the flooded hallway, shook her head and placed a hand on either side of her ashen face. Worry creased her wrinkled skin further and her shoulders hunched. 'What are we going to do, Bella? Everything'll need replaced. Carpets, sofas, curtains... not to mention the cooker and fridge freezer.'

Bella smiled. 'Don't worry, Granny, it's all insured and we'll figure something out. We'll pack up the important stuff and bring it upstairs. We could go to Mum and Dad's until they get home from holiday but this is likely to take more than two weeks to sort out, so we might have to go to a hotel after that, but hopefully the insurance company will be able to help with the arrangements.'

Isla peered up at her, her eyelids drooping, and the corners of her mouth, usually turned up in mischief, were on this occasion pointing downwards. 'But I can't take Beau to a hotel, and I'll no' be parted from him, Bella, I'd rather live on the street.'

Bella rested her forehead on her granny's. 'We'll sort something, please don't worry.'

* * *

Bella fired off a brief text message to Olivia to let her know she would be late to the castle and would explain later, then once 9 a.m. rolled around, she began making the necessary calls to sort out their dire situation. Just over an hour later, as the sun seemed to be reluctantly hanging in the sky but hiding behind a heavy grey cloud, there was a water authority van parked outside and a friendly plumber inside the house trying to figure out what had caused the flood, how to get rid of the water and, most importantly, how to set about drying the place out.

Bella instructed Isla to pack some clothes and to get ready to leave the house. The insurance company had arranged a stay at a local budget hotel rather than staying at her parents' but, as suspected, Beau wasn't welcome. The insurance company had suggested booking him into a kennels to stay until the house was habitable again.

Isla was, not unexpectedly, horrified at that thought. 'But he'll miss us. I can't dump him with strangers for goodness knows how long, Bella, that's not fair,' she said as she ran her hands over the dog's smooth black and toffee-coloured back. 'He's never stayed at a kennels before. Not since I got him from the rescue centre. He'll think I'm giving him up.' As if on cue, Beau raised his head and stared at her with those big chocolate-brown eyes, filled with love. It appeared to cement her resolve. 'No, it's not going to work. I can't do it. We'll have to go your dad's until they come home.'

Bella sighed. 'But then what? Granny, Mum and Dad just don't have the space, I'm afraid. That's why I moved in with you, remember? It's only temporary, though. I'm sure he'll be fine at a kennels, won't you, Beau?' As if the dog understood, he rolled away so his back was facing her, and he gave a deep, dejected sigh.

'I'm just not happy about it, Bella. He'll think we've abandoned him. It'll break his little heart... and mine.' Isla's chin trembled.

Bella huffed. 'I know it's not ideal, Granny. And I promise I'll try to find somewhere that'll accept dogs so you can be reunited as soon as possible. In the meantime, I could ask if Beau can stay at the castle. He gets on well with Olivia and Brodie's dogs, Wilf and Marley, and I'm sure they'd have him for a while until we're sorted.'

Isla's face brightened. 'Oh, do you think so? That would be so much better. I'd be happier knowing he's with friends instead of in some shelter all by himself.'

Bella smiled. 'I'll see what I can do. We'll call at the castle on our way to the hotel and I'll speak to Olivia.'

Isla reached out to squeeze her hand. 'Thank you, hen. I don't know what I would do without you. Did they say how long it will be before we can move back home again?'

Bella shook her head. 'No, they can't tell at this stage. I think it'll depend on how long things take to dry out. But it could be a long while. We need to be prepared.'

It was Isla's turn to sigh now. 'My lovely home.'

Bella hugged her granny tightly. 'I know, Gran... I know.'

* * *

Bella, Isla and Beau arrived at the castle at noon. Heavy rain pounded at the lush green leaves on the oak trees lining the long driveway and the clouds overhead were still a strange grey colour that threatened a storm.

In inclement weather such as this, the castle took on a bleak eeriness to its façade, the likes of which wouldn't look out of place at a Halloween attraction. Bella wondered how on earth the original occupants, hundreds of years before, had coped with the cold on the inside when it matched that of the outside. There was evidence of fireplaces in most rooms but some of those rooms were vast, with lofty ceilings, which would have no doubt been very difficult to keep warm. She was certainly grateful for their modern heating system and other luxuries that meant the stone floor was warm to the touch now, instead of icy underfoot.

'Hi! Is everything okay?' Olivia asked as she stepped back to let them inside the large double doors of the castle. 'I've been so worried.' She hugged Bella and Isla before bending to stroke Beau. Marley and Wilf appeared from the direction of the kitchen, their fluffy, pale golden tails wagging and long pink tongues lolling as they greeted Beau like a long-lost brother.

Bella huffed through puffed cheeks. 'Where to begin? There's been a flood at Granny's caused by an eroded and cracked pipe. The ground floor is currently under several inches of water.'

'Aye,' Isla added, 'and I never did fancy an indoor pool. Definitely not one that's unheated anyway.' She chuckled.

Bella smiled, impressed at how her granny was handling the situation. 'Yes, it was a bit of a shock this morning.'

Olivia gasped. 'Oh, my word! That's terrible. Can I do anything to help?'

Bella winced. 'Actually, I was wondering if Beau could possibly stay with you here until things are sorted. He won't be any trouble.

I'm going to take Granny to the hotel the insurance company have booked so—'

Olivia's eyes widened. 'A hotel? You're having to move out? It's that bad?'

Isla folded her arms across her chest. 'Oh, aye, it's that bad and worse. My carpets are ruined. My kitchen might need replaced. The wiring too according to the water chappy.' Isla's voice wavered and Bella's heart lurched. *Okay, so maybe she's not handling it as well as I thought.*

'Oh, Isla, that's awful,' Olivia said. Then she suddenly held her hands up. 'Wait a minute! You have to move in to one of the new apartments! It's the perfect solution! There's plenty of room for you in the two-bedroom ones.'

Isla waved a dismissive hand. 'Och, I shall not, don't you be worrying about us, Lady Olivia dearie. Bella and I will be fine so long as we know little Beau is being looked after.'

Olivia placed her hands on her hips and tilted her head. 'Isla Douglas, you must call me Olivia, and you will not be setting foot in a hotel, not while there's perfectly good accommodation for you here. I won't hear of it. That way Beau can stay with you, and you don't have to worry about him.'

Isla's chin trembled and her eyes became glassy. 'You'd do that for us? But... what about your business? Your income?'

Olivia reached out and patted her arm. 'Don't you worry about that. We have that author moving into one of the flats towards the end of July, and the others are up for short-term rentals but they don't start until August and September, so it'll be fine. Please let me help you.'

Bella hugged Olivia. 'Thank you so much. You're an absolute lifesaver.'

Olivia's cheeks coloured. 'Don't be daft. And in future, please ask for help,' she told her in a half-joking, half-chastising manner.

Bella tucked her hair behind her ear nervously as she felt her face warming. 'I didn't like to after what happened with the Kerr thing.'

Olivia scoffed. 'Come on, Bella, I said that was forgotten, so why are you still dwelling on it?'

Bella shrugged. 'I just didn't want to put you out.'

'It's my pleasure, honestly. Now you know where the keys are. I've earmarked apartment one for our author guest as it's a one-bedroom, so why don't you take apartment two? And let me know if you need me to come and help you pick up more of your belongings. Or perhaps I can get Brodie to pick you up some shopping while he's out. He's just in Inverness collecting some large-print copies of his book for the gift shop.'

Bella hugged her friend once more. 'Don't trouble him with that. I can go after work. Now what's on the agenda today, boss?'

Olivia grinned. 'It's gift shop stock delivery day!' She clapped her hands excitedly. 'We only had limited stuff at the Christmas market event, so we've gone all out and have some amazing things to sell. Not long to go now!'

Bella's stomach flipped, Olivia's giddiness was contagious. 'I can't believe we're only a couple of weeks away from opening. It's been so fast and ridiculously slow at the same time.'

Olivia rolled her eyes. 'Tell me about it. Uncle Innes has been desperate to get the place open so he can showcase his finds. He's become an expert on local produce, bless his heart, and he's sourced some beer from the Black Isle Brewery across the bridge, some cheese from the Connage Highland Dairy, and some honey and artisan breads from Druid Temple Farm, so I think it's only fair we should have a tasting this evening. I thought I could gather all the new staff together seeing as they'll need to know what they're selling. What do you think?'

Bella beamed. 'Count me in!'

11

Bella and Isla walked across the cobbled courtyard in the old stable block beside the castle and Bella unlocked the door to apartment number two. She stepped inside, closely followed by her granny. This one had burgundy-coloured walls and cream paintwork with old oak flooring throughout, apart from the plush mink-coloured carpet in each of the bedrooms. More of Reid Mackinnon's artwork was displayed on the walls.

Isla sighed and shook her head. 'It really is stunning. I can't believe we get to live here for a wee while, Bella, in the grounds of a real-life castle. I feel like I'm fulfilling a dream that belonged to me when I was six.'

Bella smiled as she once again took in the scheme of décor she had chosen and had helped implement. A sense of pride washed over her. 'It is a bit like a dream. I suppose if anything good can come of the flood, this is it.'

Isla chuckled. 'I might refuse to leave when my house is dried out. I'll be too used to living in luxury. And it's all on one level, which is so helpful. The stairs were getting a bit much at home,' she said as her expression morphed into one of sadness.

Bella placed her arm around her granny's shoulders. 'I know. We might have to start thinking about a stair lift. Now would be a good time to get one fitted, you know, while we're out of the way.'

Isla shrugged off Bella's arm and turned to face her. 'You'll be putting me in a home next,' she said with a bony index finger randomly pointed towards the door. 'I'm fit as a fiddle apart from my dodgy knees, a bit of arthritis and cataracts, I'll have you know.'

Bella stifled a smile. 'Of course, Granny. And don't worry; I won't put you in an old folk's home. Not unless you decide you want to live in one.'

Isla folded her arms across her chest. 'Aye, well, that won't be happening any time soon. It'd ruin my love life.'

Bella's eyes widened. 'Granny, you don't have a love life.'

'And I don't want one either, at the moment. But if I did, I wouldn't want some *auld gadgie*. And that's alls I'd find in that place.'

Bella grinned. 'Oh, so you may be in the market for a younger man, eh, Granny? You dark horse, you.'

'Aye, well, like I said, not at the moment but who knows if Tom Jones comes calling? Or that Gerard Butler. He's a looker too.' Isla pondered that then added, 'I also like that Benadryl Cumberpatch from those superhero films I watched at the day centre. He's a handsome chap.'

Bella nodded, her lips pulled in to fight a smirk. 'Oh, aye, well, we live by a castle now, so who knows who we might encounter. I'll be keeping my eye on you, Isla Douglas.'

'Well, one of us should find love in a place like this, eh?' Isla winked mischievously.

Bella giggled. 'Absolutely. Look, you go unpack your things and I'll head over to the castle kitchen. I'll scrounge us something for lunch while you get settled.'

'Bless you, hen. And if you see that Benadryl chappy on your

way, you know where to send him.' She chuckled to herself as Bella
left the apartment.

* * *

Later that evening, Isla sat in the freshly decorated living room,
watching a period drama on the brand-new flat-screen TV, with
Beau curled up on his blanket at her feet. Mr Darcy had just
emerged, sopping wet, from a lake and, along with Elizabeth
Bennet, Isla was transfixed.

Bella had dressed in jeans and a patterned top that skimmed
her curves nicely and she felt good about herself. 'Are you sure you
don't want to come with me, Gran? We're tasting all the local
produce Innes has sourced for the castle gift shop. It should be
good.'

'Och, no, hen, you go on and have fun. I'm going to watch my
programmes and have a wee glass of the sherry that Brodie
dropped off earlier. He's such a sweet young man.' Olivia had
texted Brodie to inform him about Bella and Isla being their guests
for a while and without prompting he had called in on his return
from Inverness with a bag of goodies including chocolates, sherry,
wine and flowers.

'He certainly is. Well, if you're sure, I'd better get going. I won't
be too late.'

'Don't hurry home, dearie. I'll be fine.'

* * *

Bella arrived at the gift shop that was the former games room
when the castle had been modernised in the Georgian era, and
walked inside.

Thanks to lottery funding, staff had already been employed

and trained and a raft of volunteers had come forward from Drumblair village and the surrounding area to work as tour guides. They had all been invited to the tasting event.

'Bella! Come and get a drink. I can highly recommend the Red Kite ale,' Olivia said as she beamed at her from the shop counter, her cheeks a little flushed.

The shop was kitted out with oak shelving and glass cabinets. On the shelves were all manner of tartan gifts, soft toys, books and there was a refrigerated cabinet stacked with local cheeses, bottles of wine and beer. It had a wonderful quaint ambience like an olde worlde traditional shop and Bella felt sure people would be flocking to buy souvenirs once the castle was open to the public.

'This looks amazing now the shelves are stocked!' Bella said as she took in her surroundings. She walked with Olivia over to where the other guests had gathered around the counter and helped herself to a bottle of beer and a glass. 'Evening, everyone.'

Uncle Innes raised his glass. 'Ah, Bella, here's to you and your help getting the place running smoothly. The stable block apartments are spectacular.'

Bella felt her face heating. 'I'm glad you like them.'

Brodie slipped his arm around Olivia and said, 'Aye, you're missing a trick with such a talent for interior design.'

Olivia slapped his chest playfully. 'Don't be telling her that, she might want to leave!'

Brodie glanced at her, kissed her head and laughed. 'Sorry. Hey, Bella, I've got something for you.'

Bella scrunched her brow. 'You have?'

Brodie reached behind him and retrieved something from the countertop. 'Aye, your suggestions on the book were really useful. It's turned out grand.' He held out a copy towards her. 'This is a signed copy just for you.'

Bella grinned and took the book. 'Fantastic! Thank you so much.'

The inscription read:

To Bella, thanks for reading my garbled notes and encouraging me to keep going, Love Brodie

'You just need to submit it and get it published nationwide now,' she told him.

It was Brodie's turn to blush. 'Aye, well, we'll see about that.'

As well as Sadie, Duncan and Ailsa, the gift shop retail team, there were a lot of new faces amongst the people in attendance and Olivia took hold of Bella's hand and introduced her to them all. Bella smiled and shook hands with them in turn. 'Welcome aboard. It's a lovely place to work and I hope you'll be as happy here as I am.'

Olivia walked over to the door and opened it for Mirren, who had arrived with a platter of food, closely followed by Dougie, who held another. 'Come on, folks, get stuck in. I've made sandwiches; there's Scottish crowdie and oatcakes, shortbread, and all sorts of other stuff.'

Innes stepped forward. 'Much of this deliciousness is going to be sold in the shop and it's good for us to know what it all tastes like,' he said as he grabbed an oatcake and loaded it with the soft cheese.

Bella took a couple of finger sandwiches made from the artisan bread she'd been looking forward to and munched on them while Olivia went to mingle with some of the new volunteers, leaving Bella with the new retail team. The chatter was light-hearted and friendly and she could see why each of them had been employed.

A few moments later, Olivia came back over, a crease of worry crumpling her brow. 'Erm... Bella, I don't want to alarm you, but the police are here in the courtyard outside your apartment. Brodie has just had a notification from the security camera app on his phone. And I have no clue where my phone is.'

Bella's stomach plummeted and her blood ran cold. 'Oh, shit, Granny Isla.' She placed down her glass and dashed from the shop, fearing the absolute worst.

12

Bella ran as fast as she could along the freshly laid path, closely followed by Olivia, Brodie, Mirren and Innes. What was only a few hundred yards felt like a thousand as she picked up her pace. Panic clutched at her heart, causing it to thud against her ribs. What on earth had happened? Was her granny okay? The fact an ambulance wasn't mentioned was a little comfort, but that didn't mean one wasn't needed, did it? She couldn't bear the thought of anything happening to her granny. Her eyes began to sting.

Bella arrived in the courtyard by the apartments, out of breath, her head spinning and stomach churning, and sure enough, there were two police cars parked up, blocking the entry way, blue lights flashing. Bella rushed over to the front door of their temporary accommodation and saw a man dressed in black bundled up on the floor outside the door to apartment one, which was at a right angle to apartment two. His wrists were handcuffed behind his back and a female police officer with dark curly hair tied at the nape of her neck was pinning him down as three more looked on, one of whom was scribbling in a notepad. When the female police officer looked up, Bella recognised her as Mel, the keyboard player in Coppercaillie. Beau growled his displeasure from beside his owner where Isla stood in her doorway, arms folded across her chest and an expression of what could only be described as the utmost pride on her face.

Relief flooded Bella when she saw her. 'Granny! Oh, thank goodness you're okay!' She grappled Isla into a hug. 'What on earth is going on?'

Isla patted Bella's back reassuringly. 'Stop your fretting, hen, I'm fine.' She held her at arm's length. 'I just stopped a criminal in the act, that's all.' Beau gave a single bark as if agreeing with her.

'I've told you I'm not a criminal!' the man in black insisted from his prone position.

'Aye, well, why are ye skulking around at night outside the abode of two vulnerable women? I saw you through the peephole, young man,' Isla replied. Bella stared at her granny, as a small but significant dose of reality hit; vulnerable wasn't a word she had ever associated with the woman but maybe that was a mistake on her part. The fact she was feisty didn't mean she could protect herself. 'You look like a criminal all dressed in black,' Isla continued. 'The only other person who dresses like that and hangs about near women's houses usually brings chocolates, but I don't see any on you.' A rumbled snigger travelled through the small gathered group and Beau barked again in support of Isla.

Bella wasn't sure what to say. The man was a stranger, and he was, indeed, all dressed in black, which gave him a kind of cat burglar slash Milk Tray Man appearance. She turned to one of the police in attendance. 'Can you shed any light on things?'

The male officer with short dark hair and a neatly trimmed beard, who Bella recognised as Maeve's son, Harris, and the lead member of Coppercaillie, cleared his throat and straightened his face, clearly amused by Isla's reference to the 1980s chocolate advert. 'Certainly.' He nodded, his face now a stoic mask of professionalism. 'Mrs Douglas alerted us to an intruder and, of course, we take these things very seriously. We attended the scene right away and, sure enough, this man was outside the apartments, loitering suspiciously.'

Isla tugged at Bella's sleeve. 'Arabella hen, you remember Sergeant Donaldson, don't you? He's single like you, I know him from the day centre, he's a musician, remember? He's Maeve's boy, aren't you, Harris?' Isla said as if they were in a coffee shop rather than the midst of a potential crime scene. Bella wanted the stone slabs on the ground to open up and swallow her.

Of course Bella recognised him. His performance at Olivia's birthday party had been brilliant and she wondered if he was as embarrassed as she was. The poor man must have been in his mid-thirties so definitely *not* a boy, but he smiled regardless, in spite of his evident feelings manifesting in his red face.

He nodded. 'Aye, that's right. You style my mum's hair, don't you?'

Isla smiled with pride again and patted her own purple braided hair-do. 'I do. I like to do my bit.' *Please don't say for the old folks, Granny. Please—* Bella screamed in her head. 'For the elderly, you know,' Isla finished, much to Bella's further embarrassment. Sergeant Donaldson gave a knowing smile but Isla didn't let up. She nudged Bella. 'Doesn't he look handsome in his uniform?'

Thankfully, before Bella could respond, the man in black interjected. 'Excuse me! I feel like I'm on some bizarre episode of *Blind Date* here. Can you *please* uncuff me?' he pleaded his case again, only louder this time.

'Not until we ascertain your reason for sneaking around here uninvited,' Sergeant Donaldson told him.

'I'm not uninvited. I'm just a bit early, that's all. I'm booked to stay here!' the man in black snapped.

Bella's eyes widened as she heard Olivia gasp and watched as she pushed forward. 'Aiden O'Dowd?'

'Yes!' the man replied in a strained voice. 'I *have* said so about half a dozen times now to this purple-haired woman and to the officers, but no one seems to be listening!'

'Oh, my goodness! But you're not due for weeks yet! Sergeant Donaldson, please uncuff him, he's my first paying guest and this isn't the welcome he was supposed to have.'

'But if he's a guest, why is he dressed all in black and acting suspiciously?' Officer Mel asked in her broad Yorkshire accent, a raised eyebrow told of her distrust. 'Mrs Douglas says he was talking on his mobile about *trying to get into the place*.'

Again, the detained man interjected, 'I was trying to contact Lady MacBain to explain I had arrived early due to unforeseen circumstances but there was no answer. I left messages. I didn't think it would be a problem as she did say I was going to be her first guest.'

Olivia patted her dress pockets. 'I'm sorry, Mr O'Dowd, I seem to have misplaced my phone.' She turned the pockets inside out to prove her point. 'But perhaps you should have waited until you actually spoke to me before turning up out of the blue. Then perhaps this situation could've been avoided.' Bella watched as Olivia cringed, probably realising she wasn't helping. She continued, 'We were only in the gift shop trying out the new products; you should've just popped around there.'

'I have no clue where that even is,' the man replied in a curt tone.

'Perhaps you can uncuff him, Sergeant Donaldson?' Bella asked, guilt niggling at her for her granny causing them a wasted journey. She turned to Isla and whispered, 'Granny, you could have just called me instead of bothering the police. I'd only been gone half an hour.'

Isla gasped and placed her hand over her heart. 'Och, not a chance. I *wasnae* about to put you in the clutches of a burglar, he could have been a sex-crazed lunatic for all I knew! And I'm in my nightie!' She didn't bother lowering her voice.

The man in black was pale faced, probably due to his ordeal, and looked exhausted. He gave a heavy sigh. 'I can assure you I'm not. I write about crime, I don't partake of it.'

Isla's face lit up. 'Oh, so you *are* that writer chappy.' She stepped forward and held out her hand as Sergeant Donaldson uncuffed the man and helped him to stand. 'I'm Isla Douglas and this here is Bella, my beautiful granddaughter. We'll be neighbours,' she said as if she hadn't just had the man accosted.

He glared at her. 'Great. I'll be sure to keep out of your way.'

Mr O'Dowd in no way resembled the old man Bella had anticipated the crime author guest to be. Instead of a balding head was a thick mop of dark blond hair, instead of a rotund stomach was a rather flat one and instead of an elderly face full of wrinkles was a handsome, smooth exterior aged at around thirty to thirty-five, with piercing blue eyes glaring angrily from it. He was tall and had broad shoulders, the absolute antithesis of what Bella had imagined him to be.

She really would have to stop stereotyping people.

Olivia fumbled in her other pocket, pulled out a bunch of keys and deftly removed one from it. 'Mr O'Dowd, I apologise for missing your calls but you simply weren't expected. Now that you're here, though, you're welcome to stay, of course.' She handed him the key as he rubbed his wrists.

'Thank you,' he replied sharply. 'I'll unpack my car and then, if I'm free to go, I think I'd like to go inside and collapse in a heap, if I may.' His accent was quite soft and Scottish in spite of his Irish-sounding name.

Olivia nodded. 'Of course. Absolutely. I'll have some food and drink brought down for you. Can we help you get your things from the car? Where have you parked?'

'I thought I'd be best to park out of the way, so I've left my car around the side of the block. Although I did notice someone's abandoned an old heap round there, too, so maybe I should move it?'

Bella's eyes widened. 'Ahem... the *heap of a car* happens to be Fifi, my *vintage* Citroen, actually.'

He opened his mouth to speak but closed it again, only to repeat the exercise before saying, 'Vintage? Of course, yes, sorry. I... I thought it'd been dumped. I only mentioned it in case Lady MacBain wasn't aware and needed to arrange for a tow.'

Bella gasped and opened her mouth to speak, but Olivia interrupted quickly, as if she realised a raft of insults was about to burst forth from her friend. 'Brodie will come and help you collect your things. Won't you, Brodie?'

Brodie was clearly finding the whole situation quite amusing but contorted his mouth to dull his grin and nodded. 'Aye, of course. Lead the way, sir.'

Brodie followed Mr O'Dowd past the police cars and out of the courtyard. He glanced back over his shoulder, smirking, and gave a cheeky double thumbs up signal.

After a few moments, the two men returned with a pile of boxes, two holdalls and a laptop bag. Mr O'Dowd nodded curtly and unlocked the door under the watchful eyes of the gathered group. He turned and gave a tight-lipped smile. 'I don't need any further assistance, thank you all. Rest assured I'm not about to trash the place, and I'm quite capable of walking in by myself,' he informed them.

The group mumbled and chuntered as they dispersed awkwardly. Two of the police officers climbed into their car and drove away hastily. Mirren, Innes and the others followed Olivia in the direction of the gift shop, and Bella followed her granny inside their temporary home.

Once inside, Beau, happy he had fulfilled his duties, circled several times on the rug and flopped down. Within moments, he was snoring.

'Good grief, poor Olivia. We'll be lucky if she doesn't evict us after this,' Bella said with a huff as she slumped onto the sofa.

'Don't be daft,' Isla replied with a wave of her hand. 'I was only doing what I thought was right. The last thing I wanted was to stand by and allow Olivia's property to be broken into and vandalised, or worse, after all the work you've put in.'

Bella softened. 'I know, Granny. You're right. I'm sorry. I hope there's no animosity between us and our new neighbour. I don't know how long we need to be here, but I don't want to feel awkward if we bump into him.'

'Och, *dinnae* worry, lass. I'm sure he'll calm down after he's had a sleep. He'll realise it was all a misunderstanding.'

'I hope so.'

Isla leaned forward in her chair. 'What did you think of him then?'

Bella huffed air through puffed cheeks. 'I thought he was understandably frazzled, poor guy.'

'Not him, I meant Harris, the police sergeant. Handsome close up, don't you think?'

Bella rolled her eyes. 'Stop trying to fix me up, Gran.'

Isla shrugged, clearly trying to portray innocence in her hunched shoulders and sweet smile. 'I'm asking what you thought of him, that's all.'

Bella rubbed her hands over her face. 'He was a handsome man with very kind eyes. Happy now?'

Isla straightened her spine and beamed. 'Aye, that'll do for now. He's got a good, secure job and his own house. Never been married, doesn't drink or smoke. Doesn't do drugs, doesn't go out partying.' *Blimey, what does he do?* Bella thought. 'He's musical, likes nature and being outdoors. Knows all the wild birds.' Isla was beginning to sound like a bloody personal ad. 'Husband material, wouldn't you agree?'

'Granny, how many times do I need to tell you I'm not looking for a husband? And if I was, I'd find my own.'

'Aye, I know. But if he was to ask you out, would you go?'

Bella had to end the conversation in any way she could. And fast. 'I dunno. Like I said, I can find my own boyfriend. Now can I please go back to the party?'

Isla folded her arms across her chest and pursed her lips. 'I'm not stopping you.'

Bella pushed herself up from the comfort of the sofa and stood. 'Okay, don't wait up.'

* * *

Bella closed the door of the apartment behind her and waited to hear her granny lock it with a click before she stepped outside.

The night was crisp and clear and the square horseshoe shape of the stable block acted as a shelter from the gentle breeze. Her breath formed puffs of cloud as she exhaled into the air. The lack of up light meant the display above her was rather magnificent. Tiny pinpricks of light were scattered across the inky dark sky and as her eyes adjusted, she could make out the Milky Way, a cloudy band of clusters of stars stretching across the night. For a moment, she didn't feel the cold, and all thoughts of stressed, handcuffed men and musical police officers dissipated. For a moment, she revelled in the silent wonder of the umbrella of darkness above her.

The gravel crunched beneath her feet, and she wrapped her

jacket tightly around her as she made her way back to the gift shop. When she arrived in the warmth again, the few remaining people were chatting and finishing off their glasses of beer. Fleetwood Mac's 'Silver Spring' played on the newly installed sound system and Bella began to relax.

She noticed Sergeant Donaldson and his co-worker Mel were still there, much to her dismay. She made her way over to Olivia in order to avoid him. It was embarrassing enough to have her eighty-five-year-old granny referring to another octogenarian as old right in front of her son, but to have that granny blatantly try to fix her up with that son in front of a crowd of people just added insult to injury.

'Hey, are you okay?' Bella asked Olivia.

Olivia smiled and shook her head. 'I should be asking you that. Can you believe he just turned up like that? I wish he'd let me know sooner he was coming early, like a week or so, instead of ringing on my mobile and then turning up unannounced when I hadn't approved it, and sneaking around like that. Your poor granny. She must have been terrified.'

Bella smiled too. 'Nah, she's a tough old boot. Nothing much fazes her. You saw what she did to Kerr with her handbag on the night of the fashion show. Anyway, don't worry; she was right as rain when I left her. I feel so bad for the poor guy. He must be wondering what he's let himself in for.'

'Oh no, don't be silly. I think he probably knows he made a mistake.'

Sergeant Donaldson approached them, and Bella flitted her gaze around the room, anywhere that meant she could avoid eye contact with him. He cleared his throat. 'Lady Olivia, PC Sherburn and I shall go now if you're happy everything is sorted.'

'Have you had a drink and a snack at least?'

He raised a hand. 'No, it's fine, we're heading back to the station to hand over but thank you.'

'Thanks, sergeant. I'm so sorry you had a wasted journey, but it was better to be safe,' Olivia replied.

The man nodded. 'Oh, absolutely. Never apologise for calling us out if you feel we can help.' He turned to Bella. 'Nice to meet you officially, Arabella. It's good to put a face to a name as they say. Your granny's quite the character.'

Bella laughed lightly as her face warmed to furnace level. 'That's one way of putting it. And please, call me Bella.'

'In that case, I'm Harris,' he replied with a warm smile that brightened his whole face. Apart from the night of the birthday party, he always looked quite serious. She resisted the urge to say he should smile more often then perhaps he wouldn't appear so intimidating.

'I'm Mel,' the female officer said as she held out her hand.

'Good to meet you, Mel,' Bella said as she shook it. 'That's a Yorkshire accent, isn't it?'

Mel nodded with a grin. 'Aye, it is. Well spotted. West Yorkshire, actually.'

'How come you're up here?'

'My husband Neil's job, he bought a garage, does car repairs. Glad we moved, though. Love it up here.' Bella instantly liked Mel. She had a warm smile and an accent to match.

Bella nodded. 'Oh, good. I love it too but I'm slightly biased, I suppose, as I was born up the road. Anyway, thanks again, Mel and Sergeant— I mean Harris.'

Harris smiled, gave a single nod and turned to his colleague. 'Come on, Mel. Let's get back to the station.' The female officer smiled and silently followed him out of the gift shop.

'Did you send some food down to the writer bloke?' Bella asked once the police had left.

'I did. Uncle Innes took it. He's such a diplomat, I thought it best. He says Mr O'Dowd had calmed down and was very happy with the apartment, so that's a relief.'

'Well, that's good. I hope I can keep out of his way. I get the feeling I'm not going to be entirely popular with the guy.'

Olivia nudged her. 'Don't be daft. You're popular with everyone.'

Bella smiled widely. 'Aye, if only that were true.'

13

The following morning, Bella felt surprisingly fresh considering the beer, wine, whisky and cheese combination of the night before, not to mention the drama. She had woken earlier than normal for a weekend and had lain there for a while in the cosy room, thinking the bed was way too comfy to get out of without at least giving sleep another chance.

After unsuccessfully trying to return to the dream she'd been having about being serenaded by Harry Styles, she decided to get up. She could hear her granny's loud snores coming from her bedroom; the excitement of the flood and then the police the night before must have knocked her for six, which wasn't at all like her. She was up *before* the lark under normal circumstances.

After taking a quick shower and dressing in jeans and a warm jumper, Bella pulled on her jacket, left her granny sleeping, and decided to take Beau for his morning constitutional around the grounds. He wagged his tail eagerly as she clipped on his harness. There would no doubt be deer and rabbits around and she couldn't trust the little fella not to go darting off to chase something.

As she stepped through the front door into the fresh morning air, she inhaled a deep breath and smiled. There were definitely worse places to wake up in. It was a bright but chilly July Saturday at around 7.30 and the sun was on its ascent. She could see the huge, majestic oak trees above the roof of the stables swaying gently in the breeze, making a low whooshing sound that reminded Bella of the sea. The flower-filled planters in the centre of the courtyard glistened with tiny droplets of water that resembled diamonds when the rising sun glinted on them, and even though it wasn't yet warm, the air was fresh and clean. It was a shame this arrangement was only temporary; she could get used to having this view on her doorstep and she was determined to make the most of living in such a beautiful place.

She spotted sudden movement by the entrance to the court-yard. Unfortunately, Beau saw it too and let out a high-pitched yip, at which point he yanked her forward and she tripped over her feet trying to gain some purchase on the damp cobbles. In the commotion, Beau's lead slipped through her fingers, rendering him free to pounce, and he went shooting off like a bullet.

'Beau! Come back right now!' Bella screeched.

Of course, the inquisitive canine did no such thing. Instead, he went barrelling into the figure, all dressed in grey, who cried out and fell to the floor with a loud 'Oof!'

'You should control your bloody dog!' the man shouted at Bella as he removed AirPods from his ears.

Who else but Mr O'Dowd? 'Oh, great. It had to be you, didn't it?' she mumbled to herself as she jogged over to the man, who was now sitting on the damp gravel outside the courtyard, a curled-lipped expression fixed on his face as he held the dog at arm's length while Beau tried his best to lick him. He looked like some-thing out of a boxing movie in his grey jogging pants and matching grey hoodie. A black woolly hat sat atop his head and a, not surprisingly, grey scarf wrapped around his neck. *Who does he think he is, Rocky Balboa?* This guy clearly needed some kind of colour therapy. After witnessing his all black attire the previous night, Bella observed he seemed to live his life as if in a monochrome movie from the forties.

'I'm so sorry, Mr O'Dowd. He's usually quite well behaved. I think you startled him, and with what happened last night...' she said as she picked up Beau's lead and pulled the overfriendly dog away.

'It had to be my fault, didn't it? Why don't you have me arrested again?' he replied sarcastically, with a sneer as he held his wrists together.

Fancy some salt and vinegar for that huge chip on your shoulder? 'I didn't mean... I wasn't accusing...' She sighed. 'Look, I'm sorry. We'll be on our way and get out of yours.'

Mr O'Dowd scrambled to his feet and brushed himself off but when he turned to jog away, Bella burst out laughing in spite of herself. The fabric across his rear was now a dark, wet patch from sitting on the dewy gravel.

He stopped and turned to face her, a deep furrow in his brow. 'Is it amusing to you that your dog attacked me?'

'Attacked...? I mean, he could've licked you to death, I suppose but... of course not. I apologised, didn't I?' She pursed her lips.

'Well? What's so funny then?'

Bella tried to calm herself. 'I'm sorry, it's just that... erm...' She gestured to his trouser area.

He glanced down at his crotch then looked back up at her with a horror-filled, crumpled expression as he placed his hand over the area. 'What about it?'

She gasped and widened her eyes. With a rapid wave of her hand, she said, 'Oh no! Not *there*, the – the back... your erm...

bottom?' She winced, as that wasn't exactly an appropriate talking point with a total stranger either.

He glanced down and contorted himself, pulling at the fabric until he could see the wet patch. 'Oh, great. Now I look like I've peed my pants. Just my luck to have landed in the only puddle around.'

Bella tried not to laugh but it was an exercise in futility. She placed her hand over her mouth as if it would stop the noise from escaping, but nevertheless, laughter erupted from her, loud and unrelenting.

Mr O'Dowd stood there, glaring for a moment until he smiled, and that smile turned into a deep rumble of a chuckle. 'It could only happen to me,' he said, but this time with humour. He took a few steps towards her. 'Look, can we start again? I know I haven't been the most cordial of people since we met last night.'

Bella chewed her lip for a moment. 'Well, that's not really surprising. My granny did almost have you arrested as a sex-crazed lunatic.' She held up her hand. 'Her words, not mine.'

He chuckled. 'That's true. I can assure you I'm neither sex-crazed, nor a lunatic. I'm just Aiden.' He held out his hand and Bella stepped a little closer to shake it.

'I'm Bella and this is Beau. My granny is Isla. She's actually very sweet, if a little rebellious for her age.'

'I think the purple hair was a bit of a giveaway. Anyway, it's nice to properly meet you, Bella. And you too, Beau,' he said as he bent to scratch the dog behind his ears. 'Maybe don't launch yourself at new people, eh? That goes for you too,' he said with a glance up at Bella and a glint of humour in his eyes.

'Advice noted,' Bella replied with a laugh. She was relieved he was actually being friendly to the dog, even after the incident. People who didn't like dogs had no place in her circle of friends.

She tilted her head as she watched him interact with Beau. 'I understand you're here to write a book.'

He nodded. 'That's right. My editor thought this would be a good place to get the words flowing, so we'll see.'

Bella glanced around at the trees, the cornflower-blue sky and the historic castle. 'I think your editor was right. I can imagine it being very inspirational for creative types like yourself. That's always been Olivia's intention, anyway.'

'Let's hope so. Well... I won't keep you. I'd better get jogging so my trousers dry off.'

Bella took that as a sign he didn't want to talk any more. 'Ah yes, better let this little guy burn off some of that energy.'

He gave one last handsome smile. 'Bye for now, Bella.'

'Bye, Aiden. Enjoy your run.'

* * *

Bella walked with Beau right down to the shoreline of Loch Ness by the old chapel. She stood watching the ripples on the surface of the loch as Beau ran around with a huge stick he'd collected on the way. He dropped it at her feet, and she threw it for him to fetch, then the whole process started over. The mountains visible across the loch were crowned with a hazy mist that the sun was doing its best to burn off. When Bella closed her eyes and inhaled, she could smell the fresh scent of the Scots pines that stood the other side of the chapel, a clean fragrance that always reminded her of Christmas.

Purple-hued thistles were in bloom, creating a vibrant skirt around the stone of the chapel, their tufty heads bobbing in the breeze coming in off the water. It was such a peaceful place. She took out her phone and snapped a couple of photos then a selfie to post on her social media with the word:

Bliss

to accompany it.

When she arrived back at the apartment with a panting Beau, Granny Isla was up and drinking tea by the unlit fire. 'Oh, there you are, I thought perhaps you'd been lured away by the temptation of chocolate from our new neighbour.' She laughed lightly at her own joke.

Bella smiled. 'Granny, you're terrible. Is there any more tea in the pot?'

'Oh aye. It'll be nice and strong how you like it.' Beau trotted up to his owner and rested his head on her lap. 'And have you been a good lad?' she asked the dog, who wagged his tail eagerly.

Bella poured herself a mug of tea and scoffed as she shouted through from the kitchen. 'He didn't start off that well.'

Isla shook her head at the dog. 'You didn't go chasing *babbits,* did you? You wee scamp.'

Bella chuckled at her granny's choice of words. 'No, it wasn't *babbits*. It was peoples!'

Isla lifted her chin; her eyes were wide. 'Peoples? Oh no! Who did he chase?'

Bella raised her eyebrows and gave a knowing look. 'Who do you think?'

Isla raised her hand to cover her mouth, possibly to try to disguise her amusement. 'The Milk Tray Man?'

'Maybe call him Aiden, eh?'

'Was he cross?'

'He was at first but then he saw the funny side, thank goodness.'

'He'll be regretting coming to Drumblair, thanks to us, eh, Beau?'

Bella giggled. 'In Aiden's position, I might feel the same. He's had an eventful twelve hours, that's for sure.'

'Did he seem nice? You know, once he'd calmed down?' Isla asked while tugging at her sleeve. Her attempts at nonchalance failed miserably.

'Nice enough, Granny, but remember I've told you to stop trying to fix me up with every man you come across. First that care worker, then Sergeant Donaldson, now Aiden the writer. You'll be wearing nappies and firing arrows next.'

Isla gave a deep sigh. 'I want you to be happy, dearie.'

Guilt niggled at Bella. 'I know, and I love you for it. But I don't need a man to make me happy.'

Isla waved a dismissive hand. 'Aye, I know, I know. I'm an interfering old fool. But I won't be around forever, and I want to know you're taken care of.'

Bella laughed rather too loudly. 'Granny, you'll be around for years yet, so stop saying things like that, will you? And I can take care of myself. Like I said, I don't—'

'Need a man, yes, yes. I hear you loud and clear. I'll stop. I know when my help's not wanted.'

Bella rolled her eyes, knowing full well her granny was incapable of stopping when it came to matchmaking.

There was a knock at the door and Bella went to answer it. 'Hey, Olivia. How are you doing?'

The two friends hugged. 'I'm good, thanks. Brodie has gone into Inverness to get his car serviced, and I thought I'd pop round and see if you fancy doing something. If you're not already busy.' Bella gestured for her come in and the two women walked into the living room.

Bella glanced over at her granny, who waved. 'Hi, Lady Olivia. Feel free to whisk my granddaughter away. She sees enough of my old wrinkly face.'

Bella fought the urge to roll her eyes again. 'I need to chase up the insurers and get a timescale from the builder, though.'

Isla waved her hand. 'You can do that later, or on your mobile. And anyway, it's Saturday, go on and enjoy yourselves, you deserve a break, the pair of you.'

Bella shrugged and turned back to Olivia. 'Sounds good then. What are you thinking of doing? Are you sure you can spare the time? It's not like you to be all calm with a week to go until the grand opening.'

Olivia shrugged. 'Everything's ready so I thought we could make the most of the calm before the storm.'

'I like your thinking. How about we head into Inverness too and do a bit of shopping, maybe grab a spot of lunch? I can text Skye and get her to meet us.'

'Perfect,' Olivia replied.

Bella went into her bedroom and grabbed her handbag and phone. She fired off a quick text to Skye and returned to the living room, where she kissed her granny and then the two friends left.

'I'll drive,' Bella said as she dangled her keys aloft. They walked around the side of the castle to where Fifi was parked. Aiden was there beside his own car, an expensive-looking navy-blue saloon.

'Hi, Aiden,' Bella said brightly, happy in the knowledge they had sorted out their issues.

'Oh, hi, Bella. Where's your little friend?' Aiden asked with a grin.

'Beau? He's staying home with my granny while Olivia and I go to town for a spot of lunch.'

'And you're driving *that*?' He winced as he pointed at Fifi but there was a distinct glint of mischief to his amused expression.

Bella narrowed her eyes. 'Absolutely. Fifi hasn't let me down yet.'

Olivia stepped forward. 'Is everything okay with the apartment, Mr O'Dowd?' she asked politely.

'Please, call me Aiden. And yes, it's great. Really beautiful, in fact. Whoever you had in to design them has done an amazing job.'

Bella felt her face flushing as Olivia informed him, 'Ah, you can congratulate the designer yourself.' She gestured to Bella.

Aiden raised his eyebrows. 'Really? So that's what you do for a living, is it? Interior design?'

Bella made an unladylike snorting noise. 'Me? Nah, I know what *I* like, I suppose. I'm actually Olivia's assistant.'

Olivia nudged her. 'You're way more than that. She's my right-hand woman, and my best friend. I don't know how I'd cope without her.'

'Well, you have impeccable taste, Bella. I love the navy-blue walls, and the wood panelling is a really nice touch. Very in keeping with the varied history of the castle and its buildings. I think I'm going to take away some tips on what to do with my place when I go home.'

Bella tucked her hair behind her ear, a nervous reaction she was all too aware of. 'Thank you. It's kind of you to say so.'

Aiden shrugged. 'It's true. Well, I'd better be going. Got a very important date,' he told them before climbing into his car and driving off, waving as he left.

Olivia's face crumpled. 'So, he's not single then,' she said with a hint of disappointment to her voice.

Bella scowled. 'You have the nicest, best-looking boyfriend, why do you sound so gutted that Aiden isn't single?'

Olivia whacked her arm playfully. 'Not for me, you *bampot*.'

Bella rolled her eyes for what must have been the fiftieth time that day and made another strange noise to voice her frustration.

'Urgh, not you as well? I've enough to handle with Granny Isla playing cupid and firing her arrows into every single man she sees.'

Olivia giggled. 'Bless her; she wants you to be—'

'—Happy! Yes, so she keeps telling me. Come on, let's get going.'

Fifi roared to life and Bella almost wished she had driven away before Aiden in his flashy car; she would have loved to prove him wrong about her vintage vehicle. Okay, so it was a bit rusty, and there was no Bluetooth or phone charger, no Spotify or satnav, but it was hers and she loved it. She'd had to get a CD player installed by a specialist but sometimes, when she drove over bumps, the CD shot out and she had to search for it when she parked up. But it was a piece of history and the fact it was built in the mid-eighties and was still running almost forty years later was no mean feat. She was proud of Fifi and wouldn't hear a bad word said against her.

14

Bella parked up in the centre of Inverness and the two friends made their way to their favourite restaurant in an old converted church on Fraser Street and were shown to a table by the bar. The place was very atmospheric with its vast vaulted double-height ceilings and log fire. Modern art adorned the walls and large fresh flower displays were dotted around the place, their sweet fragrance and vibrant colours adding to the beauty of the surroundings.

A tall, dark-haired waiter brought them menus and took their drinks order.

'I do love this place,' Olivia said. 'It's so romantic.'

Bella laughed. 'And yet you're here with me, not Brodie.'

Olivia smiled. 'I don't mind if you don't.'

'Have you heard anything from Kerr?' Bella asked rather tentatively.

Olivia sighed. 'Not personally. Uncle Innes saw him coming out of a pub in Inverness and warned him again to stay away. Kerr just sneered, told him it was a free country and walked away. He looked quite rough, apparently.'

'I hope he stays away, Liv. We don't want him showing up on opening day next Saturday.'

'We certainly don't.'

'And how's Brodie's divorce going?' Bella asked as the waiter placed two mocktails on their table.

'It's almost done. Not long now.' Olivia's wide, bright smile told of her happiness and relief at the fact.

Bella excitedly reached over and squeezed her hand. 'And then you'll be getting married!'

Olivia giggled. 'I have to wait for the official proposal first. This little ribbon he tied around my finger is getting rather scratty, but I won't take it off. He's wonderful, Bells,' she said dreamily. 'I feel so lucky that we found each other again. Although I had no clue he even liked me back at school.'

'Honestly, you two are so perfect for each other. The way he looks at you...' Bella said with a wistful sigh.

Olivia's expression changed to one of seriousness. 'The trouble is... I've never loved a man so strongly, Bells, and it terrifies me.'

'You have nothing at all to worry about, Liv. You're the centre of his world, it's so clear.'

Deep down, Bella wished she could find someone, too, in spite of her protestations that she wasn't bothered. She was surrounded by loved-up people, from Olivia and Brodie, Skye and Ben, even down to Mirren and Dougie. And though she didn't *need* a man to 'complete' her, or anything quite as prosaic, sometimes she thought it would be nice to have someone to go with on double dates with her friends.

At that point, Skye walked up to their table. 'Hey, girlies!' Bella and Olivia jumped to their feet and a group hug ensued.

'It's been too long since we did this,' Skye said as she took a seat and waved the waiter over. When he arrived, she requested another mocktail. 'Ben dropped me in town but it's too early for alcohol. I might fall asleep if I drink.'

'How are the wedding plans going, Skye?' Olivia asked.

'Exhausting,' Skye replied with a huff. 'I'm beginning to like the idea of escaping to Gretna, it's got so complicated.'

'Oh no, although your mum and dad would go ballistic if you did,' Bella said, remembering the way they'd had to console Skye after she had suggested a small, quiet wedding to her mum. The fallout had been ridiculous and lasted for days.

'Aye, that's true. It's getting silly now with who won't sit next to whom, and who we can't invite if we invite a certain person from that side of the family, and who can't travel from the other side of the family. I'm a bit fed up with it all, to be quite honest with you.' The waiter brought Skye's drink and she took a long swig. 'Anyway, enough about me, any news on that rat of a brother of yours, Liv?'

'I was just telling Bella that Uncle Innes saw him coming out of a pub rather worse for wear.'

Skye pursed her lips and leaned forward. 'Rumour has it he tried to get back with Adaira and she wouldn't even let him in the house.'

'Good on her!' Bella said.

'We just need him to stay away from the castle opening now,' Skye said.

'I may see if we can arrange some kind of security just in case.'

'Anyway, has that writer arrived yet? Is he an old fat guy like you thought, Bells?' Skye asked.

Olivia laughed. 'The less said about the writer guy and his arrival, the better. But I think Bells would agree he's rather cute and not an old fat guy at all, although very much taken, apparently.'

Skye curled her lip and harrumphed. 'Really? That's rubbish. If he's a hottie, I was hoping for some romantic tale of your eyes meeting across a cobbled courtyard.'

It was Bella's turn to laugh now. 'Yeah, it definitely didn't happen that way and I think you've been watching too many romance movies.'

As they giggled, Bella felt a presence beside her and Skye looked up with a quizzical glance.

'Sorry to interrupt, Bella, but I spotted you from over by the bar and thought I'd appear rude if I left without saying goodbye.'

Bella looked up to be met by the smiling brown eyes of Sergeant Donaldson. 'Oh, hi... erm... s-sergeant.' *Oh god, why didn't I call him by his proper name?*

The tall, well-built man glanced at the other women briefly. 'It's Harris, remember?' he said with a smile. 'I trust your granny is okay after her ordeal?'

Skye's eyes widened. 'What ordeal? What happened? Is Isla okay? Please tell me she's okay?'

'Oh yes, she's fine. She called the police on our new neighbour when she thought he was breaking in.'

Skye almost choked on her drink. 'The writer? So that's why you didn't want to talk about his arrival!' She laughed. 'That's hilarious! Isla's such a star. Gangsta Granny strikes again!'

Bella felt sure her face was bright red enough to light a room. She realised she hadn't answered the sergeant's question. 'Ahem, yes, sorry, Harris, she's fine, thank you for asking.' She turned to see the other two women grinning at her. 'This is my friend Skye, and of course you know Olivia.'

Harris smiled at the other women. 'Of course. Hello again, Olivia. Good to meet you, Skye.'

Bella felt a little awkward. 'So, what are you up to? I see you're off duty today.' She glanced at the black crash helmet tucked under his arm, with a red and yellow lightning strike printed on it, and noted the black leather biker jacket he wore. He looked quite handsome in his civvies, in a serious, rugged kind of way.

He nodded. 'I am indeed. Out for a lunchtime lemonade before I go for a ride. I'm heading to the Merkinch Nature Reserve to do a bit of walking and a wee bit of bird watching. The weather's just right, bright but not too warm.'

'Sounds lovely,' Skye replied. 'I've never been on a motorbike before, have you, Bella?' she continued with a pointed glance.

Bella frowned. 'Erm... no, I can't say I have,' she replied, fully aware of what her friend was doing.

'I shall have to take you for a spin sometime,' Harris said.

Bella swallowed nervously. Being pillion on a motorbike wasn't exactly on her to-do list, much like wrestling a lion or jumping into a pit of rattlesnakes didn't appear on there either.

She smiled self-consciously. 'Oh... I don't know. I'd probably be a terrible passenger.' She felt sure her face was heated to egg-frying level by now, to add to her increasing embarrassment. 'I'm more of a four wheels kinda gal.' She gave her two friends a flared-nostrilled, wide-eyed glare she hoped spoke volumes.

Harris shrugged. 'You've nothing to be scared of. You'd be in very safe hands,' he said. 'You can trust me, I'm a police sergeant.' His eyes seemed to twinkle with humour in the overhead lighting.

Good grief, he has a nice smile.

Bella shook her head to dislodge the thought. He wasn't her type. He might ride a motorbike and sing and play in a band, but he was otherwise rather dull from the things her granny had said. And she wasn't keen on his beard. Feeling a little put on the spot, she gave a nervous laugh. 'O–okay then, maybe one day.' She felt a little safer by adding the vagueness to her reply.

Harris grinned, showing a set of perfect white teeth. 'It's a date. Or at least it will be. I'll check my diary and pass a message on with Mrs Douglas next time I see her at the day centre.'

'Lovely,' Bella replied, unsure of what else to say and thinking quite the opposite.

'Right, well, I'll be off then. See you soon. Enjoy your lunch.' And with that, he left the restaurant. Bella watched him leave and tried not to notice the way his jeans stretched across his thighs as he walked.

Stop it, Bella Douglas. You're being bloody ridiculous. He may have nice legs, broad shoulders and a lovely smile, but he watches birds, for goodness' sake. He doesn't drink. He's too serious. And did I mention he watches birds?

After a few moments of making sure the man was out of earshot, Skye and Olivia squealed, causing all heads to turn in their direction.

'Shhh!' Bella said, glancing around the place with an apologetic smile. 'You'll get us chucked out!'

'Bella's got a date, Bella's got a date,' Skye chanted in a sing-song voice like a nine-year-old schoolgirl.

'Not really. It was a bit too ambiguous to call it a date,' Bella insisted.

Skye scoffed. 'You're kidding right? He actually used the phrase, "it's a date".'

Bella scrambled around her brain for a suitable retort but came up blank.

'He definitely likes you,' Olivia said with an excited grin. 'I could tell that last night, though. He kept looking at you. And he's rather gorgeous, don't you think?'

'I agree,' Skye said. 'Very handsome and that deep voice... yum.'

'Yes, but—'

Skye continued, 'And a police sergeant. That's quite sexy. Quite heroic.'

Bella scrunched her brow. 'Not really.' *Did you hear him say he watches birds?*

Olivia gasped. 'I've realised who he reminds me of.'

Bella sighed, *oh, here we go.* 'Bill Oddie?'

A crease formed between Skye's brows. 'Who?'

Bella turned to Skye and crumpled her face in incredulity. 'Really?'

Olivia continued. 'I'm being serious. He has a look of Tom Hardy when he was in that film with Reese Witherspoon and Chris Pine, only with a beard. Same cropped hair and same kind of build by the looks of him too.'

Skye nodded vehemently, wagging her finger for good measure. '*This Means War.*'

Bella again turned to Skye. 'Isn't that taking things a bit too seriously? She's entitled to her opinion.'

Skye paused for a moment then shook her head. 'No, the film is called *This Means War*, you melt. And she's right; only your sergeant's teeth are straighter. I think you're in there, Bells.'

Bella huffed and rolled her eyes. 'He's not *my* sergeant and can we *please* change the subject?' she asked sulkily, wondering if she really had just agreed to an actual date with Harris.

15

When they had finished their lunch, Ben collected Skye to visit a potential wedding venue on the outskirts of the city and Brodie arrived at the restaurant to ask if Olivia fancied seeing a show at the Eden Court Theatre; he invited Bella too but she didn't feel like interloping on their date, meaning she was left to drive back to Drumblair alone.

Thinking back to the start of her lunch date with the girls, she shook her head. How on earth had she let herself be cajoled into riding pillion on the back of a far too strait-laced police sergeant's motorcycle? Okay, the girls were right, he was quite handsome, but her granny had made him sound far too perfect with his lack of bad habits; a little boring even. *He's a twitcher, for goodness' sake!* Not that she was looking for craziness. But a little excitement wouldn't go amiss, although she didn't mean the excitement of peeing her pants on the back of a motorbike going at a hundred miles an hour along the back lanes of Inverness. She would think of an excuse to get out of it. She'd have to.

As she drove along listening to her Harry Styles CD, Bella sang along to 'As It Was', getting carried along with the lyrics, and didn't spot the huge pothole until it was too late. There was a loud thunk as her tyre dropped into the hole and she ducked as the CD shot out of the player, flew past her head and hit the rear window before disappearing out of sight.

Bella screamed, 'Shiiit!' as her heart almost leapt from her mouth and the car came to a sudden, dramatic halt. With her eyes wide, she glanced around but luckily there were no other vehicles in sight. Then she realised the car was standing at a lopsided angle. 'Oh no, no, no, Fifi, what have I done?' She tried to start the engine again, intent on moving to a safer spot, but Fifi was clearly not going anywhere. 'Come on, old girl, please!' She turned the key in the ignition again but the engine sputtered and stopped.

'I don't bloody believe this. Why can't one thing go right for me at the moment?'

She grabbed her bag and climbed from the car; steam was now billowing from the bonnet; at least she hoped it was steam. She grabbed her phone and went to dial, but of course there was no signal at that precise location. Why would there be?

'Aaaaarghhhhh!' Bella growled and stomped her feet like a toddler in the midst of a tantrum. She paced up and down, trying to decide what to do. She could walk into the next village but that meant leaving Fifi in a hazardous place. She could wait for a while but who knows how long it would be until someone came along?

She was still pacing when she heard the roar of an engine. She stepped into the road and waved her arms in the air to alert the oncoming driver of her own vehicle and its unhelpful position, and the driver came to a stop.

She recognised the lightning stripe down the side of the helmet worn by the rider and wasn't sure whether to be relieved or horrified.

'Bella, are you okay?' Harris shouted as he removed his helmet and placed it on the seat of his bike. He jogged towards her, a concerned expression furrowing his brow.

'I'm fine but I think Fifi is damaged.'

Harris glanced around. 'Fifi?'

Bella gestured at her vehicle. 'This is Fifi.'

Harris raised his eyebrows and almost smiled. 'Oh, right. I see. You... erm... you named your car.'

Bella nodded, feeling a little silly for the first time when admitting it.

'But you're not injured?'

Bella shook her head. 'Not physically, no,' she replied with a sad glance at her beloved vintage Citroen. 'Emotionally, maybe.'

'Had her a long time, have you?'

Bella appreciated his attempts to sing from the same hymn sheet. 'Since I was a teenager. She used to belong to my granny so she's very special to me.'

'Ah, I see. Well, my mate Neil is an excellent mechanic. Mel's husband from the band?' She nodded. 'I'll hop back on the bike and go let him know to come and collect her. You'll not get a signal out here. Are you okay to wait with her while I go? Then I'll go to the station and grab my spare helmet from my locker, and I can run you back to Drumblair.'

'Oh no, Harris, I can get a taxi, honestly, I don't want to ruin your day off.'

'Hey, it's not a problem. I'd rather do that than leave you stranded. And anyway, it means we get to have that ride sooner than expected.' He seemed quite happy with his plan.

Bella nodded, she was too sad to argue. 'Thanks, if you're sure?'

'Absolutely. Do you have an emergency triangle?'

Bella nodded. 'I do, in my boot.'

'Okay, put that out and stand away from the vehicle in the

grass. I'll be as quick as I can.' He put on his helmet, mounted his bike, started it and drove off at speed.

After putting the triangle out, Bella stood away from her car, looking on with a pit of sadness in her stomach. She hoped it could be repaired. If it had only been the tyre that would have been easier, but the engine was still steaming, which was a worrying sign. She couldn't afford a new car and wasn't going to ask her granny for a loan. She had given her the car in the first place, that was enough for a pensioner. She could only hope it didn't cost the earth to get Fifi running again.

* * *

A short while later, Bella heard the roar of a motorbike again and, sure enough, Harris returned. Once he had dismounted from his bike, he removed his helmet and walked towards her with another helmet hooked over his arm.

He handed Bella the helmet. 'Here you go, put that on and make sure it's nice and secure under your chin. Neil is on his way to pick up, erm, *Fifi*. What he doesn't know about cars isn't worth knowing. Anyway, he'll take her back to his and give her a check over. He's got my number so he can call me once he knows what the damage is. And I'll let you know so you can get in touch with him.'

'I really appreciate this, Harris. You didn't have to go to so much trouble.'

He smiled. 'Really, it's no bother. Come on, let's get you home.'

Once the helmet was fastened, Bella's head felt weirdly heavy. Harris held out his arm and helped her to climb on behind him.

'Put your arms around my waist and hold on. You'll be fine. I'll take it steady,' he told her over his shoulder in a muffled voice.

She did as instructed, and her heart skipped as the engine

growled to life. Harris pulled off and she gripped the man's torso as if her life depended on it... because really it did. As they rode down the narrow lanes, her hair whipped up around her neck and although she tried to watch the scenery as it whizzed by her face, she found her eyes closing and she tucked her head in behind Harris. She wanted the journey to be over and to get back to the castle in one piece. Her heart was in her mouth and her jaw was clenched tightly closed as her stomach lurched on each corner they rounded, fear she would fly off into the hedgerow knotting her guts. She was definitely not a thrill seeker, that was one thing the journey showed her about herself.

After what seemed like hours but was probably a matter of minutes, they pulled onto the long driveway leading to Drumblair Castle. Harris had slowed substantially, and Bella lifted her head to watch as the imposing structure came into view. The MacBain clan flag billowed in the breeze atop one of the towers and Bella could just about make out the outline of the wildcat in the centre.

They pulled around past the front of the castle and then along into the courtyard that opened out in front of the stables. Bella spotted Aiden sitting on one of the benches situated between the apartments with his laptop resting on the seat beside him and a mug of something in his hand. His eyes were closed, and his head rested back against the stone until he heard the bike, at which point he opened his eyes and watched their approach with apparent interest.

Bella heaved a sigh of relief when Harris pulled the bike to a halt. He held out his hand and helped her to dismount before climbing off the bike himself.

She tugged the helmet from her head with a loud 'Oof!' as she almost removed her ears and feared decapitation at the same time. 'Thank you so much for your help.' She desperately tried to straighten her hair, which she figured was probably sticking up at all angles.

'Like I said, it's no bother at all. What did you think of the ride?' Harris gestured towards the bike and smiled in a way that led her to believe he hoped she'd reply positively.

Continuing to faff with her hair, she said, 'Oh... erm... it was... erm...' *Words, Bella, use your words, preferably nice ones that don't include puke or heart attack.*

He chuckled and nodded. 'You're still a *four wheels type of gal*?'

She laughed with relief and nodded. 'I'm afraid so.'

'Noted. So, four wheels when I take you out then?'

Bella was a little taken aback. 'When you take me out?' Had she missed something? Or was that the payment he required for helping her?

His face flushed and he cleared his throat. 'Ah, erm, I forgot to actually *ask* you, didn't I? I remember having the conversation in my head but...'

'Yes, I think you forgot to ask,' she replied with a smile. 'But... to be honest, I'm not really looking for—'

He pursed his lips and nodded. 'Right, no bother. Totally fine. I'll be off. Oh, but can I have your number so I can get in touch when I hear about your car?' He held out his phone.

Bella was riddled with guilt as she took his phone and typed her number in. 'I really do appreciate your help. I don't mean to sound ungrateful.'

He shook his head. 'Hey, no, it's fine. It's not like I was asking you out as some kind of quid pro quo. I thought it might be nice to get to know you a little better, that's all. Honestly, it's fine.'

She swallowed as she noted his disappointed expression. 'Okay, well, thanks again for the help, and the lift.'

He gave a curt nod and a very brief smile before tugging on his helmet. 'Bye for now. I'll be in touch.' He quickly straddled the bike, started the engine and drove off without looking back.

16

Bella heaved a sigh. Had she been too harsh on Harris? Too dismissive? He was a nice guy, and very good-looking, admittedly. But he really wasn't her type; he seemed far too serious and strait-laced... and that beard...

'Are you okay?' came a voice from behind her. 'You look fed up.'

She turned and was greeted by the tilted head and squinted eyes of Aiden O'Dowd as he shielded his face from the sun. His blond hair was tousled as if he'd just got out of bed, in spite of the hour, and there was a distinct shadow of stubble outlining his square jaw.

'Oh, hi, Aiden. Yes, I'm fine, thanks. How are you? Getting plenty of words down?'

'Urgh, no, I'm having a bit of writer's block, hence my lack of typing and the coffee I'm drinking.' He held up his mug. 'Can't seem to get going today.'

'Ah. That's not good.'

'Nope. So, where's the vintage Citroen today? I didn't take you for a two wheels type of person.'

She scoffed. 'Why ever not?'

He shrugged. 'I don't know, you're one of those put together, never a hair out of place types. I saw the way you messed with your hair the moment you took the helmet off. And wasn't he the copper from last night?' Well, he'd certainly read her correctly.

'It was, his name's Harris. And I admit, you're right, I was terrified the whole ride home. I think my life would've flashed before my eyes if they'd been open.'

Aiden laughed. 'Ah. Can't say I'd enjoy it either, to be honest. Give me four wheels and a metal cage any day.'

'Agreed!'

'So, why were you on the back of the police sergeant's bike?'

Aren't you the nosy parker? 'Long story,' Bella lied. She didn't want to give him any ammunition to mock her poor car.

He held out his arms. 'I'm not busy. I should be, admittedly, but I'm not.'

She plonked herself down on the bench beside him. 'I broke my car,' she stated plainly with a deep exhale.

He raised his eyebrows. 'Oh! How did you do that?'

'Pothole,' she replied bluntly again. '*Very* big pothole.'

'Oh no. Is it repairable?' At least he seemed sincere.

She shrugged. 'I have no idea at the moment. Harris has had it taken to his friend's garage in Inverness. He's going to let me know when he hears anything.'

Aiden nodded. 'Right. Fingers crossed then?'

She sighed. 'Fingers crossed.'

'Are you and he...?' He wagged his fingers in a back and forth motion, but she guessed what he was getting at.

'Together? No. We're not. Why would you think that?'

'I suppose because riding pillion is a fairly personal mode of transport.'

'Well, there was nothing particularly *personal* about it. Not in the way you're suggesting, anyway.'

Aiden took a sip of his drink. 'He definitely likes you. I can tell. I'm good at reading people. I suppose it comes with writing. I spend a lot of time watching folk and observing their behaviour. Learning what makes them tick.'

'Ah, well, you're slightly off the mark this time. I only met him properly last night. I've seen him from a distance before and he played at Olivia's birthday celebration but that's about it. Didn't you hear my granny embarrass me by introducing us in the midst of the chaos?'

He scowled. 'Oh yes, of course.' He tapped his head. 'I made the *Blind Date* comment.' He chuckled. 'It must have slipped my mind, probably because I'm subconsciously trying to block out the events of last night.'

Bella bit her lip. 'Whoops, yes, sorry about that.' She paused briefly. 'Anyway, last night was the first time I'd actually spoken to the man. Although my granny has been dropping hints about him being *good husband material*,' she huffed.

'And you don't agree?'

She tilted her head. 'Is nosiness a part of being a writer too?'

He cringed. 'Okay, fair point. I'll stop prying.' There were a few moments of silence where they sat, faces tilted towards the sun. The breeze had dropped, and the only sound was birdsong. 'She's a character, your gran,' Aiden said eventually.

'People often say so. There's never a dull moment with her, that's for sure.'

He laughed. 'Yes, I can tell that's the case. She dotes on you too. Are your parents still around?'

'They are. They're on a European cruise for my dad's sixtieth birthday just now, they went yesterday. But I live with Granny because my old room was turned into an office slash gym when I first left home.'

He chuckled. 'Ah, that old chestnut. Same happened to me

except mine was turned into a room for my dad's model railway when I went off to university. Bloody massive that thing was. It had all the little trees and people. It was quite cool really,' he said with a tinge of sadness.

'Are yours still around? Your parents, I mean.'

He glanced down at his feet. 'Yes and no. My mum had early onset dementia and Dad was her carer. He couldn't cope when she'd gone and kind of gave up for a long time. He's remarried now but it's not quite the same. I don't see much of him. I don't exactly feel welcome. The new woman isn't keen on me.'

Bella's heart sank. 'Oh, Aiden, I'm so sorry.'

'Thanks. It's been a while now. Still stings, though, even at thirty-four.'

'Do you have any brothers or sisters?' Bella asked, intrigued to know more.

'Nope. Just me.'

'That must be hard.'

He nodded. 'It can be.' He rubbed his free hand over his face and gave a strained laugh. 'Anyway... bloody hell, sorry for dragging you down even further.' He laughed. 'You didn't need my sob story.'

She shook her head. 'No, don't apologise. So, where did the name O'Dowd come from? You don't sound Irish.'

'I was born in Northern Ireland, near Derry. My folks moved over to Ullapool when I was wee to run a pub, so I grew up there. I've been back to Ireland to visit a few times out of interest, but I consider myself more Scottish really. How about you?'

'Inverness born and raised,' Bella replied. 'I love Scotland. I love Inverness and I don't think I ever want to leave.'

'So, you don't fancy checking out life in any other countries?'

Bella took a long look around her surroundings. 'Can't say I do no. Not even any other Scottish cities, to be honest. My heart's here in the Highlands. I don't mind the idea of visiting other places, but I'll always want to come home.'

'Fair play to you. I love Scotland, too, but I live in London these days. Easier for the job.'

Bella couldn't imagine living in a city as big as London. Too busy, too much traffic, too much pollution. 'Is that where your publisher's based?'

'It is, yes.' He didn't elaborate and Bella felt his demeanour change a little. 'Well, I suppose I should get back to it. This book isn't going to write itself.'

Bella took the hint and stood. 'Do you write under your own name? Only I'm huge crime fiction reader and couldn't find your books under Aiden O'Dowd.'

He lifted his laptop and tucked it under his arm. 'So you Googled me, eh?' he asked with a glint in his eye.

'Only because I love crime fiction,' she replied. She didn't mention she and her friends had tried to cyber stalk him while out for lunch, but it had proved fruitless.

'Well, I write under a pseudonym. Sorry, I think I can hear my phone ringing. I left it in the kitchen. I'd better go, it's probably my editor.' Without saying anything else, he briskly walked inside to his apartment.

'Rude,' Bella mumbled. She hadn't heard a phone ringing. All she was going to ask was for the name of his books so she could check them out, but he had seemed a little standoffish.

* * *

Bella let herself into their apartment. 'Hi, Granny, I'm back.' Beau ran to greet her, and she bent to quickly rub his belly when he rolled onto his back at her feet. 'Hello, Beau, who's a good boy, eh?'

'He's in the bad books, the wee scamp,' Isla called from what now appeared to be her favourite chair by the log burner. 'Raided the bin for the paper bag the ham came in while I was in the shower. Made a *muckle* mess on the floor.'

'Beau! You little monster,' Bella said with a giggle.

'Did you have a lovely time, dearie?' Isla asked.

Bella walked over and kissed her granny on the head. 'I did until it was time to leave. I'm afraid I think Fifi is broken.'

Isla gasped. 'What happened? Are you okay?'

Bella plonked herself down on the arm of the chair. 'I'm absolutely fine but I'm not sure what damage was done to the car. I hit a pretty big pothole, so I think the wheel is knackered, and then there was steam coming from the bonnet. I have no idea what that was all about. I'm so sorry, Granny.'

Isla patted her leg. 'Don't be such a wee dafty. You're more important than that old heap.'

Bella bent to rest her head on her gran's. 'I love that old heap. Mainly because she was yours.'

Isla shook her head. 'You *bampot*. It's a hunk of metal. It can be replaced. You, on the other hand, *cannae*.'

Bella stood and walked over to the sofa where she flopped down and hunched her shoulders. 'It can't be replaced, though, that's the problem. I don't have the cash. And without a car we're a bit stuck.'

Isla waved her hand. 'Och, pish. We'll sort it out. Don't you fret. It's typical everything's happening when your dad's away though, eh? Oh, I forgot to say he messaged on the WhatsUp today. They've made it onto the boat and their rooms are very nice apparently, they're having a lovely time by the sound of it. Anyway, I told him we're both fine and they've to stop worrying and enjoy themselves and that we'll call him on his birthday.'

'Good. I'm glad they're having a good time.'

Isla went silent for a moment and then with a confused frown asked, 'Hang on, how did you get home if Fifi is broken? Taxi?'

'I got a lift; the car has been taken to a garage in Inverness.' She did her best to avoid telling her granny *who* had been her knight in shining armour for fear of building her hopes on the match-making front.

'Did Brodie bring you home?'

Bella sighed, figuring she'd find out at the day centre anyway. 'Actually no, he and Liv were going to see a show. I got a lift from... ahem... erm... Sergeant Donaldson.'

Isla's eyes widened and she placed a hand over her heart. 'He brought you home in a *polis* car? Did anyone see you? People will think you've been arrested! It'll be the talk of the day centre.'

'No, Granny, it's fine. He was off duty. He brought me home on his motorbike.'

Isla gasped. 'That's even worse! They're death traps, those things! Och, I don't think you should do that again, hen.' She fanned herself dramatically. 'They're no' safe. You hear all sorts. You'd think someone of his standing would know better than to own a death machine.'

Bella remembered the expression on Harris's face when she turned down his offer of a date. 'I don't think you need to worry about him offering again.' She decided to change the subject. 'Anyway, I've been chatting to our neighbour.'

'Mr O'Dowd? Oh, how nice. Was he pleasant with you after last night and this morning? I feel terrible now I've had time to think about it all.'

Bella smiled. 'Don't worry. I think we're forgiven. He was quite chatty.'

'Shame he sounds Scottish, though. I do love an Irish brogue. I like that singer who has a nice speaking voice. What's his name? He wears those sunglasses like Roy Orbison sometimes. I've seen him on the *Tops of the Pops* programme, though it's a while ago. I don't even think it comes on the television any more.' She gestured to the back of her head. 'He has a ponytail, which is a bit daft for a man of his years in my opinion... Bonio!' she shouted, causing Bella to almost jump out of her skin. 'Aye, Bonio, that's him. Lovely singing voice too.'

'I think you mean Bono, Granny, from the band U2?'

Her granny nodded. 'Aye, that's what a said.'

Bella smirked. 'He seems pleasant enough, although he acted a bit funny when I asked him about his books. It was like he didn't want me to know anything. Not the best way to sell them.'

'He might have thought you were a grouper. He's on a work retreat wanting a bit of peace and quiet, not to be pestered by groupers.'

Bella suddenly imagined an ugly, miserable-looking fish with her own blonde hair and had to fight the laughter threatening its escape. 'I think you mean *groupie*, Gran.'

Isla rolled her eyes. 'Aye, that's what a said.'

17

On Monday, 18 July, Bella was up early after another fitful weekend lacking sleep. Her granny's house was preying on her mind.

She showered and dressed and went to sit at the kitchen table to drink her first coffee of the day in the hopes it would wake her up. Her granny had been out sitting in the walled garden of the castle again with a copy of Brodie's book since the crack of dawn. She couldn't put it down and kept spouting off interesting facts at the most random of times. As Bella was sipping her drink, Isla came in, followed by her canine shadow.

'I'm going to the day centre after all. Maeve has sent me a WhatsUp. Harris is on his way to collect me, isn't that kind of him?'

Okay, so we're back to trying to set me up with Harris again, are we?

'Yes, that's really nice of him, Granny. Although Olivia has given me the day off so I was going to ask if I could borrow her Land Rover to take you in.'

'Oh, don't worry, Maeve says it's no bother.'

Bella decided to tease her granny. 'Maybe he'll collect you in his *polis* car and everyone will think you've been arrested.'

Her granny placed a hand on each cheek. 'Och, no, I *hadnae* thought of that.'

Bella rolled her eyes. 'I'm only teasing. I'm relieved to have a day off. The shop's ready for the opening but Olivia will need me for the rest of the week, including Saturday with it being the big day. There's a celebrity guest coming to open the event but Olivia's keeping it under wraps.'

Isla was clearly still focused on the mode of transport she would be taking to the day centre. 'I'm sure he has a car of his own as well as the bike. I'm sure I've seen him drop Maeve off at the day centre in a car that didn't have flashing lights.' She pondered for a moment then shook her head. 'Harris is off until this evening, by the way.' She gave Bella a pointed look.

'Oh, right.' Bella tried her best not to engage.

The doorbell chimed and suddenly Isla dashed towards her room. 'Get that, would you, dearie, I've forgotten my... erm... thingy.'

Bella knew exactly what game her granny was playing, and she was wasting her time. With a huff and a roll of her eyes, she walked to the door. She paused and plastered on a smile as she opened it. 'Hi, Harris, Isla's getting something from her room. Come on in for a minute.' He stood there in blue jeans, a fitted white T-shirt and a navy-blue bomber jacket. He looked handsome in his civvies again.

'Hi, Bella. Thanks.' He smiled and followed her into the kitchen. 'I was wondering if you're free at all today,' he said but held up his hand. 'Neil has been in touch about the car. He wants to chat to you in person.'

Bella's stomach sank. 'Oh, right. I'm off today as it happens.'

He nodded. 'You may as well come with us. I can take you to the garage when I've dropped Isla at the day centre if you like.'

Bella smiled. 'That'd be great, thank you. I'll grab my handbag.'

Isla and Bella passed in the hallway. 'I'm coming with you,' Bella said.

Isla beamed. 'Oh, lovely! Are you and Harris spending the day together?' The hope in her eyes annoyed Bella.

She scoffed. 'No! Nothing like that. He's taking me to see the mechanic, that's all.' Realising she had spoken a little too loudly in her frustration, she quickly glanced towards the kitchen, wondering if Harris had heard. If he had, he made no indication.

'Oh, well, that's a shame,' Isla replied rather sullenly.

Bella grabbed her bag from the chair in front of the dressing table in her room and checked her reflection. The dark circles around her emerald eyes told of her lack of sleep. She grabbed a concealer pen, dotted it quickly along the dark areas and patted it in with her ring fingers. She ran a comb through her hair that had grown rather fast since she'd last had it cut, and it now sat in waves just above her jawline. She figured her jeans and long-sleeved Florence and the Machine top would suffice, seeing as this wasn't a date. She grabbed her linen jacket, in case the bright glow of the Scottish sun she saw when she opened the front door was deceptive, and then walked back to the kitchen where Harris was chatting happily to Isla while crouched on his haunches and stroking Beau.

'Sorry, that's me ready,' Bella said.

Harris glanced up at her. 'Ah, I love a bit of Florence,' he said with a smile and a nod to her top.

Oh no, don't go giving me reasons to think we have things in common. 'Yes, me too,' she replied, immediately realising she had stated the obvious.

'Which is your favourite track? No, wait, let me guess...' He stood, tapping his finger on his bearded chin while keeping his gaze fixed on her. Her stomach felt weird for a moment until he said, 'I bet it's "Delilah".'

Dammit. She narrowed her eyes. 'It is, as it happens, but isn't that everyone's favourite Florence track?'

He shook his head. 'Nope. Mine's "Dog Days Are Over". It's a really hopeful song.'

His reply surprised her. 'Yes, that's a good one too.'

Isla huffed. 'If you two are quite finished, I've a day centre to get to.' Bella turned, ready to chastise her, but Isla winked. 'You may as well sit in the front, hen,' she said to Bella. 'I'll be out before you, and I've got Beau.'

They walked outside and Bella was relieved to see a silver Jeep waiting for them. Three on a motorbike with a dog would have been interesting, that's for sure.

* * *

Once Isla was happily ensconced with the 'old folks' at the day centre, Harris set off to take Bella to the garage.

'How are you feeling?' he asked with a brief glance in her direction.

'Terrified,' she replied.

He nodded. 'Aye, I thought as much. Neil didn't tell me anything, so, I can't even forewarn you, I'm afraid.'

They pulled into the front courtyard of Neil's garage and Bella spotted Fifi up in the air on a ramp. Her stomach flipped, seeing her beloved little car with bits missing.

Harris turned off the Jeep's engine. 'Ready?'

Bella inhaled a deep, calming breath. 'As I'll ever be.'

They climbed out of the car and were greeted by a tall, broad man with a shaved head, stubbly chin and a dirty face, wiping his oily hands on an even oilier rag. 'Harris, you ugly sod,' Neil said with a fond grin, in his unmistakeable Yorkshire tongue. 'And you must be Miss Douglas? You're far too good-looking for this numpty.'

'You cheeky wee munter,' Harris replied with a fond laugh. 'We're just friends. Bella, allow me to introduce my best mate, Neil. What he lacks in hair he makes up for in mechanical knowledge.'

The two men shook hands and slapped each other on the back. Neil turned to Bella. 'Take no notice of him; I'm actually a stunner under all this grease, just ask our Mel. Anyway, you look like you're about to face a firing squad.'

Harris told him, 'Aye, she's very fond of the car, pal. Dreading what you're about to say.'

Neil pulled his lips between his teeth. 'Aye, it's not the best news, I'm afraid.'

Bella gulped. 'Just tell me. Rip off that band-aid, as they say.'

Neil nodded. 'Right, okay, so the drive shaft is fu... buggered.' Bella found it amusing how he modified his language before the worse of the two profanities fell from his lips. He continued, 'And you'll need a new wheel, tyre and shock absorbers. Then we'll have to check the tracking and possibly adjust that. And a bit of a touch-up is needed to the paintwork too, although I think the chips might be older damage. These cars were created for farmers, believe it or not, meaning they're quite tough, so it could've been much worse.'

Bella nodded. 'Okay. So, how much are we talking?' She braced herself for the answer, clenching her fists by her sides.

Neil sucked air in through his teeth. 'Unfortunately parts aren't easy to come by wi' it bein' an old classic, and labour alone is gunna be around a hundred and twenty quid plus VAT. All in all, you're gunna be looking at somewhere around six hundred to seven hundred quid including labour, VAT and parts. But in all honesty, it'll depend on how much the parts are and where I can source 'em from. Scrappers don't always have 'em in.'

Bella felt the blood drain from her face. While it could've been much worse, she didn't have that kind of money lying around. A high excess on her insurance meant she would need to find a decent chunk of the overall amount. She had no savings after putting all her money into decorating and furnishing the flat she'd had to give up renting when she'd lost her last job, and she couldn't ask her parents because they were funding her brother until he found a suitable job now his degree was finished, and they had spent their savings on the cruise for her dad's birthday. There was no way she was asking her granny, who had taken her in and refused to accept rent money. And she had no credit card.

She nodded. 'Right, I see. Okay. Can I... can I have some time to think things through? I need to arrange the finance.'

Neil nodded. 'Aye, no worries at all. Happy to keep it here until you know what you wanna do. And o' course, feel free to get some other quotes. Although, to be honest, you have to ask yourself if it's worth havin' it fixed. I could get you a little run-around for what it's gunna cost to repair it.'

Bella shook her head. 'Oh no, that won't be necessary. I love Fifi and if she can be repaired, I'd rather do that. And as for other quotes, if Harris trusts you, so do I.' In her peripheral vision, she saw a small smile flash on Harris's face.

Harris touched her arm. 'Come on, I'll buy you a coffee. You look like you need it.'

She smiled. 'Thanks, I think I do.'

'See yous later, pal,' Harris said to Neil.

'Aye, see you later. Take care, Bella. And I'm sorry it wasn't better news.'

Bella forced a smile. 'No, thanks so much for your help.'

Bella followed Harris back to the Jeep and he opened her door. When they were both strapped in, Harris started the engine and they set off in silence into Inverness centre.

18

Harris mentioned a coffee shop he frequented when on duty, so he led the way. As they walked through Inverness, people stopped him to say hello, or they waved to him from their cars, or from across the street. Children even seemed to know who he was, waving, high fiving him or calling out to him. Bella felt like she was in an episode of a TV show, or a musical where the local copper is more like a celebrity. She kept expecting the people around them to burst into song, or for a flash mob to break out in his honour. She chuckled to herself about it and kept a look out just in case.

Harris had a smile and a kind word for everyone, and it was clear he was well respected. She hated to admit it to herself, but she really did like him as a person. When they walked into the coffee shop, the elderly lady behind the counter greeted them with a friendly smile. She wore a brightly coloured floral apron with the café name *Pettifer's* embroidered on it.

'Sergeant Donaldson. Lovely to see you on your day off. I hardly recognised you in your clothes!'

Harris feigned shock. 'Now, Mrs Pettifer, you'll be giving me a reputation I *cannae* uphold!'

The lady behind the counter turned an interesting shade of pink. 'Och, you know *verra* well what I meant, you cheeky young man.'

Harris chuckled. 'Aye, it's a good thing I did. Bella here will be wondering what I get up to!'

Mrs Pettifer's smile broadened. 'Oh, now, is this your lady friend? Lovely to meet you, dearie. We've been saying for a while we wanted to see him settled down, haven't we, Malcolm?'

'Eh?' called a man's voice from somewhere out of sight in the kitchen, but she ignored him.

'Oh no, Bella here is a friend,' Harris said with a flush of colour to his face.

Bella nodded. 'Yes, we're friends.'

The owner's smile faded and was replaced by a kind of head-tilting pity. 'Oh, that's a shame. Well, you go take a seat at your usual table and I'll bring you over a menu.'

Harris led the way to a table by the window. 'Is this okay?'

Bella grinned. 'Absolutely fine. Great vantage point. I can see why you'd choose it when you're on duty.'

He chuckled. 'Aye, I can have a wee break but make a quick getaway if needs be.' They sat and Mrs Pettifer placed a menu in front of each of them. Harris addressed her with warm familiarity. 'Thanks, Mrs P.' He leaned across the table. 'Mrs P is the best baker. You should try her Victoria sponge,' he said. 'You won't regret it, I promise you.'

Bella didn't feel much like eating but didn't want to offend him when he had been so kind as to bring her and help with Fifi. 'Okay then, you've convinced me.'

'And to drink?'

'A white coffee, please.'

'The usual times two, Mrs P!' Harris called over.

'Coming right up.'

They sat with an awkward silence hanging over them for a moment or two until Harris spoke. 'I heard you and your granny talking this morning while I was waiting on you. I gather she's still trying to sort out your single status,' he said with a grin.

She covered her eyes with her hands for a couple of seconds. 'I'm so sorry you heard that. I know my reply was a little harsh, but she's driving me mad at the moment. It's like she thinks I can't survive on my own without a man.'

He smiled. 'Hey, I get it, don't worry. I know what these old lassies are like when they get the bit between their teeth. They'd have us married off tomorrow if they could. My mum's the same, always pointing out some woman or other she thinks would be good for me.'

'I'm glad it's not just my granny.' She smiled and that strange silence descended again until Bella felt she had to break it. 'So, what made you want to be in the police?' she asked, genuinely intrigued to know the answer. She knew she could never imagine doing such a tough job.

He narrowed his eyes. 'Be careful, you might get to know me a wee bit and like what you find out.' His eyes glinted with humour.

Bella felt an unexplainable flush rise up from her chest. 'It's a risk I'm prepared to take.' She smiled.

He shook his head. 'Okay, well, you've been warned.' His smile revealed those straight teeth and a dimple in both cheeks. 'It all started when I was a kid when we lived in Edinburgh. Let's say the police were familiar with my parents, well, my dad, anyway. They were always so supportive and concerned about me and Mum. I admired how they handled things and decided when I grew up I wanted to help people like they'd helped us. We moved here when I was around ten, but things didn't really change; different location, different police, but the same situation of their regular visits. And they were still people I appreciated having around.'

'I didn't realise you were from Edinburgh. What brought your parents to Inverness?' She hoped she wasn't prying, especially seeing as she could tell there was something deeper beneath what he had told her about the police being a presence in his life from a young age. She held up her hands. 'Feel free to say no comment.'

He smiled. 'No, it's fine. It is what it is. My mum's aunt passed away and left her the house here in Inverness, so we relocated. It was supposed to be a fresh start.' He paused and Bella could sense he was reliving something unpleasant. He quickly snapped out of it and continued, 'She was an eccentric old woman by all accounts, my mum's aunt. Bought and sold antiques and weird stuff. The house was beautiful from the outside. Quite big and Victorian. But inside it was crammed to the gunnels full of her collected things. Piles of newspapers and magazines, cardboard boxes full of goodness knows what, loads of tins of out-of-date food, as if she was expecting some catastrophic event. Turns out she'd been a bit of a hoarder. It took a hell of a lot of sorting out but when it was done it made us a great home. Mum lived there right until she was struggling to get up and down the stairs. I didn't want her to go into the old folk's home, offered to get one of those stair lifts fitted, but she insisted she didn't want to be a burden with me having my career in the police and all that. So, she moved into Sunnyside a couple of years ago, and now the house is mine.' He shrugged.

'Oh, that's lovely. So, your dad isn't around any more?'

Harris fiddled with the menu and raised his eyebrows for a split second. 'No, he passed away around ten years ago.'

Bella thankfully still had her parents and couldn't imagine how difficult it would be to lose either of them. 'I'm so sorry.'

Harris shook his head. 'Don't be. He was a hard man to love. In fact, I've spent my life striving to be nothing at all like him, hence my career choice. But that's a whole other story.'

Bella didn't want to pry further and was wondering how to

change the subject but luckily, Mrs Pettifer placed a tray on their table, complete with a cafetière, a jug of cream, a sugar bowl, cups and two huge, fluffy pieces of Victoria sponge cake filled to bursting with fresh cream and jam.

'Wow, thank you. This looks delicious,' Bella said as the earthy aroma of coffee and the fruity sweetness of the jam tantalised her senses, making her mouth water. She sliced the corner of the cake and placed a forkful in her mouth. The sponge was light as air and melted on her tongue, and she closed her eyes for a moment to revel in its deliciousness. 'Wow,' she said. 'You were right,' she mumbled in between chewing. 'Best Victoria sponge ever! Just don't tell Mirren at the castle I said so.'

Harris chuckled. 'Told you, didn't I? Right, my turn. So, how did you end up working at the castle?'

She took a sip of her coffee. 'Nothing as inspiring as your story. I'd had a run of bad luck with jobs, and like you said, that's a story for another time. But anyway, Olivia inherited the castle unexpectedly and decided the best way to keep it going was to open it to the public. But that was going to take loads of work and she was still designing for Nina Picarro, a fashion house in New York, so she needed someone to help with the day-to-day running of things. I was between jobs, so she asked me to be her PA and I snatched her hand off for the chance. I mean, what's not to love? I get to work in the most stunning location and with my best friend; it's a win-win situation.'

'So how did you come to design the apartments? That's not really something you would expect a PA to do. Although I have to say you did a grand job from what I've seen.'

'How did you know about that?' She immediately knew the answer and they both said 'Isla,' in unison.

'It was a bit of a happy accident, really. Olivia knows how much

I love interior design. It was what I wanted to do for a career but it didn't work out unfortunately.'

'How come? You've definitely got a flair for it.'

Bella's stomach fluttered and for some reason she was happy he liked what she'd done. 'Thank you. Life got in the way. I dropped out of my art and design degree in the first year because my mum got ill. I couldn't focus. And I wanted to be there for my dad and my kid brother. She eventually got the all-clear but I'd already got a job by then and I'd got used to the money. I do regret it sometimes.'

'You should look at doing a part-time course online.'

'You sound like my granny.' She smiled.

'She's dead proud of you,' Harris told her. 'She talks about you non-stop.'

Bella cringed. 'Yikes, how boring for everyone.'

His mouth tilted up at one corner. 'It's really not.' He was kind of sweet in the way he tried to make her feel at ease.

'Do you spend a lot of time at the day centre?' she asked, wondering how he knew Isla so well.

Harris took a mouthful of cake and chewed for a moment. 'Aye, especially with it being connected to the residential home where Mum lives. But I tend to go in under the capacity of work if needed, and we like to be a presence around the older folks, so they're not worried about asking for help if they need it. Lots of them live alone, the ones that don't live at Sunnyside like my mum, and it's good for them to be able to put a face to a name if ever we're called out. And, of course, I do tend to drop my mum in sometimes if she's been visiting me, so I hang around for a bit. They're a lovely bunch up there. Very sweet. I've a lot of time for them. I could listen to their stories for hours, and often do.'

Bella allowed herself to like him a little bit more. 'That's very kind of you.'

He shrugged. 'I'm a good guy.' He winked playfully. 'But seriously, community policing is very important to me.'

She was realising she had got him rather wrong from the start. 'It's clear you love your job.'

'I do. It's good to feel like I'm being useful, you know? It feels like more than a job, though. It's an honour to help people get justice, and it feels good to give back.'

'You're a very compassionate man and people clearly think a lot of you. You seem to know everyone in Inverness if our walk here is anything to go by.'

He held out his hands. 'I did say I'm a good guy.' He laughed and his eyes crinkled at the corners.

Bella couldn't help laughing along. 'You did say that, more than once.'

She ate another mouthful of cake to distract attention from her flushed cheeks. 'Hmm, anyway, changing the subject, when I saw you at the bar you said you were going birdwatching, is that something you do regularly?'

Harris tilted his head and squinted. 'I gather from your expression it's not something that interests you?'

Bella touched her face with her hands, self-conscious at how well he seemed to read her. 'My expression? I mean... I can't say I've ever been interested in birds, really, so I don't understand why people find them so fascinating they'd want to sit all quiet and spy on them. But each to their own.'

Harris laughed. '*Spy* on them? I've never looked at it that way before.'

'So, what appeals to you so much about the avian population?' Once again, Bella was genuinely intrigued to know.

'I love how they look after their young, how they go about everyday life. Their sense of community and protection.'

Bella nodded. 'Well, yes, I can see why that would appeal to you specifically.'

'And I love the way each species has its own sound, its own voice, I suppose, like a different language.' He fell silent for a few moments, and he frowned, opened his mouth and closed it again as if he was unsure of divulging anything further. Eventually he continued, 'My interest started when I was wee. My dad was... how can I put it?' He looked up to the ceiling briefly as if searching for answers, then shrugged. 'Sod it, might as well tell it how it is, eh? My dad was an alcoholic and a petty thief. He'd come home most Saturday nights *pished* out of his head and belligerent with it. I'd have been around six or seven from memory but I'm sure it'd been going on long before that. Some nights the police would escort him home or to the cells at the station to sleep it off. And sometimes if he left before the police were called on him, he'd arrive home being loud and aggressive.

'On those occasions my mum would get me out of bed and walk me round to my grandad's house – her dad – with my coat over my pyjamas, and I'd stay there for the night to keep me safe. Me and my grumpa, as I used to call him, we'd get up on the Sunday morning and Grumpa would pack sandwiches for us. Then we'd get the bus to Threipmuir Reservoir outside Edinburgh. He had this wee pocketbook with photos of British birds, and we'd sit on a bench or in the hide, and tick off the ones we saw. They were special times.'

He lifted his chin, and his chocolate-brown eyes were glistening with emotion. He cleared his throat. 'Sheesh, I don't talk about this stuff usually. How did you do that?' He laughed and rubbed his hands over his face.

Bella found herself fighting back tears and she reached out to pat his arm. 'I didn't mean to pry. I'm so sorry about what you went through with your dad.'

Harris took a swig of his coffee and topped up both of their mugs from the cafetière. 'Aye, like I said, he was a hard man to love.'

'It's so sweet to hear about your grandad, though. And it explains your affinity with older people. I bet you missed your *grumpa* when you moved to Inverness.'

Harris folded his arms and leant them on the table but kept his gaze fixed on his mug. 'He died about a year before we came. That's why my aunty left her house to my mum. But you're right, I did miss him. Still do. I have his little pocketbook, though. I still use it.'

Bella pulled her lips between her teeth and tried to compose herself. She was seeing Harris in a different light now. His lack of drinking and his passion for birdwatching didn't make him boring; they simply made him sensible and sentimental. She'd been wrong to judge him. He was definitely the kind of friend she wanted in her life, and she was happy, now, she had met him. Although she might not admit that to her granny; the last thing she wanted to do was give her false hope.

'That's so lovely,' she whispered. He was quite a wholesome, caring and thoughtful man, something that caught Bella a little off guard.

He inhaled and clapped his hands together. 'Right, enough of this maudlin stuff. I've bored you quite enough with my life history.' He stood and picked up his jacket. 'I should get you home, I'm sure you have more interesting things to be doing. I'll bring Isla back later if that's okay with you?'

Bella watched as he too gathered himself. She felt she knew him a little better now, although he clearly felt uncomfortable for sharing.

'That would be great, thank you. Hang on a sec while I go pay our bill.'

Harris held up his hand. 'Oh no, it's fine, you—'

She cut him off. '—Please, it's the least I can do.'

* * *

The journey back to Drumblair was mostly void of conversation as they listened to a Spotify soundtrack. This time it was a comfortable silence, however, punctuated by Florence and the Machine singing about waiting for someone's call.

Harris pulled to a stop at the front of the castle and he turned to her. 'There you go. Home sweet home. I'll let you know if I hear any more about your car.'

Bella smiled and nodded. 'Thanks for your help.' She paused for a moment then said: 'I think you and I will be good friends,' as she climbed down from the vehicle.

He gave a brief smile. 'Friends, aye, I'd like that.' Then he drove away and out of sight.

19

Once back at the castle, Bella sat on the bench she had shared with Aiden the day before. The sun was warm on her skin and signs of summer were everywhere. The wildflower beds on either side of the entrance to the apartments were alive with bees, their little hairy legs yellow with the bounty they had collected. White candy-floss clouds floated around the blue expanse overhead and she closed her eyes for a few moments to listen to the birdsong. She could make out different tones and patterns of the chirps when she concentrated, something she had never really taken the time to notice before. Harris was right, though; it did sound as if each species had their own language.

'Afternoon, Bella,' came a familiar voice.

Bella opened her eyes. 'Oh, hi, Aiden. How are the words coming today?' He appeared to be wearing pyjama bottoms and an old faded T-shirt. Bella wondered how on earth that made him more attractive. *Get a grip, Douglas, your hormones are in overdrive!*

He nodded. 'Better, thanks.'

'That's good, you must be relieved.'

He sat down beside her. 'I am. Only another sixty thousand to go.'

Bella widened her eyes. 'Wow. That's a lot of words.'

'It sure is. It's a good thing I have no personal distractions, I suppose. Although I'm a terror for getting sucked into TikTok.'

Bella laughed. 'Not you too? I'm constantly watching cute puppy videos or make-up tutorials for effects I'll never try.'

Aiden grinned. 'Me too. Except I try *all* of the make-up tutorial effects.'

Bella laughed louder. 'I bet you look bonny with a winged eyeliner.'

He patted his hair. 'Oh, I do. And I love that sparkly eyeshadow they keep showcasing, you know, the one that's soooooo pigmented? I'll let you borrow it some time.'

Aiden was definitely funny and easy to talk to. Not to mention he was so confident and worldly. He'd shaved today and she found herself staring a little too long at the smooth skin at his jawline.

'So, how's the vintage Citroen?' he asked eventually, pulling her from her fantasy.

Bella curled her lip. 'Ugh, not good at all. Harris took me to the garage to talk to the mechanic. It sounds like a fair bit of work to get her up and running again.'

Aiden tilted his head. 'You and the sergeant are getting quite friendly then, eh?'

Bella thought she saw a glint of disappointment in his crumpled expression, and she fidgeted in her seat. 'He's a lovely guy but we're just friends.'

Aiden narrowed his eyes. 'Hmm. Interesting. He clearly likes you.'

Bella placed her hands under her chin and fluttered her eyelashes. 'Of course he does, I'm very likeable.' When he didn't respond, she dropped her hands to her lap. 'Speaking of liking people, is your other half joining you while you're here?'

Aiden frowned. 'My other half? I don't have an *other half*. I'm pretty whole by myself at the moment. Didn't you catch the comment about having no personal distractions?'

Bella raised her eyebrows. 'Oh, right. I must have got the wrong end of the stick. I heard you say something about a date the other day and put two and two together.'

He tilted up his chin. 'Ah yes, you Douglas women seem to be good at getting the wrong end of the stick.' *Ah, so he's still dwelling on his almost arrest, is he?* Bella thought. He continued, 'Sadly no, though, it was a "date" with my editor. She came up on the train and we met up for a chat about the book.'

'Ah, I see.'

There was a pause in conversation until Aiden spoke again. 'I fancy going out for dinner tonight and as you're local, I wonder if you might be able to recommend somewhere?'

She pondered for a moment. 'The Glenmoriston Town House Restaurant is lovely. Great food and they have a really nice piano bar too that serves lots of different gins and whiskies.'

'Sounds good. Shall I try to book us a table for tonight?'

Bella widened her eyes. '*Us*? You want to take *me*?' As if he wouldn't know who she meant, she pointed at herself.

He gave a laugh. 'Well, it's no fun dining out alone, is it? I thought it'd be nice to have some company, and to get to know my neighbour, seeing as we didn't exactly get off on the best footing.'

'Oh, right, yes, well, in that case I'd like that, thank you.'

He nodded. 'Great.'

Although he hadn't mentioned the word 'date', she couldn't help feeling excited about going out with him. Looks wise, he was just her type, from his fair hair to his lean body and smooth skin. There was something a little bit Hollywood about him and he wouldn't look out of place on the big screen. Add to that his status as an author and he was almost perfect. Butterflies wearing hobnail boots stomped around her stomach and some escaped to flutter around her heart.

Aiden stood. 'Glenmoriston Town House Restaurant it is then. I'll knock on your door once I've made a reservation.'

Bella was trying her best not to carry on smiling like a woman possessed but knew she was failing miserably. 'I'll look forward to it.'

Aiden left to go into his apartment, leaving Bella sitting there on the bench, fighting the urge to squeal. Once he was inside and had closed the door, she took her phone from her handbag and dialled.

When Olivia answered, Bella blurted, 'Liv, it's me! Guess who's invited me out for dinner!'

Olivia gasped. 'Ooh, ooh, Sergeant Donaldson?'

Bella huffed. 'No! Why would you think that? Anyway, no, our author friend!'

Olivia paused as if processing the information. 'Oh! Exciting! So where is he taking you?'

'The Glenmoriston Town House Restaurant!'

'Swanky,' Olivia replied.

'The problem is I didn't bring any going out clothes from Granny's. Can I borrow something?'

'Of course. Come upstairs and have a look through my wardrobe.'

* * *

Isla arrived home from the day centre around 5 p.m. with Beau and closed the front door behind her before making her way into the living room and flopping down into her favourite chair with a deep, tired sigh. As if exhausted from his day of cuddles, Beau lay down and closed his eyes for a snooze.

Bella glanced behind her. 'Are you alone?'

She pointed at the dog. 'No, Beau's with me.'

'No one else?'

Isla glanced over her own shoulder. 'I should hope not, why? Who were you expecting me to bring? My toyboy?' She chuckled. 'I'll have to find one first.'

'I thought Harris might have come in to say hello.'

Isla tugged off her shoes. 'No, he dropped me off and then left because he's on the late shift at the station. He said you'd had a nice time together today, though.'

Bella knew her granny was fishing for details. 'We did. He's an interesting man. Definitely a lovely *friend* to have around.'

Isla huffed. 'Friend? Right then.'

'So, what have you been up to today?'

Isla rolled her eyes. 'Card making.'

Bella smirked. 'You sound thrilled.'

'Oh aye, great fun, if you're a toddler.'

'I'm sure some of the others enjoyed it, though. Maybe you should suggest something to do if they keep missing the mark for you.'

Isla waved her hand like she was swatting a fly. 'You're joking, aren't you? There's more chance of me sunbathing in the Arctic Circle than them listening to me.'

Bella leaned forward. 'I have news if you're interested.'

Isla leaned forward too. 'Oh aye? Do tell.'

'Our new neighbour, Aiden, has invited me out for dinner this evening. Trouble is all my going out clothes are still at the house so I'm going up to borrow something to wear from Liv. Aiden knocked about ten minutes ago to say he's booked us a table for 7.30 this evening. He's booked us a taxi too.'

Isla raised her eyebrows. 'Oooh, very nice. A date, eh?' Her crumpled expression didn't match her positive words.

'Well... he didn't actually call it a date as such—'

'Be careful, though. We don't really know him and he's no police sergeant. I do wonder, you know...'

When Isla didn't finish her sentence, Bella queried the fact. 'Come on, you may as well say it, you do wonder what?'

Isla shook her head. 'Well, these types of people who write crime novels. How do they come up with their ideas? They must have twisted minds, don't you think? To write such graphic and gory stories.'

Bella scoffed. 'Good grief, Granny, it means they have vivid imaginations, that's all. It doesn't make them bad people and it doesn't mean they go around committing the crimes they write about. And you've never read anything by him, so you don't know.'

'Aye, well, same goes for you as far as we know! And he was rude when you asked him about his pen name. I'd watch yourself.' Isla pondered things for a moment. 'Aye, you might be better having a code word you can say when you ring me on the What-sUp, you know, just in case.'

Bella couldn't help laughing. 'And what would you do if I rang you and used the code?'

With an indignant fold of her arms, Isla said, 'I'd ring Harris, obviously.'

Of course you would. 'I'm sure that won't be necessary, but I appreciate your concern. Now I'm off up to see Liv to figure out what I'm going to wear for my non-date with the serial killer, whoops, I mean *author*.' She stood and walked away, chuckling as she went.

* * *

Bella selected a pair of tailored black trousers and a silver-grey shirt from Olivia's extensive wardrobe. That was one definite positive about having a fashionista as a bestie. She chose heels that matched her top, a black clutch bag and a black and grey pinstriped jacket.

'Oh, my word, Bells, he'll have to pick his tongue up off the floor!' Olivia said as Bella stood in front of Olivia's full-length mirror.

'Oh no, he didn't even mention the word "date", remember!'

'Wait until he sees you, the word "date" will definitely crop up then!'

* * *

Back at the apartment and once she had finished her hair and make-up, Bella made her way through to the living room, where her granny was watching a quiz show. She was blurting answers at the television and then having one-sided arguments with the show host when they – incorrectly, in her opinion – gave out the answers.

When she realised Bella was standing there, she pointed at the TV. 'They don't do their research on this programme. You look nice, dearie.'

Bella smoothed down her shirt. 'Do you think? I don't look like I'm going for an interview, do I?'

'I should hope not, you've far too much cleavage on show for an interview.'

Bella glanced down at her chest self-consciously and gave a nervous laugh. 'Gee, thanks, Granny.'

There was a knock at the door and Bella went to answer it. Aiden stood there in black jeans, a wine-coloured shirt and a black suit jacket.

He pointed down at his clothes. 'I don't look like I'm going for an interview, do I?'

Bella laughed. 'Well, if you do, we may be fighting for the same job.' It was clear by his blank expression he didn't understand what she meant. 'I said the same to my granny about my outfit.'

'Ah! You look great,' he replied, and Bella relaxed a little. 'Come on, the taxi's waiting for us. Good evening, Mrs Douglas!' He raised his hand in a wave to the elderly lady, who had appeared in the living room doorway.

'Aye, and yoursel',' Isla replied rather unconvincingly before returning to her chair.

'One sec.' Bella dashed back to the living room, kissed her granny's head, scratched a sleepy Beau behind his ears and said, 'See you later, Granny, don't wait up.'

As she reached the door Isla blurted, 'Code word banana! Did you hear me? For the WhatsUp! Banana!'

Bella closed the door, giggling to herself about Isla's choice of code word and wondered how on earth she could casually insert 'banana' into a conversation that wouldn't look suspicious if her companion saw it.

* * *

The taxi stopped outside the Glenmoriston Town House just before 7.30 that evening. It was an attractive stone building with a large bay window to the left, which glowed amber from inside with atmospheric, dimmed lighting. Bella had only ever been once before for a family birthday celebration, but it had stood out in her memory as being somewhere she would love to visit again, and now here she was.

As Bella and Aiden climbed out of the car, Bella glanced up to see Harris, in uniform and on duty, walking towards them. He was accompanied by the female officer, Mel, who had attended on the night Aiden had been detained.

'Evening, Bella. Evening, Mr O'Dowd,' Harris said with a nod of his head. His hands were slotted into his high-vis jacket pockets, his expression remained stoic, and he had an air of professionalism about him.

Bella's companion raised his hand. 'Please, call me Aiden.'

'Hi, both of you. My granny said you were working tonight,' Bella said, a strange knot of discomfort tightening in her stomach as she glanced between the two men. 'Hi, Mel, how are you?'

Mel beamed. 'I'm great, thanks. I hear you're letting my Neil loose on your car,' Mel said with a chuckle.

'I am. Just need to save up to pay for the repairs now.'

'Get a horse, they're far more reliable.'

Bella laughed. 'I'm not brave enough for transport that has a mind of its own!'

Mel laughed. 'Fair enough.'

'So, have you been busy tonight?' Bella asked out of politeness.

Harris gave a curt nod. 'Aye, there was a call to say someone had fallen in the river but turns out it was an old coat. Anyway, have a lovely evening.' He made to carry on walking, but his partner wasn't quite ready to leave.

'You've got good taste, Aiden,' Officer Mel said with a nod towards the hotel. 'It's a lovely place that. Very special. Good place for a date.' She raised her eyebrows.

'Indeed it is,' Harris said, his face still expressionless. 'Good choice. Great food.'

'That's good to know. Anyway, goodnight, sergeant, goodnight, officer.' Aiden was clearly ready for the conversation to be over. 'Nice to see you under more friendly circumstances.'

Mel giggled. 'Oh aye, that was an interesting night, wasn't it? I should think you weren't expecting to be thrown to the floor by a woman on your first night at the castle.'

Harris kept his gaze fixed on Bella. 'Well, we'll be off. Come on, Mel, back to the station; let's allow these good people to enjoy their evening.' Mel rolled her eyes and nodded her head sideways at Harris.

Bella stifled a giggle. 'Bye, Harris. Nice to see you again, Mel.'

Aiden opened the door to the restaurant and Bella walked inside. 'The poor guy's got it bad for you,' he said as the maître d' showed them to their table and handed them each a menu.

Bella scoffed. 'Don't be daft. He was on duty, that's why he was all serious.'

Aiden gave a knowing look but clearly decided to change the subject. 'So, shall we have a nice bottle of wine? What do you prefer?'

'I'm no wine connoisseur but I really like Pinot Noir.' She hoped she hadn't said the wrong thing. If she was honest, it all tasted the same to her, apart from the cheap rubbish that gave you a hangover just by looking at the tacky label.

'Pinot Noir sounds good.' The waiter came over and took their drinks order, then they sat in silence as they perused their menus for a while.

Bella took in her surroundings, something she couldn't help doing. The walls were covered in a beautiful gold damask paper and there was an ornate light fitting hanging from a circular gold leaf-effect panel on the ceiling. It was very opulent, very classy. Tea lights glowed from the centre of each table, adding to the warm intimate ambience.

Bella wondered where the evening would go and if things might turn into a date after all.

She really hoped so.

20

Bella and Aiden made small talk about their family and friends for a while but, as they finished their melt-in-the-mouth steak main courses, and Aiden topped up her drink, he asked, 'So, I remember you saying you like crime novels. Who are your favourite authors?'

Bella took a sip of the red liquid in her glass and relished the warm sensation on her tongue. She still wondered if she had inadvertently read anything by him. 'I have quite a few go-to authors, but I love Ian Rankin. Especially the *Rebus* novels. And I've read everything Lisa Jewell has ever written. And, of course, Ann Cleeves is a favourite too. I love the *Vera* series especially. But I think my absolute favourite author has to be Carrick Murphy. His writing is... ugh, amazing. He has this way of describing places so you feel like you're there, part of the story, witnessing it all play out. His books should be made into movies in my opinion. I'd be the first in the queue to see them if they did. Although he hasn't released anything in absolutely ages, which is weird as he's usually so prolific.' Realising she had waffled, and the wine was going to her head a little, she asked, 'How about you? Do you like Carrick

Murphy? What do you like to read? And who inspires your writing?'

Aiden chuckled. 'I've heard good things about Carrick Murphy but it may surprise you to hear I rarely read crime novels myself. I'm actually more into urban and dark fantasy these days. Authors like Ben Aaronovitch and Joe Abercrombie. I love their characterisation and world building.' He sipped from his glass and continued, 'I enjoy writing crime and thriller books, though, don't get me wrong, but I find it difficult to read the genre I write in. Probably paranoia about a clash of stories or something, I don't know.' He took another small sip of his drink before carrying on, 'I suppose I was initially inspired by the likes of Ian Rankin and Irvine Welsh, though. Scottish authors who write about Scottish people and Scottish places. Like I said, I may be Irish born but I have a strong affinity with Scotland.'

'The other day, you said you write under a pen name but then seemed a bit reluctant to tell me any more about it. Is it an "I could tell you, but I'd have to kill you" situation?' She grinned.

Aiden placed down his glass and his expression became serious. He frowned and glanced over his shoulder, causing Bella to worry her joke was somehow a little too close to reality.

He chewed his lip for a moment and leaned forward. 'Look, I know I seemed a bit off about that, I shot off without giving an explanation and I'm really sorry I did that. But I really do have good reason.' She watched his Adam's apple bob as he swallowed nervously. 'It's been a stressful time for me. Embarrassing, too.'

Bella widened her eyes. 'Okay. I'm sorry to hear that. Stressful and embarrassing in what way? If you don't mind me asking, that is?'

He pulled his lower lip between his teeth and closed his eyes for a few seconds. 'Severe writer's block.'

Bella leaned forward and rested her hand on his arm. 'Oh no.

That really sucks, I'm so sorry.'

He gave a swift wave of his hand. 'Oh no, it'll be fine. I'm being badgered to get the book done but I want to get it right. More pressure.' He sighed. 'This trip is a last-ditch attempt to spark something in me. The castle location is apparently meant to inspire me for the next book in the series, which has now been two years in the making. No good when I usually write three to four in one year. It all stemmed from...' He swallowed hard. 'I had some... erm... issues... it wasn't great there for a while.'

Bella's stomach knotted for him. 'You don't have to tell me anything, it's fine.'

Aiden sighed. 'It's all right. I can tell you. You might see Harris calling in on me too.'

Bella sat bolt upright. 'The police are involved?' she almost hissed. 'What happened?'

'Kind of... yes... but not in the way you might think. Look, it's better if I just explain. Shall we go through to the bar?'

Bella nodded. A waiter came and cleared their table and Aiden ordered a second bottle of Pinot Noir. Another waiter escorted them through to the bar area and swiftly placed a freshly opened bottle of wine before them. The bar was surprisingly quiet, and they had the room to themselves when they arrived.

Once they were alone again and sitting side by side on a leather couch, Aiden turned to face Bella. 'What I'm about to tell you is painful to talk about and... partly why I was reluctant to call this a date. I'm still...' He sighed. 'I find it difficult to trust these days.' He lowered his gaze and fiddled with his watch. 'I was married. To my best friend, or so I thought, but then...' He cleared his throat. 'I found out she was having an affair with someone at work. I was utterly devastated. It almost broke me. I was on the verge of a breakdown, but I realised I had to move on. I have my career and my readers to think about.'

'Oh, Aiden, I'm so sorry. That must've been awful for you.'

He gave a small smile but didn't quite make eye contact. 'Humiliating and degrading. I gave her everything. My career afforded us the best in life but even that wasn't enough.' His jaw ticked under his skin and his brow creased. 'Things descended into a rather bitter separation. As acrimonious as it gets. The other "man",' he said, making quotation marks in the air, 'became quite aggressive when I refused to give up my home. I forced her to move out instead. So, he made threats... awful, violent threats. Then he threatened to reveal my personal details online, to tear me limb from limb, to rearrange my face, amongst other things. But the police didn't want to know, seeing as there were no witnesses.'

Bella gasped. 'That's crazy.'

Aiden inhaled a shaking breath. 'It all happened months ago now, but it took so much from me at the time. My editor and my agent were amazing. They really pulled me back to my feet and this is why I'm here. I thought it had all calmed down, but I arrived early because my ex turned up on my doorstep demanding more money. It's not like we even had kids. But she thinks I should still be keeping her and her new bloke in the lifestyle she'd become accustomed to.'

'Ridiculous! What a witch.'

He laughed once. 'I could think of far stronger names for her. But anyway, I'm here in Inverness to try and rebuild my confidence. No one knows I'm here, so I suppose I'm in hiding really. I don't particularly want my features rearranging and in theory no one can bother me if they don't know where I am. That's the beauty of writing under a pseudonym, I suppose. And up to now, the bastard in question hasn't carried out his doxxing threat, even though she's clearly revealed my personal details to him. I think it fuelled him to think he can blackmail money out of me.'

Bella reached out and squeezed his hand. 'No one deserves to be treated that way.' Something else niggled at her. 'But why is Harris visiting if the police won't do anything?'

He smiled. 'Ah, that's just consultation for my work. In the past I've got the perspective of the police on procedures for whatever I've been working on. Figured it would possibly help me again. My mental health took a beating after the split, and I lost my love of writing for a while. But it's the almost-breakdown that makes me feel... less of a man, I suppose.'

Bella huffed and stared at nothing for a few moments, letting it all sink in. 'It's all so sad. But please know having mental health issues doesn't make you less of a man. Not at all. I certainly won't judge you for that.'

He smiled. 'Thank you. I'd been fighting against coming here, to be honest. I was trying to convince my agent and my editor I was fine, that I'd get writing again, but they could tell it was procrastination at its best. But when Candace turned up on my doorstep, I finally gave in to their nagging and got in my car in a strop.' He laughed. 'My agent called me a petulant child. Then, of course, I couldn't get hold of Lady Olivia and I arrived without proper notice and almost got arrested.' He laughed. 'The rest, as they say, is history. But now I've met you, I'm glad I gave in. I just hope the words keep flowing.'

Bella nodded but her heart ached for him. 'I really hope so. Thank you for telling me and please don't worry, I won't breathe a word to anyone about this. It's not my story to tell.'

He smiled and took her hand. 'Thank you, Bella. I really appreciate that.'

Her heart skipped as he caressed her skin softly with his thumb. 'You didn't have to tell me really. I shouldn't have pushed you on it.'

He squeezed her hand and leaned in. 'Something tells me I can trust you.' He shook his head and gazed into her eyes. 'I sense you're nothing at all like my ex.'

Bella's heart began to race as he closed in, his face only inches away from hers. Things were escalating rapidly, and her mind was swimming and swooshing. Should she allow him to kiss her? Especially as this wasn't even a date. What were her boundaries? What did she even know about him really? She couldn't think clearly. Instead, she watched in slow motion as his lips got closer and closer. And just as he was about to close that remaining distance, he whispered, 'By the way, my pen name is Carrick Murphy.'

Before Bella had time to let the news sink in that she was about to kiss one of her all-time favourite authors, he slipped his hand into her hair, pulled her to him and kissed her in a way that made her light-headed and brought to mind a scene from a movie where the ordinary girl gets the handsome celebrity. It didn't seem real. Her mind was a blurry fog of alcohol and confusion.

When he pulled away, he smiled. 'Just how I imagined it would be.'

'Wait... hang on... You're Carrick Murphy? *The* Carrick Murphy? Who I waffled on about earlier?'

He chuckled. 'The very same,' he said dramatically. 'So, now you've kissed your favourite author.'

Her heart hammered in her chest, and she stared at him. His eyes twinkled in the soft light of the candles and his masculine features were a little fuzzy but still handsome. Although she was still befuddled.

Aiden stood. 'I'll go grab us a night cap, eh? Single malt?' Before she could reply and say she wasn't really a whisky drinker unlike Olivia, he excused himself and she sat there utterly bewildered. She wasn't sure how to feel and gulped down the remaining contents of her glass.

* * *

After they left the restaurant, Bella had so many questions, but her head was now thumping thanks to the amount of red wine she had consumed, and the whisky she had downed to be polite. They walked along the River Ness in silence for a while until Aiden spoke.

'Get your phone out, let's have a selfie.'

It was an odd request, but she took out her phone and he pulled her into his side and smiled at the camera lens as she held the phone at arm's length.

As she put her phone away, he kissed the side of her head. 'There you go. Something special for you to keep and remind you of the evening. Just don't post it anywhere, okay?'

Bella was a little niggled by the ego that seemed to keep rearing its head. But she reasoned it away. He was a well-known author, even if people didn't know who was *actually* behind his pseudonym.

In her peripheral vision, she spotted him glancing at her until he eventually said, 'Are you in a stunned silence? Do you have questions? Because you look like you do.'

She forced a smile. 'Sorry... I'm a bit shocked.'

'Good shocked? Or bad shocked?'

She shook her head, which was a mistake as the streetlights seemed to move with her. 'Just shocked... I suppose.'

'I have a question,' he said as they walked.

'Fire away.'

'How come you live at the castle? I know Olivia is your best friend, but it all seems a bit odd.'

'Oh yes, there was a flood at Granny's house so we're there temporarily, like you.'

'Ah, that makes sense. So how long will you be there?'

'No idea. I'm talking with the builders and the insurers daily but it's early days yet.' They stopped and leaned on the wall overlooking the river. The streetlights opposite glinted on the ripples of the water that appeared black at this time of night. Bella turned to face Aiden. 'How about you? How long are you going to be there?'

He shrugged. 'As long as it takes, I suppose. And now I'll have a bit of friendly company, too, which is a nice surprise.' He tucked a strand of hair behind her ear. 'Sorry about the kiss thing. That was a bit forward of me. I hope you can forgive me.'

She breathed in a lungful of chilly night air and smiled. 'It's fine.'

'So, which books of mine have you enjoyed the most?' he asked with eagerness.

Ah, something I can answer truthfully, she thought. 'I loved your *Long Way Home* series. Maddy, the main protagonist, was such a strong woman with everything she'd been through. So inspirational.'

'I'm so glad you like Maddy. She's my favourite character too. I'll let you in on a secret, she's based on my mother.'

'Oh, wow. That's so lovely.' She took in his features, his messy blond hair, sculpted cheekbones and vivid blue eyes, and realised once again how different he looked to her mental picture. It was probably the alcohol that caused her to blurt, 'You know, because there's no author photo on your book jackets, I have to admit to having a totally different image of you in my head.'

He grinned. 'Oh, really? Come on then, what did you think I'd look like?'

She chewed on the inside of her cheek for a moment, wondering if she should actually voice her thoughts, but once again the alcohol emboldened her. 'You'll hate me. But I presumed you would be this middle-aged, balding man with a beer belly and wrinkles.'

Aiden laughed harder this time. 'Honestly? Nice, thanks. I hope the real me didn't disappoint then.'

Bella giggled. 'Absolutely not. You're more Aiden the Hunk than Jabba the Hutt.'

He slipped his arms around her waist and pulled her closer. 'Thank goodness for that. Warning, I'm going to kiss you again.' He did and she let him. She was past the point of resisting now. He pulled away. 'Come on, I should take you home or your granny will be phoning on WhatsUp to ask if you need *bananas*.' He laughed.

Bella gasped and she covered her eyes with her hand. 'Oh, my goodness, you heard that?'

Aiden grinned. 'She's got quite a pair of lungs on her, your granny.'

Bella was so embarrassed she feared her face might burst into flames. 'I can't believe it. I feel so stupid!'

He took her hand in his and interlaced their fingers. 'No, don't be daft. I'm actually relieved that bananas haven't been mentioned once throughout the entire evening.'

Bella giggled. 'I've had no reason to bring them into the conversation, thankfully.'

'Even though I told you all about my breakdown and kissed you without invitation?'

He actually had a point. 'Well, apart from that.'

He seemed to gloss over her reply. 'I have to say, though, I'm glad that, during our *getting to know each other* chat, we didn't get to talking about our favourite fruit.' He laughed, his shoulders juddering up and down. 'I'd've had to lie.'

Bella's insides squirmed. 'Honestly, my granny has a lot to answer for.'

He fiddled with a lock of her hair. 'Nah, she's looking out for you. I think it's sweet.'

'Having known her my whole life, sweet isn't a word I often associate with Isla Douglas.'

They began walking again and Aiden said, 'I think perhaps I need to pay her a visit, show her I'm actually quite normal. People seem to have this misconception that crime novel authors write about their own sordid life experiences.'

Bella froze for a moment. 'Yes, that's exactly what she was insinuating earlier.'

'Ah, well, she definitely needs to meet me properly and I'll prove to her I'm worthy of her granddaughter.' He paused and bit his lip briefly. 'Although I bet she has her sights set on Harris for you, doesn't she?'

Yup. One hundred per cent. 'What makes you think that?' Bella hoped the street lighting would hide the flush to her cheeks – a dead giveaway.

'Oh, I don't know, he's a police sergeant, trustworthy, nice guy, am I close?'

Bella closed her eyes and nodded. 'Spot on. Although even he was on shaky ground for a while when she found out he rides a motorbike.'

He wagged his finger. 'You see, that's where I gain points. I drive a very normal car. It has four wheels and everything.' He chuckled.

'With that argument, I think you might win hands down. Once she's sure you're not figuring out ways to chop her up.'

'Nah, she's going to love me, I know it. Now, let me give that taxi firm a call. I think I'm best to get you home at a reasonable hour, set the points counter on its ascent, eh?'

* * *

After kissing Aiden goodnight, Bella unlocked the apartment door as quietly as she possibly could and closed it gently behind her.

She was still trying to get her head around the evening.

'Did you have a nice night, dearie?' Isla's voice spooked Bella, who dropped her keys on the floor and almost jumped out of her skin.

She wobbled and almost fell over. 'Granny!'

'What? We waited up for you, that's all, didn't we, Beau?' The little dog gave a reluctant yip. He clearly wished he was in bed.

Bella composed herself and walked through to the lounge. 'You didn't need to wait up. I told you I'd be fine,' she said with a slight slur.

'You're drunk!' Isla exclaimed. 'I don't think that was a very good idea.' A crease of worry was evident on her face.

Bella waved a dismissive hand. 'I'm not exactly drunk... just a bit tipsy.'

'He could've taken advantage of you, Arabella!'

'Well, he didn't.' Except he kind of did.

Isla huffed. 'You young 'uns today are too quick to trust folks. You hardly know the man and you're letting yoursel' be vulnerable in front of him. He'll get the wrong idea about you, Arabella, mark my words.'

'Ugh! No, he won't at all!' Except he could. 'He's not like that. He's very nice.' *From what I can remember, which admittedly is getting hazier by the second.*

'You really like him then?' Bella didn't miss the disappointment in her granny's tone even in her slightly drunken state.

Bella nodded. 'Mmhm.'

'So, you'd go out with him again?'

'What? A man I chose for myself? You betcha.'

Isla sighed and stood from her chair. 'I do hope you know what you're doing, Arabella Douglas,' she said as she left the room followed by Beau.

21

It was all hands on deck from Tuesday morning in preparation for the big opening on Saturday, 23 July. There was a real buzz of excitement to the place. Soon the castle would be shared with everyone, its colourful history and spectacular interior there for the world to see and enjoy its beauty. Events for Halloween and Christmas were already at the planning stages and Uncle Innes was continuing on with the sourcing of local produce and funding applications. Olivia had met with local businesses and more and more bookings were flooding in, meaning Bella was constantly busy.

The old kitchen in the castle was now a swanky new café kitted out with the latest high-tech barista equipment and Bella had become somewhat fond of the lattes, so much that she'd had to switch to decaf. All the insurances were in place and the private areas of the castle were clearly indicated, meaning Olivia at least had somewhere she could escape to when she needed to.

The snagging was all complete, but Olivia was worrying about *other* matters. She had mentioned her elusive brother Kerr on more than one occasion and was clearly worried about what he may be planning. After what he had done to the corporate event, she feared he would have something more destructive in mind and the worry was evident in the dark circles around her eyes.

During the afternoon, Bella was touring the castle with Olivia, looking for any last-minute issues. Bella was feeling less than fresh and had excused herself a couple of times when she felt sure she was going to throw up the copious glasses of water she had downed in a bid to avoid the onslaught of the impending hangover. Of course, the water had only taken the edge off and she really wanted to lie down. They diverted into the gift shop to see how the new staff were getting on with their training. Olivia informed them about the new Drumblair Tartan uniforms, and they seemed enthusiastic.

As they walked away from the gift shop, Olivia asked, 'Bells, are you okay? You seem a little off today.'

Bella nodded. 'I drank too much when I was out with Aiden,' she said, a hand over her stomach. 'He kept topping up my glass but not his own.'

'Oh, right, was he trying to get you drunk?'

Bella shrugged. 'I think he was being polite.'

'So, how did it go?' Olivia asked eagerly.

Bella smiled despite the throbbing in her head. 'It was... erm, interesting. He's... interesting.'

Olivia giggled. 'Well, that's a weird word to use, *twice*. Were there any sparks?'

Bella frowned. 'We kissed.'

Olivia seemed surprised to hear that. 'So it was a date!'

Bella shook her head. 'It was all a bit confusing.' She chewed her lip. 'Especially because... it turns out...' She glanced over her shoulder and then lowered her voice. 'He's Carrick Murphy.'

Olivia gasped. 'As in your favourite author Carrick Murphy?'

Bella hissed, 'Shhh! Yes, as in my favourite author.'

Olivia's eyes widened. 'Bloody hell, Bells, that's huge!'

'I know, right?' She crumpled her brow. 'He seemed to have a bit of an ego, though. After we kissed, he commented that I'd just kissed my favourite author.'

Olivia smiled. 'Oh, come on, I think maybe you're reading too much into that.'

Bella nodded. 'Yeah, it's probably nothing. He's a nice guy. Quite funny and sweet in a way. Maybe I'm being oversensitive after the Kerr situation.'

Olivia linked her arm through Bella's. 'Hey, not all men are as rotten as my brother. If Aiden seems to be those things, it's probably because he is.'

Bella chewed her lip. 'I hope you're right. But please don't say anything about his identity, will you? He doesn't want anyone to know.'

'My lips are sealed, honey.'

'Thank you. I haven't seen him today and I haven't messaged him. I don't want to come across as desperate. But hopefully he'll ask me out again and things will be better now the cat's out of the bag.'

'Fingers crossed for you, my lovely.'

* * *

They walked back through to the main foyer to find Innes with a group of the volunteers who had been taken on as tour guides. Innes was teaching them all about the paintings and furniture pieces in the house and their connection to the family, and was putting them through their paces. As they passed the group, Innes selected one of them to talk about the large painting in the main entryway depicting the Clan MacBain at the Battle of Culloden. It had been painted by an eighteenth-century Anglo-Swiss artist, and was one of Olivia's father's prize possessions. Until recently, it had hung in Laird MacBain's former bedroom but had been relocated due to its significance to the castle and its origins in readiness for public visits.

'Have you heard from Kerr at all?' Bella asked as they walked through to the dining room. It was as if he had fallen off the face of the earth, Bella thought.

Olivia sighed. 'Not a word. Since Innes saw him in Inverness, he's literally disappeared. But it's not like him to be so quiet for so long and I must say I'm worried he's skulking in the background, ready to pounce on Saturday. Either that or he's in very deep trouble somewhere. I've had to stop thinking about it because it's driving me mad. Brodie has been keeping a look out for him on social media just in case, but no sightings.'

Bella furrowed her brow. 'I hope he doesn't attempt to sabotage the opening like he did the fashion show.'

'Same here.'

22

On Thursday, another day closer to the grand opening, flowers arrived to be displayed in the foyer of the castle – this wouldn't be a regular thing, thanks to the expense, but Olivia had decided the opening day warranted it. Bella had overseen the delivery and with Olivia's permission she had discussed the displays and her vision for them with the florist who was to arrange them. Another small but enjoyable use of her creativity.

So many people had complimented her on the design of the apartments, especially prospective clients who had visited to look at them in more detail. She was at risk of believing herself capable of making a career out of it. In reality, you didn't essentially need a qualification in order to work in the field, but Bella was aware in order to do the kind of work she dreamed of, qualifications would definitely be beneficial.

Bella absentmindedly stared into space as she sat in the castle kitchen with Olivia on a coffee break.

Olivia pulled her from her daydream. 'How are things going with your granny's house?' she asked. 'Have there been any updates?' Before Bella could reply, she added, 'Not that I'm rushing you out of the apartment, though; you can stay as long as you need to.'

Bella sighed. 'I spoke with the contractors this morning. They're at the stage of rewiring now the dehumidifiers have been removed. Then there will be plastering and decorating. It may be a couple of weeks yet, depending on when people can come in to do the work.' Bella twiddled her mug in her hands. 'I feel so bad we're taking up space.'

Olivia nudged her shoulder. 'Stop worrying, Douglas. The insurer is paying your rent now, so it's fine. I'm not losing anything. And you'd do the same for me if I ever needed help. And if I can't help my best friend, who can I help?'

'I hope you know how much my granny and I appreciate you.'

'Actually, there is one thing you could do for me.'

'Name it,' Bella said, happy there may be a way to pay her back.

'Coppercaillie are playing at the opening, but could you possibly ask Harris if he could arrange a police presence to be around too? This business with Kerr is worrying me.'

Bella nodded. 'Consider it done.'

* * *

Later that evening, Bella and her granny were watching *Singin' in the Rain* when she received a text message.

Hey Bella, it's Harris. Wanted to check yr managing ok without yr car. If not, let me know how I can help.

She hit reply.

Hi Harris. Thanks ever so much but I'm not going anywhere this week. Lots on at the castle so needed here. I hope you're well.

A few moments passed but then a reply arrived.

Good to know. I'm gr8 thanks. I may see you tomorrow as heading to
castle on business.

Bella remembered what Olivia had asked her about asking him
to be at the event.

Okay, great because I have a favour to ask. B x

As soon as she had hit send, she regretted the kiss at the end of
the message. She hoped he wouldn't read anything into it.

Sure, what is it?

Bella hit reply.

Olivia was wondering if you could ask some of your colleagues to be
around at the opening on Saturday. She wants to make sure everything
goes smoothly and feels a police presence would help so Kerr doesn't
cause trouble.

There seemed to be a long pause this time, but eventually a
reply came.

Hopefully he'll stay away. I'm off duty on Saturday and playing at the
event so will mention at station to see if I can get a patrol car to be
close by or maybe some uniformed officers in grounds. Don't worry, we
may be off duty but we'll keep an eye on things. I'll let you get back to
your evening. Bye for now. Harris.

Bella smiled. He was so willing to help and she liked that about him. Aiden popped into her head, and she wondered if all was okay with him as she hadn't heard from him since the evening of their meal, and after what he'd told her, she presumed Harris was paying him a visit to discuss his book. While she had her phone in her hand, she typed out a message to Aiden.

Hi neighbour. I hope the words are flowing. You must have been busy as I haven't seen you leave your apartment! Bella xx

About half an hour passed until she received a reply.

Hi Bella. I've had my head down working all week. Sorry I haven't been in touch. Maybe we can do coffee here tomorrow? Let's say noon if you can get away from work for a while. Aiden xx

Bella's stomach flipped and she smiled as she typed her reply.

That would be good. I'll see you at noon. I'll take it as my lunch break, so you'd better have biscuits in. B xx

She finished off the message with a winking emoji and two kisses.

'Hey, it's coming up to the best bit, Arabella, put your blasted phone away,' Isla said.

Feeling thoroughly chastised for ruining movie night, Bella placed her phone face up on the sofa beside her in case Aiden texted again. She didn't receive another reply but was excited to see him again. She was expecting Friday to be spent checking everything over one last time before opening day but felt sure she could sneak off for an hour.

* * *

On Friday morning, Bella was up bright and early. She showered and dressed in record time, called Beau and set off to take him on a quick morning jaunt around the grounds of the castle. The sun was making an appearance now and she loved feeling the warmth of it on her skin. The place was silent apart from nature; birdsong, the sound of the loch lapping at the shingle on the shoreline, and the low melodic hum of insects going about their work. The amber rays of the sun cast a golden glow over the stonework of the chapel and Bella inhaled the fresh air deep into her lungs. She still couldn't quite believe she was living at Drumblair, the place she had loved since she'd first come home for tea after school with Skye and Olivia.

The sweet fragrance of the wildflowers surrounding the chapel floated on what little breeze there was, and Bella watched for a moment as bees danced from petal to petal, deftly landing and then moving on to the next.

Across the loch, the clouds formed fluffy white crowns around the munros. To her left, she heard the water moving and watched as Brodie swam as far in as he could before standing knee deep in the water and making his way back onto the shore, closely followed by his two dogs, Wilf and Marley, who'd also been for a dip. Brodie was known for taking an early-morning swim, often when the weather wasn't quite so forgiving. Bella didn't know whether to admire him for it or think him utterly insane. He picked up his towel from an old chunk of driftwood near the water and dried his wetsuit off a little before making his way across to Bella. The two blond dogs had a good shake before trotting along behind with their tongues lolling out. As they approached Beau, they all had a good sniff of each other with tails wagging happily.

'Good grief, Brodie MacLeod, have you finally lost your marbles? I know it's a little warmer today, but the water must be freezing!'

He grinned as he rubbed the towel over his dark, shaggy hair. 'Nah, it's refreshing and it's great for your circulation. A morning swim sets you up for the day. You can't beat it.'

'It'd set me up for a cardiac arrest and a bed at A&E, I'm afraid. Anyway, how's Liv doing?'

He raised his eyebrows. 'She's been awake since five stressing about Kerr. Personally, I don't think he'll make an appearance.' He frowned. 'You haven't heard from him, have you?'

Bella shook her head. 'No, thank goodness. Although I'm probably the last person he'd want to contact. I think I bruised his ego with the help of my kung fu granny.'

Brodie laughed. 'Aye, she's a class act is Isla. I love her to bits.' He leaned a little closer and glanced around conspiratorially before saying, 'Between you and me, I hope you have to move in here permanently. It's great to have her around, you too, obviously,' he added. 'Isla's been helping in the walled garden, you know. And don't worry, I'm keeping an eye on her to make sure she doesn't do too much.'

'Thanks for that. She thinks a lot of you too.'

'Well, I should get back to Stressy McWorrywort. It wouldn't surprise me if she was grey or bald by Sunday.' He laughed.

'Tell her I'll be up soon and to take a chill pill! It's going to be brilliant. She's worked too hard for it to be anything else.'

'Aye, I keep telling her that. Let's hope you can convince her, eh?'

'Any news on which celebrity she's got to open the event?'

Brodie made a zipping motion across his lips and threw away an imaginary key. 'I could tell you but I'd have to kill you.' He made a silly face.

'Spoilsport.'

* * *

At 9 a.m., Bella found Olivia in the undercroft that had been returned to its origins as a kitchen and store room for the purposes of the public visits. It had been made to look as authentic as possible to how it would have looked when the castle was built. There were even mannequins in period costume that freaked Bella out every time she saw them, especially the male one; his eyes seemed to follow her wherever she walked in the room.

'Hey, Liv, how are you doing?' Bella asked as she kept her eyes fixed on the male mannequin, just in case.

'Hey, Bells. I think I'm finally relaxing. Not a lot left to do now but wait for tomorrow. Aren't these mannequins brilliant? So realistic!'

Bella shuddered. 'A bit too realistic. I actually had a nightmare last night the male one appeared in my bloody bedroom.'

Olivia burst out laughing. 'Really? Aww, I think he's cute.'

'Yeah, in the way crazed serial killers are cute. I reckon he'll terrify the kids. Maybe we can use that to our advantage, though. We can tell misbehaving children he'll follow them home if they don't mend their ways.' She gave a sinister, theatrical laugh.

'You cruel and heartless woman! Any news from Aiden?'

'Yes! I'm calling for coffee with him at lunchtime.'

'Oooh, I can't wait to hear all the details.'

23

Bella called home to freshen up. She checked her appearance in her bedroom mirror. Her blonde waves were nice and smooth and had a 1920s look she had achieved miraculously without even trying. Thanks to sleeping better – with the exception of the mannequin nightmare – the dark circles around her green eyes had diminished. Deciding not to change, she smoothed down her short-sleeved cream dress that had a blush-coloured flower print; it was fitted at the waist, skimmed out over her hips and stopped just below her knees, and hinted at a touch of cleavage without showing too much for the daytime. It was a particular favourite she chose when she was feeling good about herself, and today was one such day.

Isla and Beau were making the most of the sunshine and were already out in the grounds for a stroll, armed with a packed lunch and a flask of tea. Bella had made sure her granny took her phone just in case.

'Aye, don't worry yoursel', I'll message you on the WhatsUp if necessary,' Isla had told her before they left. 'But Beau'll look after me, won't you, lad?' The dog had given his usual yip of agreement looking like he understood every word and trotted to the door as if trying to hurry up his owner.

Promptly, at noon, Bella knocked on the door of apartment one and waited as butterflies set about fluttering in her stomach. Aiden opened the door but was on the phone. At first, he looked a little confused but he held up a halting finger, mouthed the words, 'Two minutes,' and then beckoned for her to come in. He was unshaven and his hair was sticking up at all angles. He was wearing the same pair of pyjama bottoms and T-shirt she had found rather yummy almost five days ago, but now found it a little disconcerting he was still wearing them, especially when she had made an effort to look nice.

She followed him through to the living room and was a bit annoyed to find the apartment she had poured her heart and soul into designing in a dreadful mess with empty wine bottles and dirty glasses on the formerly beautiful oak coffee table, along with a red wine stain in a ring the size of a bottle base; the specially selected oak coasters were still stacked at the edge of the table *unused*. There was a pile of dirty clothes on the floor by the sofa too that she had to step over.

Aiden ran his free hand through his hair then pinched the bridge of his nose as he paced the floor. 'No, I've amended that scene; it just wasn't working, so I had a rethink.' There was a long pause while Bella presumed the other person on the call was speaking. 'Oh, you know, I'm okay. I'm in the back of beyond, in the middle of nowhere. So it's not perfect. You know how I love my sushi and matcha and you just can't find it around here.' He laughed lightly. 'But it's very peaceful, unlike London. Too peaceful, really. I actually miss the noise.'

He walked through to the kitchen and lowered his voice. 'Has Candace been in touch with you?' Another pause. 'No, the message was anonymous. It just said "I know where you are".' He walked back through to the lounge, he was chewing at the skin around his thumb and his nostrils were flared. 'Maybe it was a prank. Look, I've got to go, someone's here now. Yeah, bye, Nelly, and thanks again.' He hit the end call button on the handset with a rigid index finger and threw the phone onto the sofa before running his hands through his messy hair.

'Hey, hi. Sorry about that,' he said as he walked over and slipped his arms around Bella's waist. 'I have to admit I'm not really prepared for this.' He glanced around the mess in the room.

Bella raised her eyebrows. 'I can go if—'

'No, you're here now.' He bent to kiss her and for a moment she forgot he appeared to be a bit of a slob. 'I could use a bit of distraction,' he told her as he rested his forehead on hers. 'And you're the perfect kind.'

Distraction? Is that how he sees me? She decided she was being paranoid again and gazed up at him and into those bright blue eyes, so blue they looked like contact lenses, and she closed her own eyes as he lowered his head and kissed her again; the one saving grace was he'd cleaned his teeth.

Things got a little heated this time, his hands explored her body over her clothes and found her bottom, he squeezed her firmly there as he nibbled on her lip, and he pulled her closer to him with urgency, his arousal evident as he did so. He kissed a trail up her neck, along her jaw to her ear, his stubble grazing her skin. Shivers travelled the length of her spine, but not the kind she'd expected, and her heart pounded. She could feel his heart drumming fast too but for entirely different reasons. Something felt off.

'Shall we take this to the bedroom?' he whispered as he slid her dress up her leg to her thigh.

That was the jolt she needed. A little shocked, Bella gathered her wits and pushed on his chest. 'Whoa, I think... I think maybe we should slow down a wee bit.' Panting, despite her actions to halt things, she smoothed down her dress and took a step back. She wasn't the type to rush into sex; she hadn't jumped into bed with Kerr and this would be no different.

He frowned and nodded. 'Right, right, yes, of course, sorry. But you've got all dressed up for me and you look so sexy in that dress and...' *Dressed up for you?* She hoped he wasn't insinuating the dress was an invitation of some kind, and wondered what had happened to simply kissing without expectations of it going further? Why did it have to lead to sex? He held up his hands. 'But you're right; we haven't known each other long. My bad.' He took a deep breath. 'Can I get you a coffee? I have biscuits. That nice woman from the castle kitchen gave me some homemade shortbread.'

They had known each other for a split second in the great scheme of things, and even considering their heart-to-heart, she knew very little about him. Looking back, she realised he knew even less about her. An awkward atmosphere hung in the air, and she replied, 'Coffee would be good, thanks.' In order to lighten the mood, she added, 'And Mirren's shortbread is delicious. You're in for a treat.'

'Good to know. Have a seat while I pour the coffee. I have a fresh pot on.'

Once again, Bella stepped over things; a laptop bag, a pile of books, a used coffee mug, pages ripped from a notepad with illegible scrawl covering them. She sat on one of the two-seater couches. 'Looks like you've been busy,' she called to Aiden in the kitchen. It was the most diplomatic thing she could think of saying without calling out his slovenly ways.

'Yeah, sorry about the mess. I'm a bit of a boor when I'm working. Can't let my mind get diverted off course when the ideas strike. With the exception of a pretty woman, obviously.'

Bella cringed, finding his comment a little condescending, and began to wonder if other 'pretty women' had distracted him recently. She pushed the thoughts aside. 'Is everything okay? You sounded concerned on the phone when I arrived.'

Aiden walked back into the living room with two cups of coffee and handed her one. 'Oh, it's nothing. I was just catching up with my editor. She's a friend too.' He sat on the sofa opposite her, clearly keeping his distance now.

'Ah, I see.' It was obvious there had been more to it than that, but she didn't pry.

'So, have you seen much more of the police sergeant?' he asked, before taking a sip of his coffee and appearing to be doing his best to appear nonchalant.

Bella was confused by the question. 'Why do you ask?'

He shrugged. 'Like I've said before, I think he has his sights set on you, that's all.'

'We're friends, he's a nice guy.'

'I suppose.' He took another sip of his coffee. 'Seems a bit boring to me, but if you like that sort of thing...'

Bella scowled. 'That's unkind, Aiden, and uncalled for.'

Aiden nodded. 'You're right, I'm sorry. I'm a wee bit jealous, that's all. I suppose I'm used to getting what, and *who*, I want, but you seem different and that's good.' *Ego much?* Alarm bells rang in her mind; he had nothing to be jealous about when they had shared one night out that wasn't even technically a date, but before she could voice her concerns, he carried on, 'I'm sorry, okay? Forgive me? I'm a bit useless when I really like someone. I say all the wrong things.' It wasn't a good excuse, but it was a reason. 'Anyway, the words have been flowing today and I have you to thank for that.'

She was intrigued by his comment. 'How so?'

He glanced down at his bare feet and smiled coyly for a

moment. 'It's like you're my muse or something.' He grinned. 'I think about kissing you and the words flow.'

That was kind of romantic, she supposed, although did kissing her make him think about killing people? It wasn't like he was Nicholas Sparks! With his comment clattering around her head, she decided to try to get to know him a little better.

'So how long have you been writing? I know you've got lots of books out there so I'm guessing it's been a while.' *Ugh, now you sound like you're interviewing him.*

'My first book was published when I was twenty-two. I'm writing book number twenty right now. Once the words are flowing, I usually get things done quite quickly.'

'Wow, that's what you call prolific.'

'Yeah, I suppose you could say that.' Aiden fell silent but it was clear to Bella from his fidgeting and the way he kept opening his mouth and then closing it, following this with a frown, that he had something to say. Eventually he leaned forward, resting his elbows on his knees. 'I... I hate to ask this but... that photo you took of the two of us when we went out for dinner the other night... Did you share it around at all?'

Bella raised her eyebrows, a little perturbed by his question. 'Did I share it around?'

He scratched his head. 'Erm... yeah. Did you?'

'Absolutely not, Aiden. Not after what you told me. I wouldn't do that. And I wouldn't share something of you, or anyone for that matter, without permission.'

With his eyes firmly fixed on her, he asked, 'And you didn't snap any photos of me before you knew my situation?'

Bella gave a humourless laugh. 'Why would I take photos of some guy I'd just met and share them on my socials? That'd be weird.'

He sighed. 'You can be honest with me. I won't be upset. I mean you weren't to know the weight of the situation; you don't live in the world I live in. I mean you're not... erm...'

'Famous?' she scoffed. 'No, Aiden, but I have empathy and I do know how to behave.'

'Oh yes, of course, I wasn't suggesting anything to the contrary. It's just you have quite a presence on social media, and you share photos *very* frequently. You seem to photograph a lot of what you do on a day-to-day basis, so I thought I'd ask.'

Bella flared her nostrils and tightened her jaw, she felt a little foolish knowing he had been checking up on her. 'Well, if you've seen my social media accounts, you should know I haven't posted the photograph, shouldn't you?' She was aware of how defensive she sounded, but the churning in her stomach told her it was justified. 'And might I remind you the photo of us was your idea?'

He smiled fleetingly. 'You're angry with me. I wasn't suggesting any malice, but people like you don't often get it and sometimes act without thinking.'

Bella's heart began to race again, only this time it was for completely different reasons. 'People like *me*? What's that supposed to mean? And how dare you say I would act without thinking? You don't know me well enough to make such a bold assumption.'

He placed his cup on the coffee table – without a coaster. 'You're getting quite hostile, Bella.'

'Is there any wonder?'

He huffed. 'Look, everything's coming out wrong. I didn't mean it to sound so negative. I've been in this business for a long time and because I'm writing under a pseudonym, people don't always take it seriously when authors like me receive threats because they don't see my fame the same as, say, a popstar or an actor. But the truth is the fame is just as real. And along with the ones who adore us come the less savoury ones who don't. I just... I received a message that led me to think you may have—'

Up yourself much? Bella forced herself to calm down, inhaling deeply through her nose. 'I can assure you, Aiden, people *like me* have a good understanding of the world and the common sense not to announce the whereabouts of someone who's operating under an alias, and to be honest, I take offence at you insinuating I'd do such a thing. And frankly, I'm surprised you'd try to sleep with someone you deemed to be so incredibly dim. Or does intelligence not factor into things when you're looking for gratification? Especially when you clearly see someone as an easy lay?'

The doorbell chimed before Aiden could respond. He stood and dashed for the door, his face rather red. 'Ah, Sergeant Donaldson, come on in,' she heard him say. 'Bella's here.'

Harris walked into the living room after Aiden, and after a pause where he seemed a little confused to see her, he gave Bella a nod. 'Afternoon,' he said in a stern tone. It was interesting how his demeanour changed when he was on duty. He was the epitome of stoic professionalism.

She plastered a positive expression on her face. 'Hi, Harris, what a nice surprise.'

A fleeting smile flashed across his features. 'Aye, good to see you, Bella. I hope your granny's well. Please pass on my regards.' He turned to Aiden. 'Sorry I'm a bit late. I know I was supposed to be here at ten past twelve, but I got stuck behind a tractor.'

Bella glanced at her watch; it was only twenty past. Aiden had invited her for noon, so she was surprised to hear he had arranged for Harris to arrive so soon after her, especially after he'd tried to get her into bed moments after she had arrived. She wondered considering his enquiries about her and the sergeant, if that had been the plan all along; for Harris to turn up while they were in bed and for Aiden to have the opportunity to let Harris know what was going on. He had commented on her relationship with Harris a few times since they had met now, and had said he was used to getting what he wanted, so maybe he felt he needed to somehow mark his territory. He clearly didn't know her at all, she was no man's property, and now she felt a little queasy at the notion he could be so possessive after only one night out.

She stood. 'I presume you guys have got things to discuss, so I'll leave you to it.'

Harris's eyes widened. 'Oh no, please don't leave on my account. I can always come back.' He smiled widely but the expression seemed forced and didn't reach his eyes. 'Far be it from me to interrupt a blossoming relationship.'

Bella turned towards Aiden. 'Oh no, it's fine, isn't it, Aiden?' Again, before he could respond, Bella turned to Harris. 'Bye, Harris. I'll be sure to pass your regards onto my granny, that was very kind of you.' And with that firm assertion of neglect towards her host, she left, closing the front door quietly behind her, even though deep down she was seething.

She stopped off at her own apartment and quickly changed into jeans and a T-shirt – her lovely dress seemed sullied somehow now – grabbed a cardigan in case the temperature took a nosedive as it sometimes did in the Highlands, and left again.

She needed some air.

* * *

Bella found Isla and Beau in the walled garden. Isla was chatting to Brodie's father, Dougie, about plants, and Beau was enthusiastically digging a hole in the dirt, his tongue lolling out as he worked.

'Beau! You're going to need a bath before you're allowed in any of the carpeted rooms when we get back,' Bella said. 'Sorry, Dougie, he's making a right old mess of your borders.'

Isla turned her attention to the dog. 'Oh, bloody hell, you wee scamp, you're no' meant to be doing that! You'll get us evicted!'

Dougie stood and swiped sweat from his brow with his forearm. 'Hi, Bella, nice to see you, and don't worry, he's actually digging in a place where I'm going to plant a rosebush.' He laughed and scratched his nose, creating a muddy patch on his face. 'Take no notice, wee Beau, you're doing me a favour.' His phone pinged and he took off his gardening gloves to check the screen. 'Ah, that's my other half. The Cullen Skink's ready so I'd better be off afore I get into strife wi' the wife.' He chuckled. 'Enjoy the sunshine, ladies.' Marriage certainly seemed to agree with Dougie, he'd had a spring in his step since his wedding to Mirren and could often be heard whistling these days.

When they were alone again, Isla turned to Bella. 'How come you're back so early? I thought you'd be busy gazing into that murder writer's eyes.'

Bella folded her arms. 'Hmm, the least said about that situation the better, Granny.'

'He didn't admit to a grizzly plot to chop you up, did he?' Isla chuckled.

'Thankfully, no. But he did make me out to be some kind of airhead with no social etiquette.'

'That's nearly as bad. Why would he say such a thing?'

Bella realised even though he had peed her off, there was little she could say under the circumstances. 'Oh, don't worry about it. I don't think he'll be wanting to take me out again any time soon.'

'Ah, well, that's no great loss. I mean, he's not from around here and long-distance romance is a hard thing to deal with.'

Her granny had a point. 'That's true. Anyway, are we going to call my dad and sing happy birthday to him?'

24

By 9.30 on the morning of Saturday, 23 July, the sun was out, and people had started to arrive for the castle opening day. Bella stood with Olivia in the gift shop, where the castle tours and grounds passes were to be purchased. All three gift shop staff were in with it being the first day, smiles on their faces and an almost palpable excitement radiating from them.

'How are you holding up?' Bella asked Olivia, knowing it would be an emotional day for her.

Olivia sighed, linked her arm through Bella's and rested her head on her shoulder. 'I'm okay. I keep thinking about Mum and wondering what she would have made of all this.'

Bella squeezed her. 'I think the fact the sun came out is all the reply you need, my lovely.'

Olivia lifted her head, and her eyes glistened as she looked out of the window. 'Brodie said the same thing. It's amazing.'

At 10 a.m., Olivia stood at the front of the castle on a small podium. A red ribbon had been strung across the main entrance way. Brodie stood in the crowd, his eyes scanning everywhere, no doubt for the elusive Kerr.

The crowd quietened and Olivia cleared her throat. 'Good morning, everyone, I'm so happy to welcome you here to Drumblair Castle for our grand opening.' Applause rang out. 'We have some fantastic events planned throughout the day, such as face painting, the obligatory bouncy castle, stalls selling crafts from some extremely talented local artisans, food and drink and, of course, live music.' The crowd cheered again. 'Now, you may have heard rumours we have a special guest here to open the event and I'm excited to introduce a Hollywood actor who you will no doubt know from the box office hit and award-winning movie *The Girl and the Rose*, please give a warm Drumblair welcome to Ruby Locke!'

A collective gasp travelled the crowd, followed by a raucous applause as the stunning, fiery-haired, heavily pregnant woman walked up onto the podium, a wide smile on her face as she raised her hand to wave to her fans. 'Hi there, everyone!' Ruby said in her soft Yorkshire accent. 'It's absolutely wonderful to be here today to help celebrate the opening of this stunning castle. I heard about Drumblair from some very good friends of mine and when I was told they needed a celebrity to carry out the official opening, I said, "Ooooh, if there are giant scissors involved, will I do instead? I've always wanted a pair of them!"' Laughter rumbled through the crowd. When everyone had quietened down again, she continued. 'Seriously, though, it's an absolute honour to be here.' Innes stepped forward with the giant scissors and handed them to the star.

'I know Lady Olivia and her team have worked so hard to make this place a venue for weddings, open-air concerts, tours and school visits to name but a few of the events on the agenda, and I'm sure her parents would be so proud of what she's achieved. So without further ado, I'd like to officially declare Drumblair Castle... open to the public!' She cut the red ribbon with the comedy scissors and the crowd erupted once more with cheers and applause. 'Right, I'm nicking these babies!' Ruby said as she pretended to run off with the scissors and everyone howled with laughter.

* * *

Bella found Olivia with Ruby, surrounded by visitors, as the actor signed autographs and posed for selfies, even Granny Isla got one. When Ruby was ushered away by a burly security guard, Olivia was free and Bella hugged her.

'She's so lovely,' Olivia enthused. 'Her security detail has whisked her away to get a drink and have a break. She's seven months pregnant so he's being extra vigilant with her. They're heading back to Skye later on today.'

Bella gave an incredulous laugh. 'Here you are talking about Ruby Locke as if she's just some ordinary woman you know! And here I am thinking *how the hell did you get Ruby flipping Locke?*'

Olivia tapped her nose. 'It's not what you know...'

'So you're not going to tell me?'

Olivia rolled her eyes. 'Okay, okay, so Nina designed a dress for her to wear to the Oscars and during their design sessions they got talking about castles with her movie being set in one. Nina was telling her about me inheriting this place and she said there should be a movie about it, then she told her we were looking for someone to officially open the castle. Never in a million years did I expect Nina to call me to say Ruby had agreed to do it. It was a huge surprise and I've been desperate to tell you, but I had to keep it quiet. Forgive me?'

'Totally forgiven! It's incredible!' Bella said. 'I need a selfie with her before she leaves!'

* * *

Olivia was set to take the very first castle tour with the public and Bella could see she was visibly shaking.

'You do know you'll be great, don't you, Liv? It's your home. If anyone can make this work, it's you.'

Olivia lifted a shaky hand and tucked her hair behind her ear. 'I've never been so terrified.' This was followed with a nervous giggle, something Olivia was rarely seen to do.

Bella squeezed Olivia's arm. 'Look at the queue, Liv. People are so excited. I'm absolutely made up for you.'

Brodie walked in and came over to wrap his arms around Olivia. He planted a kiss on her cheek. 'My gorgeous Liv. This is all down to your genius, you know. And your courage to take a chance. It looks like it's definitely going to pay off. Not that Bella or I doubted it for a second, eh, Bells?'

'Not a single second,' Bella replied with a smile. They made such a wonderful couple, and Bella couldn't help the twinge of envy for what they shared. She shrugged off the thought and remembered how many times she had insisted to her granny she didn't *need* a man to make her whole. Although neither did Olivia, but it certainly made her happy.

* * *

During the morning, Bella hung around the gift shop, handing out site maps and directing people to the café and toilets and telling them about the renovations while Duncan, Sadie and Ailsa were busy serving at the till and replenishing stock on the shelves. In the scant moments when things quietened, Bella posted to the castle's social media accounts – another of her roles.

Soon Bella bumped into Olivia, who was returning from her

first castle tour; she was beaming with happiness. The smile on her face and flush to her cheeks told of the buzz she was feeling. It appeared her achievements were finally beginning to sink in.

'So, how was it?' Bella asked with eagerness.

Olivia clasped her hands in front of her heart. 'Oh, my word, Bells, it was incredible! I had a group of fifteen. Some were locals and some were here on holiday, and they were all so lovely. They asked lots of questions and I really enjoyed talking about my ancestry. The favourite room was the Georgian bedroom with the collapsible four-poster bed. They all loved the blue and white hand-painted wallpaper too. There were lots of positive comments about the fact we've been able to span the time since the castle was built up to more recent eras with the rooms, to show it across the ages. And the old kitchen was another favourite. But you were right about the mannequins.' She laughed. 'One wee toddler cried when he saw the male one. Poor lamb. We may have to get another one made.'

'I told you! He still visits me in my nightmares.' Bella laughed. 'I'm so glad you had fun. Did you see any of the other tour guides en route?'

Olivia nodded. 'Yes! They looked so happy and enthusiastic. I'm so proud I could burst.'

Bella hugged her. 'It's all coming together.'

* * *

Bella and Olivia wandered around the grounds together during the afternoon. Innes was directing traffic to the overflow car park in his high-vis vest and the café was bustling with customers; Mirren's home baking was going down a treat. People were enjoying the grounds and Dougie's gardening team were receiving lots of praise for the flower beds. Skye and Ben had been spotted trying their luck at one of the games stalls and subsequently Ben was seen carrying a rather large teddy bear. Brodie was acting as a guide in the gardens and proudly pointing to the gardening team when anyone had questions about the plants. Wilf and Marley were sitting by him, patiently and obediently waiting for him to walk to another spot. Olivia wandered off to see Brodie and Bella carried on. The place was alive with the most incredible atmosphere. It was akin to a summer festival like Glastonbury or Belladrum, only with less alcohol and thankfully less mud!

The small stage set up out front on the grass had attracted quite a lot of attention. Coppercaillie were playing a set and Bella stopped for a moment to watch as Harris sang Dougie MacLean's 'Caledonia' in front of a rapt crowd. He was definitely a man of many talents, Bella surmised. As she gazed around at the smiling faces and listened to Harris's husky voice singing about her beloved Scotland, observing the culmination of months of hard work, a sense of pride washed over her. It felt amazing to be a part of something so special and at that exact moment, Bella couldn't think of anywhere else she'd rather be.

Isla and Beau were sitting on a bench outside the apartment and Beau was relishing all the cuddles he was receiving from visitors. And on more than one occasion Bella overheard her granny telling people her granddaughter was part of the management team and she was in charge of the interior design. Bless her; she was very proud but maybe needed to stop inflating Bella's importance.

Seeing everything was under control, Bella decided to walk down to the loch. She passed the place where Aiden had parked his car and noted it was there, but he hadn't surfaced from his apartment all day.

She stood on the shore and watched the sunlight dancing on the surface of the water and thought about what had brought her to this point. The compliments she had received since she had decorated the apartments caused her to wonder how different her life might have been if she had returned to her degree course. Because as much as she loved working at Drumblair as Olivia's assistant, nothing had invigorated her like working on the apartments. She had felt herself come alive with each design decision she had made and had been so grateful to Olivia for giving her free rein when she had no qualifications to prove that she was good enough for the job. The thing that saddened her was there was no chance of further work using her design flair at the castle, as the apartments were finished and Olivia would no doubt want to change her rooms in the castle to her own and Brodie's tastes. But she had a job she enjoyed and, for the time being, a beautiful place to live. She decided she had to be grateful for what she had and not dwell too long on a dream that was out of reach.

* * *

On her return to the castle, Bella spotted Harris. Now he wasn't on a stage in the distance, she could see him a lot clearer. It was warm enough for him to be without a jacket and she couldn't help but notice the breadth of his biceps. She surmised it was a good thing he had a beard, and she didn't find him in the least bit attractive, because she found him quite intriguing in every other way. He was standing by the bench where Isla was, and another elderly lady was sitting beside her. She recognised her to be Harris's mother, Maeve.

'Bella, look who's here!' Isla said, pointing to Harris. 'They've been on the castle tour, haven't you, Maeve? Have I told you my granddaughter's an interior designer and the assistant to the castle owner?'

Bella loved how proud her granny was but every time she told anyone about her role it became more complex and increased in importance. 'I'm Olivia's PA, Granny, and I'm not really an interior designer,' Bella said before she turned to Maeve. 'Lovely to see you, Maeve.'

'You *designed* the *interior* of the apartments so what else would you call it?' Isla asked with an incredulous huff.

Maeve patted her hand. 'Aye, don't sell yourself short, hen. Isla says you've done a fabulous job.' She leaned forward and lowered her voice to a theatrical whisper. 'Although my Harris says the writer chappy next door to you isn't looking after his apartment too well. Apparently, his dirty undies were on the floor when he called in yesterday.'

Isla's face lit up with intrigue. 'Ooh, why were you calling on our murder writer neighbour, sergeant? Is he suspected of something?' She turned her attention to Bella. 'I told you he was dodgy.'

Harris glanced at Bella; a distinct smirk emerged on his face. 'I'm afraid I can't divulge information, Mrs Douglas. Police confidentiality and all that. Although to put your mind at rest, I can tell you he's not suspected of anything.' Then he mumbled, 'Except being a slob, that is.'

'I was going to get some drinks for the ladies, Bella, would you like one?' Harris asked.

Bella nodded. 'That would be lovely. I'll come and give you a hand,' she said and they set off walking towards the catering marquee.

As they walked, Harris asked, 'Are you okay? You seemed a little angry when you left Aiden's yesterday. I... I don't mean to pry, it's a sense I got that all wasn't well. Was it because of the state of the place? Because I was a little disgusted myself. Your beautiful designs need to be handled with a lot more respect.'

'No, it's not that, although I did feel annoyed he's created such a mess. But the real reason I was unhappy is something else I can't really talk about.'

'You should know I know who he is, if it helps. I know he's Carrick Murphy. He told me he's kind of in hiding.'

'In that case... I was angry because he pretty much accused me of giving up his location on social media because I don't understand quite how famous and important he is.'

Harris chuckled. 'He said that? What a dobber.' As if realising he'd spoken out of turn, he added, 'Sorry... I mean... not a dobber but... well, you know.'

'He really hurt my feelings, Harris. I would never knowingly put someone at risk like that.'

'So he's told you about what's going on then?'

Bella nodded. 'He has. It's awful and I would never divulge anything about him.'

'Aye, I know you wouldn't and I'm sure he does too really. But... he's under a lot of pressure from his publisher, I think. Maybe his slight untidiness is his way of coping, I don't know.'

Bella was quite surprised by his words. '*Slight* untidiness?'

Harris chuckled. 'Aye, okay, maybe I'm cutting the man too much slack there. He's worse than most teenagers.'

They arrived at the front of the queue and Harris ordered four cold drinks. They turned to walk back towards the bench and before she could say any more about her and Aiden, Harris said, 'Changing the subject. Have you ever thought of doing an online interior design course?'

'I have thought about it, but I don't want to let Olivia down. We're a great team and working here is wonderful so...'

'Aye, I get that, but you've got talent. You should do something with it. I bet there are online courses you can do in your spare time to fit around this place. I can imagine you going into business for yourself.'

'Really? Thank you.' She felt thoroughly boosted by his comment. Now that a few people had commented on her designs at the apartments, she wondered if perhaps she might have a potential new career ahead of her. Maybe she could realise the dream she had been chasing for so long.

When they arrived back at the bench, Isla and Maeve shared a knowing look.

'What took you so long?' Isla asked.

'Never you mind, Granny,' Bella said with a wink towards Harris.

25

When the final visitor had gone, the tills had been cashed up and the staff had left for the day, Olivia and Bella flopped onto the squashy burgundy velour sofa in the castle's private drawing room. Peace at last.

'What a day,' Olivia said with a sigh.

'It's been crazy busy. You must be so pleased.'

Olivia smiled and rested her head on Bella's shoulder. 'I am now I've got over how daunting it all seemed. It was weird, though, seeing so many strangers walking around my childhood home. Who knew so many people would actually be interested in the old place?'

'Oh, I think it was clear from the start it would be a popular attraction, Liv. There's so much history here. It's one of those places people drive by and think, "Ooh, I'd love a nosy around there." And now they can. And it's a stunning location too. When I was walking around earlier, I got the impression people are grateful to you for opening up your home to them.'

'That's good.'

'Have you heard from Brodie this afternoon?'

'Yes, he messaged after we closed to say he's taken the dogs for a run down by the loch to get rid of some of their pent-up energy.' Olivia sat upright. 'They've been so good today, don't you think? Even Wilf has been on his best behaviour and that's not an easy thing for him.'

Wilf was, to all intents and purposes, still a puppy and he had that well-known golden retriever exuberance that shone through in everything he did. But Brodie was training him so well. And he followed his 'big brother' Marley around like a shadow.

Bella grinned. 'Yes, he's been a star, bless him, and I think Marley has enjoyed all the attention. They say dogs can't smile, but when you look at his face, you can see that's absolutely not true.'

'Totally agree.' Olivia turned in her seat to face Bella. 'Anyway, now we've got five minutes to chat, how's it going with you and Aiden? He seems quite smitten.'

Bella knew she couldn't explain everything in detail, but she did her best. 'We had a bit of a disagreement yesterday about something, and I saw him in a very different light. Although, according to Harris, I was a bit hard on him.'

Olivia gasped and held up both hands. 'Wait a minute, the man who is crazy about you defended the *other* man who is crazy about you? What are the chances?'

'Neither of them are *crazy* about me, Liv. I've known them both for such a short time.'

Olivia narrowed her eyes. 'Have you never heard of love at first sight?' Bella scoffed and shook her head, but Olivia continued, 'Bella, take it from me, I've seen the way they both look at you.'

'Hmm, well, I think I'll agree to disagree.' She glanced at her watch. 'Anyway, I should get back to Granny. I'm sure she'll want a nice relaxing evening after the bustle of today. I sense a movie night coming on.'

Bella went to stand but Olivia grabbed her hand. 'Thank you,

Bells. Your help has been absolutely invaluable. Today and in the run-up to the opening. I honestly don't know how I'd have coped without you by my side. My mum would have been very proud of us both.'

Bella swallowed a lump of emotion that had found its way to her throat. 'She definitely would have been proud of *you*, Liv. You've created an amazing legacy here. Something people will enjoy for years to come, and it'll keep your mum and dad's memories alive.' She reached over and hugged her best friend.

Olivia cupped her face and fixed her with a stern gaze. 'Now tomorrow you can relax. Brodie and I have got this.'

Bella stood. 'Another day off? You can't keep doing that. I have to earn my keep.'

'You've put loads of extra hours in, and taken on things that don't really fall under the remit of PA, so not tomorrow you don't. It's Sunday and I don't want to see you unless you're taking a casual stroll *without* your iPad. I mean it, Bells. You deserve a rest.'

'So do you! I'm worried you'll run yourself ragged with the grounds being open four days a week.'

'Yes, but the castle is only open for tours on weekends at the moment, so it's not that bad.' Bella wasn't convinced and her expression must have spoken volumes, as Olivia smiled and said, 'Honestly, don't worry, Brodie won't let me run myself ragged. He's been checking on me all day. He even sneaked me away for an ice cream down by the chapel. And now the staff have been thrown in at the deep end, I think they'll be fine. I might take a step back tomorrow anyway. I'm always on site if anything happens but I really do think they'll manage. They've impressed me today. They've really pulled together as a team, and I mean everyone, from the shop to the guides to the café.'

Bella agreed wholeheartedly. 'Right, I'll probably see you tomorrow at some point, during my *day off*.'

Olivia stood too. 'That's my girl. I'm off to see if there's any food on the go. I haven't eaten since that ice cream and I'm famished.'

* * *

Bella took a steady walk back to the apartment. The sky was a little overcast now and drizzle hung in the air – this was more like the Inverness weather she knew and loved. The castle still looked magnificent as the stone darkened with the moisture and the bulbous grey clouds overhead created an ominous backdrop. The windowpanes appeared painted black now, as most of the lights in the castle were off for the night. Bella shivered and made a dash for the front door as the heavens opened and she managed to get inside without getting too wet.

'Come on, hen, and get warm,' Granny Isla said as she met her in the hallway. 'I've made a pot of tea. You must have sensed it.' She smiled and reached up to kiss her cheek. 'I bet you're exhausted after today.'

Bella slipped off her shoes and it was only then she realised her feet were throbbing. 'I am now I've stopped, Granny. But it's been so good. It was amazing to see the crowds of people in the grounds. I think all my work on social media must have helped. And the castle tours have been very well received. The local paper even came and took some photos, so that will be good publicity too.'

'Olivia must be over the moon.'

'She is. She was so worried Kerr would turn up and sabotage things but thankfully he was nowhere to be seen. Which is worrying in itself.'

'Ugh. That's the last thing she would've needed, Kermit showing up. He's probably off somewhere with Miss Piggy.' She sniggered at her own joke. 'So, what are we watching tonight? I'm thinking *Gone with the Wind*. I do love a bit of angsty passion.'

Bella smirked. 'Angsty passion? You're such a dark horse, Granny.'

Isla smiled innocently. 'Aye, never judge an old lady by her sweet manner, eh?' *Says the sweet old lady who whacked Kermit in the head with a handbag,* Bella thought with a grin. 'So, what do you think?' Isla asked. 'Rhett Butler and homemade popcorn, and we can put our feet up.'

Bella narrowed her eyes. 'When you say *homemade* popcorn, do you actually mean we should open that bag of Butterkist we have in the cupboard and put it in a bowl?'

'Well, obviously,' Isla replied with a chuckle. 'Who actually makes popcorn these days?'

'In that case, you've got a deal.' Bella went to her room and changed into jogging bottoms and a hoodie and returned to the living room, where there was a large bowl of sweet, buttery popcorn waiting for them. Her granny was searching on the smart TV for the movie. For an eighty-five-year-old, she did amazingly well with technology and Bella couldn't help but be impressed.

Bella had just got comfy and breathed a sigh of relief when there was a knock at the front door.

'Oh no, who can that be?' Isla said, her voice tinged with disappointment. 'I was looking forward to Rhett and Scarlett.'

Bella pushed herself up from the sofa and walked to the front door. When she opened it, she was greeted by a giant bouquet of flowers with a man's body poking out from beneath them.

'Please forgive him, he's a dick and he knows it,' came a fake, high-pitched squeaky voice from behind the brightly coloured, sweetly fragranced display of roses, alstroemeria, green bell and freesias.

Bella tried not to be amused but couldn't help smiling. When she didn't reply, Aiden's face appeared. 'I was an idiot. I misread signals that weren't even there and I was horrible to you. You didn't deserve that. Please accept my apology, even if you don't want anything to do with me any more, which I would totally understand. Although I really hope that's not the case.'

Bella sighed. 'You were a bit forceful, if I'm honest, and then quite mean, and you made me feel so stupid. It changed the way I saw you and I didn't like the new view.'

He nodded and, to his credit, his eyes were filled with regret. 'I know. I genuinely am sorry. But I got these pretty flowers and I hope they will go some way to making it up to you.' He handed them over and she took them.

'They're beautiful. Thank you.'

'So how has today gone? I could see lots of people when I went out to my car earlier.'

'It's gone really well, thank you. Everyone seems to have enjoyed it. I thought you might have come along to do the tour.'

He scratched his head. 'Ah, yeah, sorry about that. I've been really busy writing. But maybe you can give me a private tour sometime?'

'Maybe,' she said.

'Look, I don't suppose you fancy coming for a glass of wine next door, do you? I'd love the chance to talk to you, maybe grovel for your forgiveness a little.' There was a glint of humour in his eyes.

Bella was determined not to let him off too lightly. 'I'm sorry but I have a date.'

He swallowed, lowered his head and rubbed the back of his neck as if unsure how to behave now. 'Ah, okay. No problem. Is it with the police sergeant?'

Here we go again. 'No! It's with my granny. We're watching *Gone with the Wind.*'

He lifted his head and smiled; relief was now evident in his brightened eyes. 'Ah, oh, that's good. I can't say it's my cup of tea

I'm more of an arty film noir person, but enjoy and maybe I'll see you tomorrow.'

Bella shrugged. 'Maybe you will.'

He tilted his head. 'You're not going to make this easy for me, are you?'

'Nope,' she said and with that she closed the door.

'Was it the Black Magic man?' Isla called. 'Did he bring chocolates?'

'It was and no, but he brought me flowers instead.'

Isla huffed. 'He should have brought both. I could eat a piece of chocolate fudge. Anyway, I hope you sent him away with his tail between his legs.'

'I did, Granny. The flowers are beautiful, though. I'll put them in some water while you get the film ready.'

* * *

The following morning, Bella had luxuriated in her bed a little longer than normal while she searched online interior design courses on her phone, with Harris's words about her wasted talent ringing in her head. She found several possibilities and sent for more information, although in the back of her mind she knew it might come down to a difficult choice between repairing her beloved Fifi and chasing her dream.

Her granny had taken Beau for his morning walk. Although Bella had given strict instructions she shouldn't stay out long, as an early glance between the curtains on the way back from the bathroom told her rain was on the way once again.

'Och, I'll no' wash away, you know. I've been out in much worse, hen.'

'Even so, we don't want you catching a cold. Let him do his business and come back.'

'Yes, Mum,' Isla had replied. Bella chose to ignore the sarcasm.

She picked up her book from the bedside table and opened it up to the last page she had read the night before. She had read a couple of lines when her phone pinged. It was a WhatsApp message from Olivia.

Hey you! Dinner tonight? Warning! I'm cooking! No need to bring anything, just yourself. Say 7pm? Love you, Liv xx

Olivia had been desperate to have a dinner party since she got back from New York but had been far too busy. Bella was keen to accept, so she hit reply right away.

Sounds great. See you then! B xx

Bella got out of bed and grabbed her robe; she went to the front door and stepped outside. Rain was lashing down so hard it was bouncing up from the ground and Isla was still not back. It had been around forty minutes since she had gone out and Bella was beginning to get rather concerned. She lit the log burner in the living room so her granny could warm up and dry off on her return and made a fresh pot of tea. She was at the point of considering heading out to look for her when the front door opened.

'Only me!' Isla called in a sing-song voice.

'Thank goodness. I was starting to worry,' Bella told her.

'Aye, sorry about that. I got chatting to a couple who were going to the café for brunch. They have a beagle like Beau, he's called Bailey. Nice people, lovely wee dog. I think the two of them liked each other judging by the wagging tails. Then it started raining and I *didnae* have my rain hat or my waterproof coat. And poor Beau *wasnae* happy being out in that, I can tell you. It's getting busy again out there. The car park is filling up.'

'Come and get warm and dry off by the fire,' Bella told her. 'I'll bring you a mug of tea.' She poured two mugs full and took them through to the living room where Isla had already taken off her coat and sat in her favourite chair. 'There you go. Do you need a towel? Or a blanket?'

Isla waved a hand. 'Stop fussing, hen. I'm fine. You need to stop worrying about me so much.'

Bella's heart suddenly ached and she sat down on the arm of the chair and put her arm around Isla's shoulder. 'I do worry about you, though, Granny. I don't want you getting ill. You're precious to me.'

Isla reached up and placed her hand on Bella's. 'Hen, I'm not going to be around forever, that's a fact. You *cannae* wrap me in cotton wool. And I'm an independent woman like you are; don't forget where you got it all from.' She chuckled. 'But when my time's up, it's up. So, stop your fretting and live your life, eh? A bit of rain won't hurt me.'

Bella's throat constricted. She was absolutely not ready to talk about losing her best friend in the world. She remained silent.

'I've upset you, haven't I?' Isla asked as she twisted in her chair to look up at Bella. 'I'm sorry, love. I just don't want you spending your time worrying about an old codger like me. There's no need, really.' When Bella couldn't manage a reply, Isla reached up and touched her cheek. 'I do love you. You're the apple of my eye.'

Bella cleared her throat. 'I love you, too, Granny. Now can we change the subject?'

'Aye. What are you doing this evening? You should get out somewhere. Why don't you see if Olivia and Skye are free?'

'Actually, Liv has invited me for dinner upstairs. Is that okay with you?'

Isla nudged her. 'Of course it is. It means I'll get the snacks all to myself for a change when I watch my film.' She grinned.

'Charming. So, what will you watch this time?'

'Ooh, I don't know. I might watch that *Fifty Shades of Grey* again.' She chuckled. 'I like that Jamie Doorknob.'

Bella gasped. 'Granny Isla, you will not!' Then realisation hit. 'And what do you mean *again*?'

* * *

Bella walked along the driveway in the rain to get to the bus stop that stood along the main country road. Buses were infrequent in the area, and even more so on Sundays, but she had decided to head into Inverness and have a wander around the shopping centre in the hope of buying something new to wear for dinner that evening.

Once in Inverness, the rain stopped, and Bella was able to shop without getting drenched. Eventually, shopping bags in hand, she found herself on the street where the coffee shop was that Harris had taken her to and was surprised to see it was open. She pushed through the door and went to the counter.

'Hello, hen, you're the young lady Sergeant Donaldson came in with, are you not?'

Bella was happy she had remembered her. 'That's right, Mrs Pettifer, I'm Bella.'

'Well, it's lovely to see you again. His table is free if you're staying.' She glanced at the clock and then at the door. 'In fact, you've timed it right for meeting him.' She nodded at the door as it opened and in walked Harris.

'Bella, this is a nice surprise. I wasn't expecting to see you,' Harris said with a wide, handsome smile.

'I wasn't intending to come, if the truth be told. I'm out shopping and thought I would pop in for some delicious Victoria sponge.'

'Me too,' he replied. 'Come and join me?' He gestured to the table in the window where they had sat before. Bella nodded and Harris turned to Mrs Pettifer. 'Two of the usual, Mrs P, please.'

'Coming right up, have a seat.'

Bella followed Harris to the table and they both sat.

'So, what brings you out shopping on a Sunday?' he asked, taking off and placing down his jacket.

'I'm going to Olivia's for dinner tonight, so I thought I'd treat myself to something new to wear.'

'You deserve it. Yesterday was a massive hit. Although I'm surprised you're not working again today.'

'Olivia made me have the day off. But even though it's Sunday, I feel like I should be working, and I most definitely shouldn't be buying new dresses. I need to save up to get Fifi repaired.'

Harris sighed. 'I hope every time you see me you're not reminded about the car. Neil said there was no rush and he meant it, so please stop worrying, okay?'

She smiled. 'I'll try. It was lovely to see Maeve yesterday.'

He rolled his eyes. 'Oh aye, she wouldn't shut up about you after we left. I reckon her and Isla have been conspiring to get us together. Anyway, I put her straight. '"Bella and I are friends, Mum, and that's what we'll remain. She has a boyfriend," I told her.'

Bella shook her head. 'Well, he's not technically—'

Harris continued, glossing over her attempted protestation, 'Speaking of which, did you make up with Aiden?' he asked as Mrs Pettifer placed cake and coffee in front of them.

They both thanked her and when she had gone, Bella said, 'He brought flowers and apologised. I think I forgive him.'

'Well, I bet he'll be on his best behaviour tonight.'

Bella frowned. 'Oh no, it's just me, he hasn't been invited. I think it might be a girls' thing.'

'Ah, well, that should be fun. It's good to have such strong friendships.'

'How about you? Are you going out tonight?'

'Aye, I think I might go out with Neil tonight for a couple of lemonades.'

'Don't you drink alcohol at all?' Bella asked.

He smiled. 'Very rarely. Weddings and Christmas, but I've made sure I know my limits.' Her expression must have been questioning so he continued, 'I've seen what alcohol does to people. Not only with my dad but road traffic accidents, fights, falls. I like to have my wits about me. It doesn't mean I'm boring, though.' He winked. 'I like to have a laugh as much as the next guy. And you should see me dance. I've got the moves, you know.' He held up his arms and did a wiggle in his chair.

Bella giggled. 'So I see.' She ate a mouthful of cake then rested her fork on the side of the plate.

'Did you get anywhere with the interior design courses?' he asked.

'I did, as a matter of fact. I found one that might work. It's a pay monthly thing, so I could study in the evenings while I work at the castle.'

His eyes lit up. 'That's brilliant. I'm so glad.' Something about his enthusiasm and genuine happiness for her made her heart race a little faster. 'So is Aiden really your type then?' Bella was taken off guard by his question and as if he realised he was prying, he scratched at his beard. 'Sorry, that was blunt; you don't have to answer that.'

'I... I don't know that I have a type as such. I mean, he's attractive, sure. But the other day when he made those comments, I was reminded a person's looks aren't enough to make them partner material. Although he did try to make amends so...' The truth was she didn't know any more. A handsome face didn't last; a person ality and sense of humour are the things that stick around. But there had to be some physical attraction there, too, surely? She wasn't usually one to be so superficial and had questioned if, in fact, her attraction was more likely down to being star-struck by her favourite author.

'I agree about the looks part. They're not enough on their own. Someone who makes you laugh, and who you know you can trust implicitly, is what counts. And someone who trusts you and really cares about you is far more important in my book.'

She tilted her head. 'Oh, so you have a book?' she teased.

He chuckled. 'I could definitely write a book. A dating horror stories book.'

'Have there been a few then?' She realised that question was possibly asked a little too eagerly.

Harris rolled his eyes. 'More than I care to admit since I split up with my long-term girlfriend a couple of years ago.' He paused and then wagged his finger. 'But there was this one woman who sticks out in my memory for all the wrong reasons.'

Bella was more intrigued by the mention of a long-term girl-friend but nevertheless she leaned on the table, ready to hear the gossip. 'Do tell.'

'She had about six cats.'

'And you don't like cats?'

He shrugged. 'Love them. But I'm ridiculously allergic. I spent the whole date sneezing and wheezing because of her clothes. I never even set foot in her house. So, I was allergic to *her* because of her closeness to her cats. Couldn't see her again.'

Bella giggled. 'Oh no. That's terrible.'

'Aye, then there was someone I met on a dating app. She had such a strong accent I could hardly understand a word she said to me the whole night. By the end of it, I was sort of nodding and saying, "Oh aye, that's funny," and laughing at everything. I got a message from her the day after to say she didn't want to see me again because I'd laughed when she told me about the death of her pet budgie.'

Bella laughed louder this time. 'You didn't?'

He shrugged. 'I have no bloody clue! Then there was the woman who cried the whole way through dinner because we bumped into her ex and his new girlfriend at the restaurant. That was one uncomfortable date, I can tell you. After that, I kind of gave up, hence my mum trying to fix me up with every female who so much as smiles in my direction.'

'Aww, that's a shame. You should get back out there.'

He smiled but shook his head and played with his fork. 'Nah, I think I'll wait patiently for the right woman to find me this time. I'm sure she's out there.'

Bella smiled. 'I'm sure she is too.'

He kept his gaze on her for a moment but then she noticed an infinitesimal shake of the head and he said, 'So, did you get something to wear for tonight?' He was clearly ready to change the subject.

She nodded. 'I did, as it happens. I got a lovely blue maxi dress; very fresh and summery looking. So, it's as well I'm only going to be outside for two minutes with the traditional Scottish weather we've been having today.' She took a sip of her coffee and glanced out of the window.

'I bet you'll look beautiful.'

She turned back to find his gaze fixed on her again, and her face warmed, no doubt she was bright pink now, she guessed. 'Thank you, Harris.'

He didn't speak for a few moments, as if lost in a daydream. 'Well, I should get going, the criminals of Inverness aren't going to catch themselves,' he said as he stood rapidly and grabbed his jacket. 'Nice to see you again, Bella.'

'And you too,' she replied.

He turned to Mrs Pettifer. 'Put these on my tab, Mrs P, and I'll pop back tomorrow to settle up.'

'Aye, no bother, sergeant,' she replied.

He turned back to Bella one last time. 'Have a lovely evening with your friends.'

'Thanks. Say hi to Neil for me.'

He nodded, raised his hand in a half wave and left the café.

26

At 6.55 p.m., Bella picked up the flowers she had bought for Olivia, left the stable block courtyard and turned to the castle. She glanced over to see Aiden at the main entrance door, clutching a bottle of red wine. He looked ridiculously handsome in beige jeans and a blue checked shirt, his hair tousled and his face clean-shaven.

'Oh, hi. I didn't know you were coming,' she said, realising she sounded a little disappointed.

'Hi. Yeah, I saw Brodie this morning when I was out jogging. He was coming back from a swim in the loch. We got chatting about writing and he told me about his book. I thought it sounded like it should be published generally, not only for the castle gift shop, and I told him so. Anyway, he invited me for dinner. Apparently, another couple are coming? Skye and... someone.' He shook his head.

'Ben,' she said with a nod. 'Skye and Ben. They're good friends of ours.'

He smiled warmly. 'That's it. By the way, you look lovely.'

She glanced down at her outfit: the cornflower-blue maxi dress and a white cardigan she had bought in the city earlier. 'Thanks. You look nice too.'

He stepped closer. 'Look, before we go in, I wanted to apologise again. I think we had the start of something good and I don't want to ruin that. Are we... are we okay?' He took another step and ran a thumb softly down her cheek, causing a shiver to travel down her back. Or maybe it was the chilly evening air, she couldn't be sure.

She was still a little confused about what the 'we' entailed, considering his temporary stay in Scotland, but nodded. 'We're good.'

His eyes brightened and he leaned forward and kissed her tenderly and she allowed herself to get a little lost in the kiss. When he pulled away, he glanced down at their clothes and said, 'We're quite coordinated, aren't we?' He chuckled. 'Looks like we planned our outfits together.'

Before she had a chance to respond, the door opened and Brodie stood there with a bright, warm smile. 'Hi, guys, come on in. Ben and Skye are already here.'

Aiden stepped inside first. 'I brought some wine. I have no idea if it's any good, but I was assured by the man in the shop it will be,' he said as he passed the bottle to Brodie.

'Ah, cheers, mate. That's very kind of you. Come on through. Liv's in the kitchen. We thought we'd eat in there, a little less formal and intimidating.'

The kitchen was where Bella had enjoyed eating when she visited Drumblair Castle after school with Olivia. Mirren had been the one to cook back in those days, and it had always been a fun experience. Mirren was still a fantastic cook but back then there had been something magical about eating her meals in a real castle.

As Bella walked into the kitchen, the aroma of Italian herbs and tomatoes drifted into her nose and her mouth watered. She hadn't eaten since the sponge cake at the café. 'Wow, something smells lush,' she said.

'It's nothing fancy,' Olivia said, as modest as ever. 'It's *parmigiana di melanzane.*'

'Bella's right, it smells amazing,' Aiden said as he casually rested his arm around Bella's shoulders. She glanced at his arm and then up at him. He smiled and kissed her cheek. She wasn't sure how to feel. In fairness, she had said they were fine, but this still felt rather sudden and verging on possessive, which made her hair stand on end a little. He definitely seemed like an *all or nothing* kind of man.

'Hey, honey! You look gorgeous,' Skye said as she walked into the room with Ben, glass of wine in hand, and hugged her. 'I was showing Ben the drawing room where we girls used to watch movies when we came here after school.'

'Aye, I had no idea while I was kicking a half-deflated football around on the village green you girls were living it up in a castle,' Ben said with a grin.

Bella hugged Skye and then Ben. 'You both look great. Engagement clearly suits you. And I love that top.'

Ben tugged at his patterned shirt. 'What, this old thing?' He laughed.

'She was talking to me, you numpty,' Skye said with a good humoured nudge of her fiancé. 'Thanks, Bells, it's new. I got it from that gorgeous boutique on Post Office Avenue in Inverness.'

Olivia joined them. 'My girls back together. It's so good to see you.' The three friends hugged as a group.

'This is something you have to get used to with these three,' Ben informed Aiden. 'They're like sisters from another mister and all that.' He laughed. 'Joined at the hip by invisible thread. Egg beans and sausage. The Three Musketeers.'

'I think he gets it, Ben,' Skye said with a giggle.

'Aiden, this is Ben, and of course Skye,' Brodie said. They shook hands.

Bella got the distinct impression this was intended as a 'couples' dinner party but she and Aiden hadn't really known each other long enough to be worthy of that label. And there was that whole issue with the photograph and the accusations that had gone along with it. Thinking back to that situation caused her to bristle again. And when Aiden's temporary situation at the castle was added into the mix, Bella wasn't sure what the future held, or if they even had one.

* * *

The group sat around the table and Olivia placed a large dish in the centre along with a plate of homemade garlic bread. 'Tuck in, everyone. No standing on ceremony.'

Aiden didn't need telling twice. 'This really does look delicious, Olivia, thank you for inviting me.'

As if she could read Bella's mind, Olivia glanced across the table and gave an apologetic smile. 'So, Bella,' she said. 'Any news on Fifi yet? I've missed seeing her around.'

Aiden laughed. 'Oh yeah, what's happening with the old rust bucket? Is she beyond repair?'

Bella scowled at him. 'Fifi isn't a rust bucket. She's vintage and a rather beautiful piece of machinery. They're actually really rugged and don't rust that easily.'

He must have realised she was annoyed by his comments as he began to backtrack. 'Oh yeah, I know, I'm only jesting. I think it's great it's still running. Well... *was* still running, anyway. It's great you look after it... I mean *her* so well.'

Bella chose to ignore him and returned her focus to Olivia. 'She can be fixed once I sort out the cash. But Neil at the garage is holding her there for me until I can do that.' She purposefully didn't use the phrase 'I can't afford to have her repaired' because the fact was embarrassing, and she didn't want offers of financial aid, which she knew would happen thanks to Olivia's good nature.

Bella was aware Olivia knew her well enough not to talk about money with her in front of people. Instead, Olivia smiled and simply said, 'It'll get sorted, lovely. It won't be long.' Bella read between the lines and knew exactly what Olivia meant. She would need to talk to her after the meal and explain she would deal with Fifi herself. Olivia had done enough for her by employing her and giving her a place to live.

Aiden reached across and took Bella's hand. 'She's right. Fifi will be back before you know it.' *Oh, good grief, not you as well.*

Ben topped up everyone's wine glasses. 'Aiden, Brodie tells me you're a writer. What kind of stuff do you write?' he asked.

'I write crime novels mostly,' came his curt reply.

Ben's eyes lit up. 'Ooh, I love a good whodunnit. Might I have read anything of yours?'

Bella watched as Aiden's jaw ticked. It was a strange reaction. He held up a finger as he chewed and then replied with a strange smile, 'Actually, I write under a pseudonym. And I like to think my work is a little more complex than *whodunnits*. I pride myself on the depth of my research, and I like to insert elements of true crime in there too. Unsolved cases and solved ones alike. It adds to their realness.'

Ben was undeterred by Aiden's apparent pretentiousness. 'Ooh, a bit like that author I like, what's his name, Skye? Ugh, I'm useless with names.'

'Carrick Murphy,' Skye replied.

Ben wagged his fork. 'That's it! Have you read anything by him?'

Aiden wiped his mouth with his napkin and glanced at Bella, his lips pulled into a thin line. 'Do they know?'

Bella scrunched her brow. 'What do you mean?'

Aiden gave that weird smile again. 'Do they know about me? Have you told them? It's fine if you have.' He squeezed her hand her little too tightly. 'It'd be a relief, to be honest.'

Bella sighed and placed down her fork, suddenly bereft of appetite. 'Not this again.'

Brodie broke the heavy silence that had descended over the table. 'What's wrong? What do you mean, do we know about you? What is there to know about you?'

Ben sniggered. 'Yeah, are you Carrick Murphy in hiding or something?'

Aiden took a large swig of his drink and placed his glass down with a thud. 'Okay... Yes, I'm Carrick Murphy. The cat's out of the bag.' He held up his hands in a kind of *Tadaaaa* gesture and everyone stared blankly at him – with the exception of Bella, who couldn't bring herself to look at him.

Ben burst out laughing. 'Good one! You had me going for a minute there!' When Aiden returned his stoic gaze to Ben, his smile disappeared. 'You're not joking, are you?'

Aiden shook his head. 'I am *not*.'

Ben ran his hands through his hair. 'Shit! This is awesome. I loved that one...' He clicked his fingers. 'What was it called? *The Long...* something?'

'*The Long Way Home*,' Aiden replied.

'Aye! That's it. Man, that had me gripped from start to finish. Bloody well done, pal! I'll have to get you to sign my copy before you leave.'

'So how come you didn't say who you were? It seems a bit weird,' Skye said, eyes narrowed.

Aiden sighed deeply and closed his eyes for a moment. 'The

fact is... I had a difficult break-up. My wife cheated on me and her new partner is quite possessive. There were threats and I lost my writing mojo for a while. I'm here to get away from all that.'

'Oh no, that's horrible,' Skye said, placing her hand over her heart.

Aiden swallowed hard and stared at the table, the matter was clearly still difficult for him. 'It almost ruined my career.'

'Bloody hell, mate, that's scary,' Ben said with a shake of his head and a quick glance at everyone else.

Olivia – whose hand had been over her mouth since Aiden's admission – now chimed in. 'Well, I can assure you no one at this table knew anything. I'm your host and I had no clue.' She gave a brief glance to Bella, who was grateful for her discretion. 'Although I'm more of a romance reader myself, but even so, I can assure you no one here will give your whereabouts away. Your identity, and secret, are safe with us, I promise.'

Bella's stomach churned and she stood. 'Can you excuse me for a moment, please?'

She left the room and met Wilf and Marley in the hallway. They wagged their tails and she bent to give them both a quick scratch behind their ears, then, satisfied with that, they returned to their comfy-looking furry bed by the kitchen door.

She made her way to the front door, opened it and stepped outside. It was raining again now, and she was grateful for the stone canopy sheltering her from the downpour. As she stood there, the door opened.

'I've done it again, haven't I?' Aiden said.

Bella shivered and her teeth chattered. 'I think we should stop talking. Because every time you open your mouth, I think you're going to accuse me of something.'

Aiden closed his eyes. 'I'm an idiot. And I'm sorry I jumped to conclusions again. You have to understand the position I'm in. I've tried to keep my two lives separate for so long but maybe it's time I came right out and admitted who I am. It would be one less thing to worry about.'

'I think that's probably a very good idea, Aiden, instead of being paranoid around the people who actually like you and want to get to know you.'

He closed the gap between them. 'You still want to get to know me?' he asked with an air of hope as he gazed into her eyes.

'I don't know, Aiden. You're not making it very easy. I feel like you don't trust me, even though I've done nothing to warrant that. Fair enough, we don't know each other that well, but if you start a relationship off on shaky ground and there's already mistrust, it doesn't stand a chance.' Harris's words about trust echoed in her mind. He'd been right.

Aiden nodded and rested his forehead on hers. 'You're right. I'm so sorry. And I'm glad you like me, because I like you too. I mean really, *really* like you.'

She might like him, but was that enough? 'Then you need to start believing me when I say I've kept your secrets. If you don't believe that, we may as well stop and take things no further.'

He slipped his arm around her waist. 'I really do want to take things further. Much further.' He raised his eyebrows and she glared at him. He chuckled. 'Oh, come on, you can't be mad at me for finding you irresistible, surely?'

'Look, Aiden, things between us aren't going any further until we know each other a hell of a lot better, and until I know you aren't going to blame me anytime something happens you're not happy about.'

'I promise I won't. I promise that's all done. I'm going to speak to Nelly about revealing my identity.'

Bella nodded. 'That's a start.'

'Can I kiss you?' he asked but before she gave her consent, he lowered his mouth to hers and did it anyway.

She gave in and allowed his passionate onslaught for a moment. But all the while, Harris's words rattled around her head. 'Someone who makes you laugh, and who you know you can trust implicitly, is what counts. And someone who trusts you and really cares about you is far more important in my book.'

With a gentle push to Aiden's chest, she stepped back. 'We'd better get back inside. They'll be wondering where we are.'

At the end of the evening, Aiden and Bella made their way down to the old stable block. 'Do you want to come in for a coffee? Or maybe a nightcap? I look rather fetching in a nightcap,' he joked, but Bella was still feeling a little on edge.

'No, thanks. I'm really tired. I think everything's catching up with me and tomorrow is Monday, so I have work.'

He nodded and smiled, but his face didn't seem to relax. 'Okay. Another time maybe.' He bent to kiss her but she turned her face so his lips landed on her cheek.

'Goodnight, Aiden.'

'Goodnight.'

27

The following morning, before Bella got out of bed, she checked her phone. There was a WhatsApp message from Olivia.

Hey honey. Are you okay? Last night was a little odd but I want you to know I hadn't said anything to anyone about Aiden. Not even Brodie. Aiden is a strange character and I think you should maybe watch yourself there. I know it's really none of my business but he came across as quite possessive.

Bella replied right away.

Hi. I'm fine. And I appreciate you standing up for me last night. But I agree about Aiden. Not really sure what to do. He's really attractive on the outside but I need to see past that, don't I?

A fast response came.

Absolutely. Something about him doesn't sit right.

Olivia was very perceptive usually and the fact she had raised concerns sent shivers through Bella's body.

To take her mind off things, Bella completed the online application for the interior design course and paid the small deposit to secure her place. A ripple of excitement travelled through her at the prospect of doing something creative. Of finally following her dream and daring to hope it might one day become a reality. She wasn't sure why she had left it so long and felt excited at the idea of her materials arriving in the post. She needed to make the tough decision about Fifi now. Maybe she needed to say goodbye and save up for a new car?

No public castle tours were being run on weekdays for the foreseeable future; however, Olivia had agreed to allow the local schools in during Monday afternoons. Bella showered and dressed in smart black trousers and a teal long-sleeved top before making her way into the kitchen for a quick breakfast. Olivia had okayed a later start to the day for her as she was set to meet up with the builder at Isla's house to assess the progress and discuss what needed to be done, how much longer things were going to take, etc. Bella had asked to borrow Olivia's car and, of course, Olivia had agreed immediately.

Isla was already sitting at the kitchen table. 'Morning, hen. I've made tea, it's still warm in the pot and there's some toast on the rack too. Cold, how you like it, although I've no idea why.'

'Thanks, Granny,' Bella said before placing a kiss on Isla's head. 'And I like it cold so it doesn't get all soggy when the butter melts into it.'

'That's the best bit!' Isla replied.

'Shall I drop you off at the day centre on my way to the house to meet the builder?'

Isla smiled. 'That'd be grand, hen, thank you. It saves Harris coming all the way out here.'

'Are you ready because I need to go pretty soon so I can get back to work? There's a lot of new enquiries for the apartments for me to go through.'

'Aye, but I need to take Beau for a quick walk. I *shouldnae* be too long.' Isla made to stand up. 'Come on, wee Beau.' Beau stood from under the table and gave his body a good shake.

Bella glanced at her watch. 'Why don't I take him while you get your shoes on?'

'Oh, if you don't mind, dearie. Thank you. Come on, Beau, Bella's taking you for a wee walk. Isn't that nice? Yes, it is, isn't it?' The dog tilted his head and wagged his tail as she talked to him in a baby voice. 'Go see Bella, go on.' Beau turned and trotted to Bella to have his lead clipped on.

Bella munched on the last of her slice of toast, eaten at lightning speed, then grabbed her jacket from the back of one of the kitchen chairs. 'Won't be long,' she said as she left the kitchen and opened the front door.

* * *

Bella was disappointed to find her granny's house was still not quite ready, but research had told her it could take weeks, if not months, for these types of things to be dealt with completely. And even once it was ready, she would need to help her granny shop for new furniture, kitchen appliances, carpets and so on, and so on. The list felt endless but at least the insurer had agreed to pay out.

Feeling a little disheartened, she left the house in the capable hands of the building crew and drove the short distance back to the day centre where she had dropped Isla an hour before. Her idea was she would call in briefly in the hope perhaps Harris might be there. He always had a positive effect on her mood and at that moment she needed it.

Luckily for Bella, Harris was exiting the day centre as she climbed out of her car. She almost didn't recognise him and was rather taken back to see his beard was gone. In fact, she only knew it was definitely him, from that distance, by his purposeful walk and the police uniform. She waved at him, and he waved back, a bright smile on his face. His eyes lit up and crinkled at the corners when he smiled and seeing him without his usual thick mask of facial hair was a little distracting.

As they got closer to each other, he slipped his hands into his trouser pockets. His beard had been replaced by a light smattering of stubble. 'Hey, Bella, we'll have to stop meeting like this.' He gave her his undivided attention, fixing his chocolate-coloured gaze on her, and folding his arms across his broad chest, made broader by his stab-proof vest. Today he wore a police-issue baseball cap, and it suited him more than the usual custodian helmet.

She tucked her hair behind her ears and felt her face warming and her pulse rate increasing. 'I know! You'll be thinking I'm stalking you. Anyway, you look different,' she said, and immediately felt rather silly for stating the obvious.

He reached up and stroked his chin. 'Oh, the beard? Yeah, I shave it off every so often, keeps everyone on their toes.' He laughed. 'Mum likes to pretend she doesn't recognise me when I've shaved.'

Bella pouted. 'I was just about getting used to your beard and now it's gone.'

'You're not a fan of the old facial hair then?'

She winced. 'Not especially, no, sorry.'

'No bother. If I'd known that, I'd have shaved it off sooner,' he replied with a glint of humour in his eyes. 'Anyway, are you here to pick up Isla? Because she may be relieved if you are. Mum's got her doing a jigsaw of baked beans. That's all it is, *just* baked beans. It's enough to drive anyone batty. I had to stop trying to help because it sent my eyes squiffy.' He laughed and Bella was struck by how different his features were without the hair to disguise them. His smile was incredibly handsome, his jaw angular, and she could see his nose had a slight bend where it appeared to have been broken at some point in the past; strangely she hadn't noticed before today. His resemblance to Tom Hardy was uncanny, and now she could see what her friends had meant. He looked a little younger too without his signature beard.

Realising she was staring, she shook her head. 'Has Neil said anything about the car? I'm worried about Fifi overstaying her welcome.'

'Hey, I've already said you've nothing to worry about. She's safe, she's secure. It's really not a problem.'

She nodded. 'Okay, thank you. If you're sure.'

He bent his knees slightly so he could look into her eyes. 'I am, so no more worrying. Right, I'd better get going. If people see us meeting like this, they might get the wrong impression. It's like I'm a New York cop and you're my informant.' He laughed.

She glanced around but theatrically this time. 'Yeah, *now I'd bedda ged oudda here before dey see me,*' she replied in an absolutely horrendous attempt at a Bronx accent, and her face almost spontaneously combusted with embarrassment until he burst into laughter.

'Oh god, Bella, I do love you, you're absolutely hilarious.'

Bella watched as his shoulders juddered and his eyes watered. Seeing him laugh like that, and knowing she was the instigator, gave her a thrill that flipped her insides upside down, along with her world. What on earth was going on?

Strangely, his words didn't register until he'd gone and climbed into his car, and when his use of the 'L' word finally sank in, the butterflies in her stomach suddenly woke up again.

* * *

That evening, as Bella and her granny were almost at the end of watching the latest movie – *Forrest Gump*, which always made her cry – the doorbell sounded, and Bella's heart almost skipped a beat. *Could it be Harris?* But this thought was immediately followed by, *although why would he be here, you dufus?*

Isla interrupted her bizarre internal monologue. 'Are you going to answer that and find out who it is, or are you keeping us in suspenders on purpose?'

Bella shook her head. 'I'm sorry, keeping us in...? Never mind sorry, yes, I'll go.' She stood from the sofa and on the way to the door checked her reflection in the hallway mirror. Her blonde hair had that kind of *dragged through a hedge* appearance and her eyeliner had smudged, thanks to Tom Hanks and his amazing portrayal of the titular character in their movie.

She plastered on a smile and took a deep breath as she enthusiastically flung the door open. 'Oh, hi, Aiden.'

He was leaning on the doorframe like some jock in a teen movie from the eighties. 'Hey, gorgeous. I do love an eager welcome. I was wondering if you fancied some company.'

Bella glanced back towards the living room and then to the visitor at the door. 'Oh, erm, sorry, we're having a movie night. We have them quite regularly.'

'Oh, well, if you have them regularly, I'm sure your gran won' mind me coming in and hanging out in your room instead.'

Bella shook her head. 'Sorry, but the second movie is about to start.'

He pushed off the doorframe and peered over her shoulder into the apartment. 'Okay, great. What are you watching?'

'We've just finished *Forrest Gump* and next we're watching *Local Hero* for about the hundredth time.'

'*Local Hero*? I don't think I've seen it.'

She smirked. 'You've lived in Scotland since you were a kid and you've never seen *Local Hero*?'

'Well, now it sounds like I really *need* to watch it. I brought wine.' He held up the bottle. He whispered, 'And this would be an excellent time to get to know your grandma.'

'Come on in, then. I'll get an extra glass. Granny and I have already had a bottle of rosé.' She lowered her voice. 'It's her favourite but in my opinion it's like drinking flat pink lemonade.' She shivered at the memory of the syrupy sweet drink her granny had won in a raffle at the day centre.

'Ah, well, this is Merlot, I'm afraid,' Aiden said, pointing at the bottle.

Isla appeared in the hallway. 'Ooh, have you brought decent wine? You can come again.'

Bella raised her eyebrows. 'Hang on, you love rosé! It's what I always get for you.'

Isla scrunched her face and made an unpleasant gagging sound. 'No, you *think* I like it because you've never asked otherwise! I drink it because I don't want to hurt your feelings. It's like drinking melted-down boiled sweets. Bleurgh. Give me a good Merlot any day. Or a Cabernet Sauvignon. I'll drink a Shiraz, too, at a push.'

Bella grinned. 'I'm so sorry, Granny, I never realised you were such a wine connoisseur!'

Isla folded her arms across her chest. 'Aye, well, you do now. Anyway, come away in if you're coming, I've a date wi' a very handsome Scotsman who isn't related to Lewis Capaldi!'

Aiden gave a confused, questioning glance to Bella.

She replied with, 'Long story.'

* * *

At the end of the evening, Aiden stood and stretched. 'Well, it's been a lovely evening. Thank you for having me, Isla.'

Isla dryly replied with, 'I *didnae*.'

Bella walked him to the door. 'What did you make of the film?' she asked, eagerly waiting for his reply.

He pursed his lips. 'It was okay. A bit too bland for my liking. Although I can understand why Isla likes it. I mean she has a connection with the location. But I think I prefer films with a bit more going on.'

'Says the man who watches arty-farty film noir,' Bella replied with a smirk.

He raised his eyebrows. 'Each to their own.'

'Indeed,' Bella replied. 'Oh, well. I'd better not keep you. I imagine you've got work to do on your new book tomorrow.'

'Hmm, and a conversation with my publisher. There's something lacking in the marketing of my last release. It's a bit ridiculous when the likes of Darian Parkins and Helga Becker are higher in the chart than me with their limited vocabularies.' He scowled and his top lip curled upwards. Green wasn't the best colour on him.

'I happen to really like both those authors,' Bella replied indignantly.

He slipped his arms around her waist and pulled her close. 'But you like me better, don't you?' He didn't give her a chance to respond; instead, he planted a long, lingering kiss on her mouth then released her, turned and left.

She found him so confusing. He'd say things to annoy her, then kiss it all away, and stupidly she'd let him.

It can't be healthy, can it?

By the time she returned to the living room, Isla and Beau had gone to bed.

28

'I'm so glad you decided to look into the interior design course, Bells. I think you could really make a go of it,' Olivia said after Bella had filled her in on the details as she and Bella sat in the castle study on Wednesday afternoon, going through some orders and invoices. 'After what you did with the apartments, it's clear you've got a real creative flair.'

'Coming from you, that's a huge compliment. It's only going to be a hobby, though. Don't worry; I know you need me, so I'm not planning on going anywhere. And it's a year-long course anyway, so I can work it around my job here.'

Olivia cringed and then sighed. 'I'm sorry I made you feel that way, honey, it was unfair of me. If you do decide you want to go and do something else, you know I'll support you, don't you? I'm all for people chasing their dreams. I did it, remember. I need to get Brodie to believe in himself now too.'

'It's brilliant his book is selling so well. I bet he's over the moon,' Bella said.

Olivia beamed with pride. 'He is. Aiden has offered to take a copy to London with him when he leaves. He thinks someone at his agency might be interested in representing him.'

Bella gasped. 'That's incredible. I'm so happy for him.'

'Speaking of our author friend, a little bird, i.e. Aiden himself, tells me he spent the evening watching movies at your apartment with Isla the other night. How did that go?'

Bella decided to go for the positive response. 'It was good, we watched *Local Hero* and drank Merlot.' The flutter she had been used to when discussing Aiden was absent.

'What did he make of the film?'

Bella shrugged. 'He said it was a bit bland, but he could understand why we liked it with Granny having a connection with the place it was filmed at.' Positivity flew out the window and took hope along for the ride. 'I mean, who doesn't like *Local Hero*? And is he trying to say we're boring?'

Olivia placed the back of her hand on her forehead dramatically. 'You must dump him at once!'

Bella squinted at her friend. 'Haha, very funny. Seriously, though, I'm not really sure what we have in common. Apart from books, and even then, he doesn't read crime novels, he just writes them, so in reality, what *do* we have in common?'

'What did Isla make of him?'

'She was a little quiet when he was there. And she hurried off to bed when he left. I haven't really spoken to her about why yet.'

Olivia thought for a moment. 'Do you think it may be because he lives in London and she's worried about you leaving with him, or going to live with him eventually if things go well, something like that?'

Bella's heart sank. 'Oh, heck, I never even thought of that. I'll have to put her mind at rest. I don't see any of that happening. To be honest, he's a bit full of himself. He was badmouthing some other authors after the film. Authors who I really like. Saying things like their vocabulary is limited and he has no idea why they're higher in the charts than he is. It was a bit off-putting.'

'Hmm, maybe the shine has worn off? Is there a reason for that maybe?' Olivia gave her a knowing look.

'What do you mean?' Bella knew exactly what she meant, of course.

'Oh, I don't know, I think maybe a certain recently shaven-faced police sergeant might be going up in your estimations.'

'How do you know about his beard being gone?'

'I saw him yesterday when he came to see Aiden.'

Bella raised her eyebrows. 'I didn't see him.'

'No, that's because you were showing a young couple the long gallery as a potential venue for their wedding.'

'Oh, right.' Bella was, once again, surprised to find she was disappointed at missing Harris.

Bella borrowed Olivia's car during the afternoon to take some mail into Inverness, including some of Brodie's signed books. After leaving Drumblair, she followed the road that skirted the edge of Loch Ness and could see fishing boats off in the distance. In some places the road narrowed and every so often she had to pull into a passing place to allow for oncoming traffic. She gazed out at the loch and tapped the steering wheel in time with Queen's 'Crazy Little Thing Called Love' on Radio Highland.

As she left the village of Dores, the road veered away from the loch and at that point the scenery changed from water and mountains to bracken-hedged lanes that led towards the city. She passed by little white-painted houses, some of which had laundry flapping on lines in their gardens in the gentle breeze, and she spotted Highland cows with their long russet hair munching on grass in the lush green fields. Every so often the light would dim as the trees thickened at either side of the road; copses of firs reaching towards the sky and its life-giving sunlight. Overhead the canopy was pale blue and dotted with cumulus clouds and aeroplane contrails, and Bella absently wondered where the passengers were jetting off to.

Take That's 'Never Forget' came on the radio and Bella sang rather too loudly, considering her window was cracked open, making the most of the balmy summer day. She almost gave a poor cyclist a heart attack as she passed him as the chorus hit. In her own mind, she could've been a brilliant backing singer for the band. It was a shame they had absolutely no clue Bella and her voice existed.

Once Take That had preached to the choir – Bella was never likely to forget where *she* came from – it was the turn of Florence and the Machine and 'Dog Days Are Over'. Harris immediately sprang into her mind; his smiling eyes and his wonderful laugh after her terrible impression of a 1940s Bronx gangster's moll. There was something about him, she had realised, something that made her smile and feel safe simultaneously.

Harris wasn't the boring, strait-laced man she had presumed him to be when she first met him. And she found him popping into her mind more and more frequently. But she wasn't attracted to him, was she? It was simply that he was a nice guy, good company and very warm-hearted, that's all.

* * *

Bella posted the parcels she had brought with her and as she was leaving the post office, she spotted Harris and Mel speaking to some young guys across the street. She pretended to be looking in a shop window and watched them in the reflection, waiting to see if he spotted her. After a few moments, she decided she had hung around too long staring at the window display of what turned out to be a vape shop when she didn't vape and had no intention of ever taking it up. She made to walk away and noticed Mel nudge Harris and gesture towards her.

'Bella! Hang on!' She stopped in her tracks and turned to see Harris jogging towards her. 'I've just finished, fancy a coffee?'

Her body flooded with a rush of heat and what she could only presume was serotonin, a sensation that immediately lifted her mood. 'Sure, why not?' She hoped Olivia wouldn't mind her being a little delayed.

'Great, usual place? Or do you fancy somewhere else?'

'Pettifer's is absolutely fine.'

He turned to wave to Mel. 'See you tomorrow, Mel! And tell Neil I'll drop him a message later.' Mel waved and headed off in the direction of the police station.

Bella and Harris set off walking away from Queensgate and through the busy streets filled with bag-laden shoppers, tourists with street maps, and suited businesspeople alike, heading towards Bank Street. The afternoon sun glinted off the River Ness and the buildings on the opposite side reflected in the water. Bella adored Inverness, it was the northernmost city in the United Kingdom and was known as the capital of the Highlands too. Bella loved the history of the place and especially the architecture. The oldest building in the city was built in the sixteenth century, a fact that blew Bella's mind.

'So, what are you doing in the city this time? Not more shopping?' Harris asked.

'No, work this time.'

'Ah, I see. I came to the castle yesterday to see Aiden to catch up with him on some procedural questions he'd emailed with for his book. Olivia said you were busy and I should hang around to say hi, but I had a bit of a manic day.'

'Yes, Olivia said she'd seen you. I hope you're enjoying your work as a consultant on his book.'

'Aye, things are getting interesting, that's for sure.'

They arrived at Pettifer's and took their favoured window table. Mrs P brought their usual order across without them needing to request it.

Once they both had their coffees and of course the obligatory slice of Victoria sponge, Bella asked, 'So, how come you're finishing work early today?'

He kept his focus on his coffee, as if he couldn't look her in the eyes. 'I'm, erm, heading west for a couple of days. I'll be back on Friday.'

'Ooh, going anywhere interesting?' Bella asked as she cut a sliver of the moist cake and placed it in her mouth.

Harris sipped on his coffee but still didn't meet her gaze. 'Aye, Glentorrin on the Isle of Skye.'

Bella had never visited Glentorrin but had seen photos of Skye when she was small and remembered the jagged rocks of the Quiraing and the Old Man of Storr and how scary and otherworldly they seemed to her at the tender age of five, like something out of a sci-fi movie. Plus with her procuring Reid Mackinnon's artwork, she felt like she knew the place.

'You're kidding, aren't you? That's where the artist lives whose paintings I acquired for the apartments!'

'Small world, eh?'

'It really is.' Something felt strangely serendipitous about the situation, but she wasn't sure why. 'It will be lovely. Is your mum going with you?'

'Ah, no. It's not a holiday, it's... it's actually a work thing.'

Bella was surprised to hear the Inverness and Skye police needed to work together and wondered why. 'Oh gosh, that's a long way to go for a collaboration.'

He reached up and scratched at his chin. 'It's for an interview, actually. The area's current inspector is retiring early due to ill health and the position is open so I thought I'd apply. That was a couple of months ago now and my next in-person interview is tomorrow. I've already had several phone calls, an online interview via Teams, passed the necessary tests and done all the other bits and bobs of paperwork, checks and such I need to do. Tomorrow is mainly about meeting the chief from Portree there and getting to see the station and visit the area. I didn't expect to get this far, to be honest.'

Bella wasn't sure what to say or how to feel for that matter. 'Oh... wow... That's...'

Harris smiled. 'Daunting? Aye, it is. I'm not prepared to leave Mum, so I'm taking some time out to look at accommodation for her while I'm there, you know, just in case. She's all for it, she says, so long as she goes into something similar to Sunnyside. She reckons she'll have company that way. I can see her point, but I still felt a bit guilty at first. She seems to have gotten quite keen on the idea, though.'

For some strange reason, Bella's heart sank and a wave of sadness washed over her. 'Gosh... It's a big step.'

'It is. I've not made up my mind yet whether I'll take the job even if they offer it to me. But I've nothing really keeping me here, so...' He glanced up at her, as if assessing her reaction, but she was too stunned to find the right words.

A strange, heavy atmosphere came over them and Bella lost her appetite. 'Well, good luck, if it's something you really want to do.'

'It'd be a step up for me career-wise. There's a house that comes with the job too. It's on the outskirts of the village in a little old bothy that's been renovated and become the new police station, and the house has been built beside it. It's not massive but it'll be fine for me. The pictures look good; the house is what you'd call a blank slate. It's funny but it's the dream job I never realised I wanted. And Skye is so beautiful. Great roads for the bike. Have you ever been to Skye?'

Bella shook her head. 'No. It looks beautiful from the pictures I've seen, though.'

'It's absolutely stunning. You should visit there sometime.'

'Yes, maybe I should. What will you do with your family home, though? I'm surprised you'd want to leave that behind.'

He nodded. 'Aye, it will be hard, but I've decided I won't sell it. I'll rent it out, you know, if I go. But I haven't got the job yet.'

Why did he keep reiterating that fact? 'I don't think you have anything to worry about on that score,' Bella replied, knowing full well they would snatch him up, quick smart.

After they had finished their coffee and cake, Harris walked Bella back to her car. 'It's been good to see you again, Bella.' His cheeks flushed and he gave a small smile. 'I sound like a broken record, don't I?'

She couldn't help smiling too. 'At least you're consistent. Anyway, good luck with your interview. I'm sure you'll nail it. Although... I have to say I'll miss you if you do go. I've enjoyed our coffee meet-ups.' She tried to be as light-hearted as possible, even though she felt the absolute opposite.

'Aye, me too. We have the beginnings of a good friendship, eh? But you'll have to come and visit, bring Aiden, maybe?'

Bella was shocked when her eyes began to sting, and she knew she needed to leave as soon as possible. It had taken until now, the completely inappropriate time, to realise her feelings for Harris had been growing. Even though he hadn't been offered the job, she knew deep down it was only a matter of time. Why wouldn't they want him? He was good at his job, he was great with people, he was smart, funny, professional, reliable, trustworthy. What more could they possibly want?

He cleared his throat. 'Well, I'll see you Saturday. I presume Isla's going to the day centre tea dance?'

This was news to Bella but, then again, she hadn't really spoken at length to her granny since Aiden came for movie night. 'She hasn't mentioned it, actually, but no doubt she'll be going. She loves a good boogie.'

'Right, well, I might see you after if you'd like me to bring her home.'

She smiled and gave a nod. 'That would be really helpful, thank you. And good luck.' Before she could stop herself, she stepped forward and hugged him. He smelled clean and fresh like the air of the Inverness-shire outdoors. He wrapped his arms around her and the sinking feeling she had experienced earlier came back with a vengeance.

He pulled away and fixed his gaze on hers. 'See you soon, Bella,' he said, his voice almost a whisper. He leaned forward and kissed her cheek, lingering a little longer than she expected. She closed her eyes and relished the closeness. But it was too late. She couldn't say anything now, not now his dream job was on the horizon.

When he had gone, Bella climbed into the car and started the engine. As she pulled out of the car park, Cyndi Lauper's 'Heading West' came on the radio. 'Oh god, Radio Highland, you're killing me,' she said to thin air. And as she listened to the lyrics, she fought back the tears over something she didn't realise she wanted until it was potentially too late to do anything about it.

* * *

Thursday was wet and Bella spent the day in the castle library typing up correspondence for Olivia. She hadn't left the room all day, even though the sun had been shining in between showers.

'Hey, honey, isn't it time you were going home?' Olivia asked as she poked her head around the large oak door.

Bella glanced at her watch. It was almost six in the evening. She rubbed at her eyes. 'Sorry, I'd totally lost track of time.'

Olivia entered and sat in the chair opposite where Bella sat at the desk. 'Is everything okay?'

Bella nodded. There was no point saying anything now. She had missed her chance with Harris. A chance she didn't even realise she wanted. 'Oh yes, you know me, fine and dandy.'

Olivia tilted her head. 'You should tell that to your eyes, missy.'

Bella quickly changed the subject. 'Any news from Kerr?'

Olivia huffed. 'Innes received a text message from him finally this morning. All he said was he's fine but he's not coming back. When pressed, he refused to say where he is. I can't be bothered with the worry. Brodie says I've to let it go and I'm beginning to think he's right. While he's not here he's not causing upset, which is an awful way to think about my own brother, but sadly, it's a fact. Oh, and he is still renting the house out, so at least I know where he's getting his money from!'

'And at least you know he's still alive.'

'That's true. Anyway, get yourself home; Isla will be thinking I've kidnapped you.'

* * *

'I thought you'd disappeared into Bolivia,' Isla said as Bella walked through the door.

Her granny always had those inadvertent ways of cheering her up, usually with her malapropisms. 'No, Granny, sorry, I lost track of time.'

'Well, come and sit down, I've made a beef stew and kept it warm. I hoped we could eat together.'

'Thank you. I'll go and change.' Bella went to her room and changed into yoga pants and a baggy old Fleetwood Mac T-shirt that had once belonged to her dad. She returned to the kitchen and found a bowl of stew waiting for her.

'Tuck in while it's hot, hen. You look like you need it.'

Bella chewed a mouthful of the meat which melted on her tongue. 'Granny, is everything okay? You've been quiet since we had Aiden round.'

Isla sighed and placed down her fork. 'Aye, hen. Fine.' Her tone was unconvincing to say the least. She paused and then continued, 'It's... that writer chappy doesn't seem right in my mind. There's something about him. Something Kermit-like.'

Bella was aware she wasn't referring to the actual muppet. 'He's not like Kerr, Granny. He's just a bit... I don't know...'

'Full of his own self-importance? Too big for his boots?'

Bella placed her own fork down. 'What makes you say that?' She couldn't disagree with her.

'The way he talked about *Local Hero*, the way he talked about those other authors. I mean sure, he's entitled to his opinion, but his opinion left a bad taste in my mouth.'

So Isla had heard everything he'd said. 'I thought you had gone to bed.'

'I was on my way, but I was listening at the door of my room.'

'In all honesty, I don't see things going anywhere with him anyway, Granny. And he lives in London, which is very far away.' Bella hoped this would put her granny's mind at rest. 'Someone very wise once told me that long-distance romance is too hard.'

'Aye, that was a very sensible person. She must be an absolutely amazing woman. Certainly one to listen to.' Isla winked and Bella reached to squeeze her hand.

29

Saturday was bright and once again the grounds of the castle were busy with people enjoying the sunshine that Drumblair had been blessed with.

Bella's brother Callum had messaged her in the early hours of the morning to say he and their parents had landed back in Glasgow at midnight after their two-week cruise. She was looking forward to hearing all about it and seeing the gazillion photos that had no doubt been taken. She also needed to discuss plans with Callum to have a belated family birthday do for her dad, seeing as she hadn't been there to celebrate his sixtieth.

It was the day of the tea dance that Harris had mentioned, and Isla had dressed up for the occasion in a lilac frock that complimented her freshly re-purpled hair. She'd been quite excited about going and Bella had enjoyed helping her with her make-up.

'I don't want too much on my eyes, hen, I don't want to look like one of those drag racers,' Isla had insisted.

'Don't worry, Granny, I won't make you look like a drag racer,' Bella had assured her whilst trying not to giggle as she imagined

RuPaul driving an elongated car at speed on a track as other drag queens cheered him on.

Isla's expression changed. 'I forgot to tell you, Maeve says she might be relocating to Skye with Harris. I'm heartbroken. She's my best friend in the world, well apart from you, that is. I don't know what I'll do without her. And it's a good thing Harris isn't your type after all, isn't it? You would have lost him as soon as you'd found him. I mean Skye is only a few hours away, but it's not the same as being in the same city.'

Bella hadn't replied. Instead, she'd stepped back and admired her handiwork. 'You look very glam, Granny.'

Isla had lifted up her old-fashioned handheld mirror with the mother-of-pearl inlay on the back and patted her hair as she took in her reflection. 'Perfect! And not a drag racer in sight.'

* * *

Later that day, Bella was standing in the castle foyer admiring the artwork, as she often did when she had a spare five minutes. She hadn't heard from Harris and kept wondering what was happening with the Skye job, so being at work was the best distraction.

She heard the door open. 'She's there, mate,' she heard Brodie say.

As she turned towards the entrance, she saw Brodie standing next to Harris, who was in his uniform; a concerned expression crumpled his brow.

She smiled briefly but her stomach knotted. 'Hi, Harris. Is everything okay?'

'Bella, could you come with me, please?'

She giggled. 'Ooh, am I under arrest? Is it for my criminal records?' When he didn't smile or reply, she elaborated, 'As in... my CD collection... in case you didn't get my meaning. Although the

Barry Manilow is my gran's, honest. So not guilty there.' The way his expression was unchanging, and his gaze remained fixed on her, told her to stop messing around.

'Bella, I'm sorry but you really do need to come with me,' he said as he held out his hand.

Her insides plummeted as if she was on an elevator with broken cables. 'What is it? Have I done something wrong?' She racked her brain for answers. 'Or has something happened?'

'It's best if you come with me. I can explain on the way.' He extended his hand again towards her.

A shiver travelled down her spine and her stomach churned. 'Harris, you're scaring me. Tell me what's happened.'

He walked towards her. 'Your granny's had a nasty fall. She hit her head and—'

Bella heard a whine and glanced down to see Brodie had a hold of Beau's lead. She felt the colour drain from her face and everything began to spin as her eyes welled with tears. 'And what?' She almost stumbled and Harris grabbed for her, steadying her with both hands. 'She's not... I mean she hasn't...'

He clenched his jaw and glanced sideways at Brodie before returning his attention to her. 'She's hurt quite badly. She was unconscious when the ambulance arrived, and there was some mention they would need to take her to theatre. The paramedic said they thought her hip was broken. She's at Raigmore. I'm here to take you to her.'

Bella gasped and her legs weakened again but thankfully Harris had a strong hold on her. 'Oh my god. Is she going to be okay? What happened? She will be okay, won't she?'

Harris moved to put his arm around her. 'I hope so, Bella, but... I can't make any promises, I hope you understand. I'm no doctor. I wanted to make sure you get to her fast.'

Bella nodded; the action caused tears to spill over onto her cheeks. 'I... I need to let Olivia know that I—'

Brodie interjected, 'I'll let her know, don't worry.'

'Now, do you want Aiden to come with you?' Harris asked as he led her to the door.

Bella scrunched her brow. Why would he mention Aiden at a time like this? 'But why would I... I don't...'

'I don't think you should be alone. Come on, we'll call down for him on the way.' Harris guided her to the stable block apartments, making sure to stay close enough in case her legs gave way.

He knocked on Aiden's door. A few moments passed until Aiden answered and when he did, he was bare-chested and his hair was a tousled mess. He scowled. 'Why are you here together? What's wrong?' His cheeks paled and he took a step back.

Harris held up a hand. 'Aiden, it's Olivia's granny, she's had a bad fall and is at the hospital. Bella's in bits about it, and wondered if you'd accompany her to the hospital for moral support.'

Aiden opened and closed his mouth a few times like a goldfish. 'Oh... erm... no, it's okay, thanks, I don't do hospitals. It's a... it's a phobia type of thing. They make me feel ill. I can't really say I'd be much help.'

Harris glanced at Bella, who was finding it hard to form sentences due to the worry and emotion clogging up her throat. She watched his lips form a hard line for a moment before he said, 'Aiden, she needs some support, pal. Can you maybe put your ick aside for your girlfriend on this occasion?'

I'm not his girlfriend! Bella screamed in her mind, though she was too worried about her granny to voice her frustration.

Aiden shrugged. 'Why can't you stay with her?'

Harris replied through gritted teeth. 'I'm on duty. I only came to make sure she got to Isla as soon as possible.'

'She'll be okay on her own, won't you, sweetheart?' Aiden said in a sickly, patronising tone. 'She's tough, aren't you? Tougher than me. I don't do needles and bleeping and the smell.' He visibly shivered.

If she hadn't been so terrified of losing her granny, Bella would have been appalled with his attitude. 'Forget it, Harris, let's go, please. I want to see my granny,' Bella whispered as more tears spilled over.

'Aye, okay. Thanks for nothing, Aiden,' Harris said before he turned and held out his arm to Bella. She linked hers through it and they headed to the patrol car parked just in front of the castle.

A crowd of onlookers had gathered, and Brodie stood with Beau's lead gripped in his hand and a crumple of worry in his brow. 'Don't worry about Beau. He'll be fine with us,' he told her.

Bella nodded, grateful. The tears cascading down her cheeks had now soaked into her blouse. 'Thank you, Brodie.'

* * *

Bella sat silently staring out of the window as Harris drove her to the hospital. The sky overhead was cloudy now, and the grey matched her mood. Even the water in the loch appeared dull and there was no one around. The distant hills were shrouded in mist, their colours muted by it.

Once they arrived at the hospital, Harris dashed around to her door to let her out of the police car.

'Come on, I'll take you straight up. There may be a wait as I don't know how long she'll be in surgery.'

She grabbed his arm. 'Thank you, Harris. I really appreciate this. I really appreciate you.'

He placed his hand on hers and fixed her with a sincere and compassionate gaze. 'No thanks needed, Bella. Come on.'

They made their way up to the ward and were greeted by a

nurse behind the desk. 'I'm sorry, but she's still in surgery. She may be a while. Why don't you go on home and call later?'

Bella's heart thudded at her ribcage and her throat restricted but she straightened her spine and spoke assertively to the nurse. 'I'm sorry, no, I won't go home. I can't leave. I need to be here. And I'd like an update as soon as possible, please.'

'But she—'

Bella held up her hand. 'Will be in surgery for a while, yes, I get that. And I appreciate all you're doing but I won't be going anywhere, so please come and inform me when there's any news.'

The nurse nodded. 'Of course.'

Harris put a hand on her arm. 'Look, why don't we go the café and get a coffee? I can call your mum and dad for you, if you'd like.'

Survival mode kicked in and even though her face was damp with tears, she said, 'Thank you for the offer, but it's best if I call them. Although coffee sounds like a good idea.'

Harris nodded and smiled briefly before holding his arm out to gesture he would follow her.

* * *

After breaking the news of Isla's fall to her dad, Bella sat for what felt like hours, staring into her coffee cup. It was still full to the brim. Her mind was assaulted by memories of her granny's smile and that glint in her eyes. The way she would mix up her words and giggle at things she shouldn't. The way she'd always looked out for Bella. The way she had clobbered Kerr when he had dared to disrespect her. Her heart sank and she covered her chest with her hand. How would she cope if anything went wrong during the operation? How would she cope without her wonderful, vibrant best friend? She couldn't bear to think about losing her. It made her heart ache and her eyes sting. Her stomach was one tight knotted ball of emotion, the pain was all too real and she began to replay her last conversation with Isla. Had she told her she loved her? She couldn't quite remember. She hoped so.

She remembered again about Harris's interview. She inhaled a deep breath and plastered on a smile, now wasn't the time to be a damsel in distress. 'How did it go, at the interview, I mean?'

Harris swallowed hard and a crease appeared between his brows. 'I'm... erm... I was offered the position.'

Bella stared at the table and squeezed her eyes shut, willing the threatening tears to dissipate. 'That's... that's great news. Well done. When will you be leaving?'

'There's a two-month notice period, but...' He cleared his throat. 'I haven't accepted it yet... I'm—'

Bella's mum, dad and brother, Callum, rushed into the café and over to where she sat. She stood and almost fell into her dad's arms.

'Hey, shhh, it's okay, love. She's a tough old bird, my mum. Shh, it's okay.' He stroked her hair and she sobbed hard into his chest. 'We're here now. Shhh.'

Harris stood and greeted them. 'Isla's in surgery, it could be a couple of hours yet. We keep checking,' he informed them.

Bella's mum reached out and shook his hand. 'Thank you so much. How do you know Bella?'

'I know Bella through Isla, actually. Isla and my mum, Maeve, are friends. My mum lives at Sunnyside.'

'Oh yes,' Bella's mum replied. 'Where the day centre is.'

'Aye. I'd called in to drop some things off for my mum when the ambulance turned up.'

Bella gathered herself and straightened up, doing her best to regain her strength.

Her dad shook his head. 'She doesn't usually go on a Saturday;

how come she was there, Bella?'

'They were having a special event. A tea dance. From what Harris said, Granny tripped over a chair and fell quite badly onto her side but hit her head and was knocked out too.'

Bella's dad sighed. 'That's why they called me. We were unpacking from the holiday, and I missed a call from Sunnyside, but I presumed it was a mistake with it being Saturday, so I didn't ring back. Poor Mum.' He ran his hand over his face as the colour left his skin.

Callum gasped. 'What about Beau? Where's Beau?'

Harris held up a reassuring hand. 'Don't worry. He's at the castle with Brodie, Olivia and their dogs.'

Callum breathed an audible sigh of relief. 'Thank you.'

'I'm so worried, Dad,' Bella said as she chewed her thumbnail. 'A fall at her age can be drastic. But she has to be okay.'

'She will be, love. Like I always tell you, she's tough. We have to be patient now. She's in the best place.'

'I should probably go. But I'll be back later,' Harris said, placing a hand on Bella's back. 'If you need anything at all, don't hesitate to call me, okay?'

Bella turned and grappled Harris into a hug. 'Thank you. Thank you so much.' He smelled so good and familiar, and his arms felt safe and right.

He hugged her back and when he pulled away, he placed a hand on either side of her face and kissed her forehead. 'Take care, Bella.' There was something in his eyes that drew her in. She didn't want him to leave. She always felt so much better when he was there. Although she daren't let herself get used to that feeling, seeing as he would be relocating to Skye soon. Over a hundred miles away. Thinking about that caused tears to threaten again but she pushed the pain down, labelling it as being caused by her heightened emotions.

30

Eventually Bella and her family moved closer to Isla's ward and sat in a small family waiting room. Orange fabric chairs skirted the walls and a coffee table in the centre of the room was scattered with magazines and books. A faded artificial flower arrangement sat in the middle, looking about as cheery as everyone in the room was feeling. Bella's dad paced the floor and Bella sat with her head on her mum's shoulder, staring at the beige tiles on the floor. Callum sat, eyes closed and head leaning against the wall.

Eventually Bella stood and walked to the window. The mist had gone and now, from this high vantage point, you could see right across Inverness to the mountains where the sky was beginning to turn a dusky orange as the sun sank in the sky. Her phone beeped and she glanced down to see there were several messages that must have come through when her phone was on silent. Olivia, Skye and Harris, all checking she was okay. Nothing from Aiden. It figured and she didn't really care anyway.

After another two hours and several cups of vending-machine coffee, the door opened. 'Isla Douglas's family?' asked the doctor as she stepped inside, still in her scrubs.

Bella's dad stood, his holiday-tanned face somehow pale with evident worry. 'Aye, is she okay?'

The doctor smiled. 'Surgery has gone well. We had to replace the hip due to the nature of the fracture, she'll need extensive physio, but she should be fine. She's tough and a real character.' The doctor smiled. 'She had been knocked out when she fell but was conscious when she arrived here. She was insisting she'd be fine after a couple of paracetamol and a lie-down,' the doctor said with a light laugh.

Bella and her family were able to laugh too at this. 'Aye, that sounds like Granny, eh, Bells?' her brother Callum said as he put his arm around her shoulder.

Bella wiped her eyes and grinned. 'It certainly does. But don't be surprised if she moans about being on the *gyratics* ward.'

The doctor chuckled. 'Ah, yes, we've already had that. She also asked if there were any handsome young male nurses to look after her.'

Bella covered her face with her hand. 'Good grief, she's incorrigible.'

'Anyway, she's back on the ward in a side room at the moment. Room two. She's in and out of consciousness, so please don't overcrowd her. I know you're worried, but she needs her rest. And don't be alarmed by the bruising on her face. She's elderly and these things tend to appear quite horrific. Just think about her comment about paracetamol and you'll remember she's a tough cookie.' And with that the doctor left.

'Go on, Bells, you go see her first, love. Put your mind at rest.' Bella's dad said.

Bella hugged him immediately. 'Thanks, Dad.' With trepidation, she walked along a white corridor, past crammed notice boards housing pamphlets about various illnesses, and thank you cards from former patients and their families, towards room two

She took a deep breath and gingerly opened the door, a fresh tissue clutched in her hand in readiness.

Isla was lying with her eyes closed and attached to various pieces of medical equipment that were blipping and beeping the rhythm of her heart. It was steady and strong, which was a positive sign to Bella. Numbers were flashing on a screen by the bed and a drip of clear liquid was also attached to her somewhere under a bandage around her arm. The side of Isla's face was swollen and purple and she looked so tiny and frail. A sob escaped Bella's mouth and she immediately covered it with her tissue. Seeing her granny like this was horrendous. Bella's stomach ached, the pain dull and nauseating, and her chest tightened to the point she had to remind herself to breathe. She pulled up a chair and sat, tears once again streaming down her face, but she simply let them fall.

She reached out and took Isla's hand. Her skin was mottled and wrinkly but soft to the touch. Bella had painted her nails that morning in a soft lilac to match her tea dance dress. Her hands were so familiar and held Bella's regularly; sometimes during their movie nights and sometimes when they were out walking together. Bella had no shame about that whatsoever, regardless of her age. She adored her granny. She was her best friend, and being faced with the knowledge she could have lost her was devastating, heart-rending. Bella's pain was a physical and emotional gut-wrenching agony that twisted her insides and almost took away her breath.

She lowered her head and rested it on her granny's hand. 'You have to get better, Granny. I'm not ready to let you go yet.'

After a few silent moments, punctuated only by the noises of the equipment in the room, there was movement. 'Hello, hen, what's the matter?' came a weak, slurred voice that caused Bella to lift her head.

'Granny, you're awake,' Bella said with a sniff and a smile as relief flooded her whole body.

Isla blinked and frowned. 'Aye, I am. What's the matter, hen? Why are you crying? Is it that murder writer? Has he upset you again? I'll be having words if he has.'

Bella giggled through her tears. 'No, Granny, I've been worried about *you*.'

Isla gave a weak smile. 'You *bampot*, I'm fine. They've put a new hip in, you know. I'm like the bionic woman now. There's not many of the gyratics at the day centre can say they've got a uranium hip.'

Bella pursed her lips. 'Aye, and neither can you, Granny. I think it's titanium, actually.'

'Aye, that's what a said. I'll be giving that Eugene Bolt a run for his money now.' She glanced towards the floor, a look of panic in her eyes. 'Where's my Beau?'

'Don't worry, he's with Wilf and Marley at the castle.'

Her features relaxed. 'Ah, that's good. He likes running around wi' his wee pals.'

Bella's heart skipped and she clutched Isla's hand. It was so good to hear her talking like her old self, even if she sounded a little weak. 'How are you feeling? Are you in pain? Do you need me to get the nurse?'

'Oh no, hen. I'm not too bad considering they've chopped bits out of me. It was a lucky break if you pardon the pun. I was wanting to go home anyway. It was a rubbish tea dance, so there was nothing spoiling there.'

Bella grinned. 'Oh, that's a shame.'

'Aye, can you believe they actually served *tea*? I thought it was just a name and there'd at least be a glass of sherry in it. But no, blooming tea. And not even Earl Grey. It was the usual stuff they serve that was scraped off the floor at the tea factory. So, I can't even blame alcohol for my tumble.'

Bella giggled. 'Oh no. Did you manage to do any dancing?'

Isla rolled her eyes. 'Aye, I danced wi' Reg Anderson but he's no

Craig Rebel Hardwood. In fact, I blame him for my falling. We were dancing a two-step, but it was as if Reg didn't know his left from his right and he kept standing on my feet. Next thing I knew, I was waking up in an ambulance. I'm fine, though. You don't need to worry. I had a slight percussion when I came in but they're keeping an eye on me. I'll be home before you know it.'

Bella stood and kissed her granny's head. 'Thank goodness because it won't be the same without you.'

'Did they phone you from Sunnyside to get you to come here? Because I told them not to bother you, you know. I told them you were an integral cog in the wheels of Drumblair Castle.'

Bella stifled a laugh. 'It's no bother. Harris came to Drumblair to collect me. And I'm glad he did. He arrived at the day centre as the ambulance got there so he was at the scene and able to speak to the paramedics.'

Isla's eyes lit up. 'Oh, he's so nice, isn't he? Very considerate. Did that murder writer come with you?'

Bella gave her granny a pass for the name on this occasion. 'No, Granny, he couldn't come. He was... erm... busy.'

'Ah, well, at least Harris brought you. Are your mum and dad home from their 1830 cruise? And Callum?'

'They are. They're here at the hospital. I'll go get them. They'll want to come and see you too.'

Her granny gripped her hand and looked her straight in the eyes. 'I do love you, Arabella. I hope you know that.'

Bella's chin trembled. 'Of course I do. And I love you too. I'll see you later.' She bent to kiss her granny's head again and left the room.

Once she had closed the door behind her, she leaned on the wall as more tears came; this time they were tears of relief. She composed herself and made her way to the waiting room.

* * *

Bella arrived back at the castle at around 9 p.m. after her dad dropped her off. She was unlocking the door to the apartment when headlights flashed, causing her to squint. Harris's Jeep pulled to a halt, and she waited for him to climb down from the vehicle.

'Hi, Harris, is everything okay?' Bella asked as he approached her.

He was out of his uniform now and in black jeans, a light-coloured top and his leather jacket. As he got closer, the overhead security lights illuminated him, creating his very own halo. He really was gorgeous, and Bella couldn't believe she hadn't realised this before now. But it wasn't just his physicality that drew her to him. It was his nature. His kindness and his strength.

He smiled and stuffed his hands in his pockets, a thing she had noticed he did mainly when he was in his civilian clothes and felt unsure of himself. She found it quite endearing.

'I came to ask you the same thing,' he said with a crumple of concern to his face.

'You really are sweet. Thank you. Granny was comfortable when we left her but I'm not sure we're out of the woods yet. She's eighty-five and this fall and the surgery have taken their toll on her. It's all so worrying. I can't thank you enough for your help. Do you want to come in for a coffee?'

'Aw, no, I don't want to keep you. You must be wiped out from the events of today.'

'Honestly, I know I probably should be, but I think I'm running on adrenaline and possibly all that coffee at the hospital, so maybe I should have a camomile tea instead. Come and keep me company for a while?'

He nodded. 'If you're sure.'

He glanced towards Aiden's apartment and a strange expression washed over his features before Harris followed her into her apartment.

Bella walked around quickly turning on lamps. 'So, tea?'

'Aye, that'd be grand, thank you.'

She set about making the drinks and then took them through to the living room. She placed the mugs on the coffee table and sat; Harris took a seat beside her on the sofa.

'I'm so glad everything's okay. I've been worried about you,' he said with a light laugh.

'I'm okay now I know my granny's being taken care of. I don't know what I would do without her, and at this stage, I don't know what the future holds.'

He nodded. 'Aye, I totally get that. That's why I'm taking my mum to Skye with me.'

Bella's heart sank. 'You're definitely going then?'

He nodded. 'I am. I had to make a decision and Mum's signed up for a sheltered housing scheme in Broadford. I went and had a look around while I was there, and video called her so she could see. It's a lovely wee place and only fifteen minutes from where I'll be, so I think she'll be happy there. I'd still rather have her at home with me but she's having none of that.' He chuckled. 'They get more stubborn with age, don't they?'

'They certainly do.' She paused and searched for the right words to express how she felt but instead said, 'I'm really happy for you.'

'Thanks, Bella. It's a fresh start, not that I was looking for one really, but it's a good opportunity. A wee bit scary, but I'll cope. I'm big enough and ugly enough to take care of myself, that's for sure.'

She wanted to say, 'You're anything but ugly,' but instead remained silent.

'So, how is the interior design course application going?' he asked as he reached for his tea.

'All done. The materials should be arriving any day now.'

'Fantastic. I'm really glad you went for it.'

'Me too. I have you to thank for planting the seed.'

His face brightened. 'Really? That makes me so happy.'

His arm was resting along the back of the sofa and his fingers were so close to her she could turn and touch them, but she didn't.

She lifted her chin and found his gaze fixed on her. 'Skye isn't so far away, you know,' he said in an almost whisper. 'I do hope you'll visit. And bring Isla when she's on her feet again. My mum will miss her.'

'Definitely,' Bella said, her eyes locked on his. Heat flooded her body and she swallowed. Neither of them spoke.

'You can bring Aiden too.' Bella watched his jaw clamp firm and tick under his skin, and she felt sure he was going to say something more. But instead, he stood. 'I probably should go. It's getting late and you must be tired.'

Bella stood too. 'Don't go,' she whispered.

31

Harris frowned, clearly confused by her request, and he shook his head. 'But... I don't understand. I didn't think for a minute you'd want me to stay. I thought you'd prefer to be alone.'

She took a step closer to him. 'The place feels strange, it's not my home and without my granny it feels less so. To be honest, I definitely don't want to be alone. If I'm alone, I know I'll think too much and end up in dark places, and I really don't want that tonight. I can't let myself go there.' Her chin trembled.

His face relaxed. 'Ah, I see.' He chewed his lip for a moment as if contemplating his next words. 'I get it. I really do. It's been an upsetting day and I know how worried you must be. But how would it look? I mean, I don't think Aiden—'

She huffed and turned away, running her hands through her hair. Maybe she had misread the signals. Maybe he had been playing along with his mum and Isla and he didn't feel anything for her. Maybe she had mistaken his compliments for something other than the way they were intended?

Without turning around, she said, 'Why do you always have to mention Aiden? I thought *you* liked me. And I don't feel for *him* the way I do for...' She stiffened, realising she had almost said too much. If she had been wrong about his feelings for her, she would end up looking incredibly stupid and ran the risk of sounding self-centred and vain. 'I mean... I don't feel as strongly about him as people seem to think.'

There was a moment of silence where something in the air changed. It was almost palpable, and Bella's heartrate picked up.

Harris took a step closer so the front of this body was dangerously close to the back of hers. 'What were you going to say, Bella? Before you corrected yourself, what were you going to say?' She could feel the heat from him radiating through her clothes and she had to fight the almost overwhelming urge to throw herself into his arms. He persisted.

She turned and gazed up at him. 'Do you really want to know?' she asked, knowing it was probably pointless.

He cupped her cheek and closed his eyes for a split second before fixing her with a stern gaze and shook his head. 'No. I don't think I do. Because in two months I'm leaving Inverness to start a new life on Skye, and a long-distance relationship, even though I'll only be a few hours away, would be pretty difficult considering my role. I can't live here and run a station in Glentorrin. Which means, in a way, we're already facing an impasse. And I've been there before.'

Her glance must have been questioning because he sighed deeply and continued, 'My ex, Alba, was promoted to detective superintendent and moved to Glasgow. She was so driven. She asked me to go but I didn't want to work in such a big city. It's not me. So I said no and we tried long distance but... it was too hard. Eventually she broke things off with me because she thought I lacked ambition. But it's not that, it's just community policing is where my heart lies, and the job on Skye is exactly where I see myself being happy. And I know you don't want to leave Inverness and I completely respect that, especially under the current circumstances. But... maybe I could stay...'

A horrible realisation washed over Bella, and she closed her eyes, pausing to choose her words very carefully, and as much as she didn't want to say them, she opened her eyes and said them anyway. 'Harris, I can't be the reason you don't relocate. I imagine opportunities like this for your career won't be a regular occurrence, so realistically you have to take that job. You'd regret it if you didn't. And I don't want to be the cause of you having doubts about all of that. We haven't known each other long enough for those kinds of huge decisions.' *Keep going and you might convince yourself, Douglas.* 'The thing is, if we did become an *us* and things ended I would never forgive myself for causing you to turn down your dream job. And not only that but you may end up resenting me if you do. And, as you said, I can't leave Inverness. Not with what's happened to my granny. She means so much to me and the thought of not being here for her, even if it's only a few hours away...'

Sadness became evident in his furrowed brow. 'I totally understand. You don't need to explain. And I don't want to put pressure on you either. Long distance is never easy. It puts unnecessary strain on things, and this would be a new relationship that doesn't need extra pressure.' He sighed and ran a strand of her hair through his fingers. 'But you've probably noticed I'm already falling for you, and I don't want to fall deeper and then have it all come crashing down around us if I leave.'

Bella's eyes began to sting. '*When* you leave. You have to leave.'

He closed his eyes and nodded then rested his forehead on hers. 'And you have to stay. So... as much as I don't want this, maybe it is better certain things remain unsaid. And in that case... friends?'

Tears spilled over from Bella's eyes, and she repeated, 'Friends.'

The word felt like poison on her lips. Why hadn't she been honest? Why hadn't she told him exactly how she felt?

He clenched his jaw and lowered his face to hers then paused before placing a gentle, almost chaste kiss on her lips. She inhaled the scent of him and realised how being this close to him affected her. Her heart ached as it hammered at her chest.

Before she could stop herself, she wrapped her arms around him and pulled him close again, kissing him once more with all the desire that had been building inside of her, but she had tried to ignore. She poured her heart into that kiss in case it was the last time it ever happened, and he kissed her back with as much urgency.

She knew it was selfish but the feel of his lips on hers sparked something deep inside of her. A switch had been flicked and it felt right. She wanted him and although her heart and head were in conflicting positions, her heart was winning the game this time.

He pulled away and fixed his gaze on her, a crease of confusion furrowing his brow as he stared in evident bewilderment. 'But...'

She knew she had to explain. She gripped his hands and pleaded at him with her eyes. 'Okay, so maybe I lied. I don't *want* to be friends. I want *you*, Harris. I know this is totally out of the blue, probably completely pointless and incredibly selfish, and I know I'm possibly going to regret this when the time comes for you to leave, but could we try? Could we see where this goes? Because regardless of everything I've just said, the things about us failing and you resenting me, and what you said about long distance being hard, I don't care. Because this feels right. Am I crazy? Or do you feel it too?' He didn't reply. 'Harris, what I'm trying to say is I'm falling for you too, and if that's how we both feel, surely we can make it work, can't we?'

He stepped back but kept his eyes fixed on her. He didn't speak but still he stared. Her heart sank and she felt light-headed. He was going to say no. He was going to stick to his guns and be strong for them both. He was going to demand they remain friends and her heart was going to break because she wasn't falling at all. She had already plummeted headfirst into love with him, and that fact had only just completely sunk in, like a lead weight on her heart.

What had started as a friendship had rapidly changed, and she hadn't recognised it for what it was. The times she had looked forward to seeing him, the times she had been disappointed when she had missed him, the times she had been boosted by something he had done for her, or something he had said, the way she had found herself looking at him, secretly imagining what it would feel like to kiss him. Well, now she knew, and she wanted to fight for it.

She wanted more.

He shook his head, but the crumple to his forehead didn't disappear. 'But we *just* agreed this wouldn't work.' He ran his hands over his hair and laced his fingers on top of his head as if doing so would stop him from wanting to touch her. 'And we'd have to live apart. We might not see each other very often.' He removed his hands from his head and held them up in a halting motion. 'I don't want you to get hurt and I certainly don't want to be the one responsible for hurting you.'

A spark of hope spurred her on. 'But that's it, Harris, I'll be hurt more if we don't give us a chance, won't you? Because that way we'll never know if we could have been something amazing. And we have two months to see what happens. What if we try to be friends but lose each other anyway because it's too hard? Wouldn't you rather see where things go? A lot can happen in two months. We of all people should know that.'

He needed no further encouragement. With one swift move, she was in his arms and his lips were on hers in a kiss that took her breath away and sent shivers through every fibre in her body. Nothing had ever felt so right. Not kissing her favourite author and

not even kissing her childhood crush. This kiss was the stuff o
dreams, of hopes, a manifestation of everything she never realisec
she wanted until now.

She slipped her arms up around his shoulders and into his hai
as the kiss intensified. But she slowed down and pulled away a
little. With her eyes closed, she breathed, 'Will you stay with me
tonight... please? I can't... I can't offer anything more than close
ness for now but... I don't want to be alone. I want to sleep in you
arms and wake knowing you're there.' Although she wanted him
physically, too, she knew her mind was clouded with worry anc
she wanted to have a clear mind the first time they made love, anc
she had every intention of that happening. Just not tonight.

He didn't speak and she worried she had said the wrong thing
She closed her eyes. 'I'm... I'm sorry, I know I'm making no sense
and my signals are all over the place. First I kiss you like my life
depends on it and then I say I can't offer anything more but... today
has been so hard and emotional, and you're the only one I want to
be near. And I should make a clean break with Aiden; I suppose it'
only fair to do that before you and I... But I... I want to know you're
here with me because I don't think I'll sleep if you're not. Is tha
incredibly selfish of me?' When she opened her eyes, she founc
him gazing at her, a smile on his full lips.

He lifted his hand and smoothed his thumb across the apple o
her cheek. 'Bella, I'm here, aren't I? For whatever you need. So lea
the way,' he whispered.

* * *

Bella fluttered her eyes open as she felt gentle circles being draw
on the fabric of her T-shirt. She sighed and stretched befor
turning her face and seeing Harris gazing down at her.

'You smile in your sleep,' he told her. He was fully clothed and had lain on top of the covers all night long.

'You've given me something to smile about,' she replied.

'Likewise,' he said before placing a chaste kiss on her shoulder.

'What time is it?' she said as she rolled onto her back. 'I need to call the hospital.'

'It's around 7 a.m. But there should be someone on the desk if you want to put your mind at rest.'

She climbed from the bed in her old sleep T-shirt and knickers and picked up her phone. Her heart hammered as she waited for her call to be answered.

Once she had spoken to the nurse and had been assured her granny had had a good night's rest and had already eaten breakfast, relief flooded her body and she slumped back onto the bed. 'Don't you need to leave to get ready for work?' she asked but realised it sounded like she was trying to get rid of him. 'Not that I want you to go, of course.'

Harris sighed but kept his gaze fixed on her. 'I do really, but at this precise moment I'm too busy thinking how beautiful you are when you've just woken up.'

She smiled. 'Oh yeah, with my bird's nest hair and dog breath.'

'To me you've always been beautiful.'

* * *

Half an hour later, Harris glanced at his watch. 'I really do need to go,' he said before gulping down the rest of his coffee. He was still fully dressed and Bella had slipped on some yoga pants. They were in the kitchen and had just finished eating some of Isla's pastries, the French ones she called *crescents*. Bella had welled up as she had put them onto plates and when Harris had seen her wipe at her eyes, she had explained all about her granny's name for croissants.

'She's quite literal without realising it,' she said with a smile as she finished her explanation and wiped her nose with a tissue.

Harris held one aloft. 'From hereon in, they will be forever known as crescents.' Bella had loved that. She wasn't quite ready for him to leave and was almost regretting her decision to keep things PG the night before. But she needed to get ready herself and deep down she knew it had been the right way to go.

'Can I see you tonight?' he asked. 'Although I don't get off until 11, all being well, but I could come here after.' He placed down his mug and then his eyes widened. 'I-I don't mean for sex; I don't want you to think that. And I know it'll be late and you'll probably be asleep by the time I get here but I'd... I'd like to fall asleep with you again.'

She stood and snaked her arms around his neck. 'I'd like that very much. And I may not be that tired.'

He smiled and kissed her but then she watched as his jaw ticked under his skin. 'What about Aiden? Does he still think he has a chance of something with you?'

Guilt niggled at Bella, and she took a step back. 'I honestly don't know. I'll have to speak to him. Make sure he realises whatever it was, it's over.'

'I think he'll be hurt, Bella. Be careful, okay?'

She nodded. 'I will.'

'I presume you're going to visit Isla today?'

Bella picked up his mug and her own and took them to the sink. 'I am. Olivia wants to come too so we're going together. Which is good because we can go in her car.'

'That's good.'

Harris walked over and slipped his arms around her waist. 'I'll see you tonight then. Walk me to the door?' He bent and kissed her neck, sending shivers throughout her body and she had to resist the urge to stop him from leaving. He took her hand.

When they reached the door, she opened it and he stepped outside. She followed and he turned and pulled him to her. He kissed her one last time, a long, lingering kiss she didn't want to end. When the kiss ended, she spotted Aiden at his front door in his jogging gear.

'Oh, h-hi, Aiden,' she said as she felt the colour drain from her face.

Harris stepped in front of Bella. 'Aiden, mate, before you go jumping to conclusions, I was here to comfort Bella over the situation with her granny.'

Aiden folded his arms across his chest. 'As opposed to what, exactly?' Neither of them answered. 'Right, nice. Very classy. Good to know where I stand. And I knew you were playing us both, Bella the innocent. Pfft.'

Bella stepped around Harris, determined, as always, to stand up for herself. 'That's not true, Aiden. I wasn't playing you both. Harris and I only slept together...' Realising what she had said, she shook her head. 'I mean *actual* sleep. I'd had an emotional day and he understood that. And anyway, I wanted to speak to you first about us... and I'm sorry, but you and I were never going to work, you must know that.'

He sneered. 'No, but what I do know is you have double standards. You wouldn't sleep with me but clearly couldn't wait to get PC Plod into bed.'

'Hey, come on, Aiden, don't be crass,' Harris said with a step forward. 'You heard Bella say that's not what happened.'

Aiden smirked. 'Oh and of course we *alllll* believe everything *sweet Bella* says, don't we?'

Harris held up a hand. 'Aiden, I suggest you get back inside and calm down, pal.'

Aiden snorted. 'Or what? You're going to resort to police brutal-ity, is that it?'

Harris shook his head. 'Just leave it, eh. I'm sorry you found out this way but it's for the best.'

Aiden's grin became sinister. 'Funny how she wasn't in the least bit attracted to you a few days ago. In fact, she seemed pretty incredulous at the suggestion you might have a thing for her. Seemed quite disgusted from my memory. You had a chance of something with me and you ditch that for a boring copper, Bella, really? Don't look so shocked, that's what you thought about him until yesterday.'

Bella gasped. 'I never said—'

'But now your granny's in hospital and you're lonely and sad, he'll do, is that it? What's the female equivalent of any port in a storm?'

'Aiden! There's no need for that!' Bella exclaimed.

'*Away an' boil your heid,* Aiden,' Harris growled. Aiden slammed his door and Harris turned back to Bella. 'See you later,' he said. She could have sworn she saw hurt in his eyes and when he walked away without kissing her again, her stomach knotted.

Had Aiden ruined everything out of jealousy?

32

Oh, my word, Bells, you're in love with him!' Olivia said with an excited bounce in the seat of her car as they travelled the lanes towards the city hospital. 'I *knew* you had feelings for him. You forget how well I know you. It was obvious to me but you're so bloody stubborn you wouldn't admit it. And I think it's because you'd have to admit your granny had set you up.' She giggled.

Images of Harris played through Bella's mind as she stared blankly out of the passenger window. 'I didn't think he was my type, that's all. Although I'm not entirely sure I even have a type when you consider how different Kerr, Aiden and Harris are.' She turned in her seat to look at Olivia. 'But it really did hit me like a ton of bricks last night. It sounds so farfetched. But it feels right. Like it was meant to be.'

'And he stayed over to look after you. How sweet is that?'

Bella felt a flush of heat rise from her chest as she remembered the feeling of his body next to hers. 'I know. I felt awful for giving him mixed messages, but my head was so messed up with what had happened I couldn't sleep with him feeling like that. But I definitely wanted to.' She placed her hand over her heart and felt it racing. 'Then it all fell apart this morning.'

'How come?' Olivia asked without taking her eyes from the road.

'Because as he was leaving, we saw Aiden.'

Olivia's eyes widened and she gasped. 'Oh no! I bet that didn't go down well. How did he take it?'

'He was awful, Liv. Although I don't suppose I can blame him. But he was very unkind. And the awful thing is he told Harris I had been disgusted at the thought of being with him until I was lonely, which is a complete lie.'

'The rat bag!'

'Yes, and what makes it worse is I think Harris may have believed him. He left quickly and I haven't heard from him since.'

'*You* could message him, Bells.'

Bella sighed. 'I don't want to be one of those needy women who does that whole "I miss you already" thing when I only saw him a couple of hours ago.'

'But it would ease your mind. And anyway, I'm sure after the night you shared and the conversation you had, Harris won't have any reason to believe Aiden.'

'No, but the other problem is Aiden has to work with Harris on the whole consultation for his book thing. It's going to be very uncomfortable for both of them. I feel like such a harlot.'

Olivia smiled. 'You didn't have sex with either of them. You're definitely no such thing. Try not to worry.'

'He said he was going to come over after his shift, so I'll talk to him and make sure he knows Aiden was lying.'

'Absolutely.'

* * *

Isla was propped up in bed when they arrived but the bruising on her face looked slightly worse. 'Ah, my girls. It's lovely to see you!'

'Isla, you're looking much better than I expected. It's a good thing you're a tough cookie,' Olivia said as she kissed her cheek.

'Och, I'm not too bad. Bored *oot ma heid,* though.'

'I brought you some romance novels from the supermarket so they should keep you going for a wee while,' Bella told her as she handed the books over.

'Ooh, these look good,' Isla said as she glanced over the pretty covers featuring couples. She seemed intrigued by one with a blue cover featuring a woman standing on a beach with a dog. 'Ooh, this one's about the Isle of Skye. I do love Skye. It's such a beautiful place. I've fond memories of visiting with your grandpa Caelan. We almost moved there at one time,' she said with a sad smile. 'Maeve's moving away to Skye, you know,' she said with glassiness to her eyes. 'I'm going to miss her. She's my only real friend.'

Dammit, I didn't read the title of the book. 'I know, Granny, but I'll take you to visit her, don't worry.'

Isla sighed. 'Aye, but it won't be the same, will it? It won't be as easy. She won't be just up the road any more.'

'Try not to think about it until you're better, eh?' Bella replied with a squeeze to her arm.

'It's a shame, really. Before my fall, I was beginning to think it might be a good idea for me to move into Sunnyside and it helped Maeve was there already.'

Bella gasped. 'You're not serious, are you?'

'Aye, hen. I'm no' getting any younger and my house has the stairs. What if I'd fallen there when you weren't home?' She shivered. 'Your mum and dad have no room for me, and their house has stairs too. And we *cannae* live at the castle forever. And let's be honest, hen, one day you're going to want to move in with a man and get married. And if I'm still here, you'll no' want me around then.'

Bella's eyes welled with tears at the thought. 'Granny, that's not going to happen any time soon, so please don't worry. I'm not leaving you.'

Isla took her hand. 'Arabella Douglas, I'm an eighty-five-year-old woman. I'm not going to be around forever but I'm not going to have you putting your life on hold in the meantime. Do you hear me?'

That dreaded lump of emotion threatened to close up her throat again. 'Seriously, Granny, stop talking like that. I'm not putting anything on hold. There's no one waiting in the wings for me so I'm all yours,' she lied and caught Olivia looking at her with a crumpled, sad expression.

'Aye, well, I'm beginning to think about my future, and my options.'

'But you've always been so determined to stay independent, Granny.'

'Aye, hen, but I wasn't being realistic.' Her expression showed defeat and Bella's stomach knotted with sadness. 'I'm a stubborn old boot. I'm where you get it from.' She laughed.

'But you love your house. All your memories are there. How could you bear to leave it?'

'No, hen. All my memories are in here.' She pointed to her head. 'And if that fails me at some point, they're in here.' She pointed to her heart.

The drive home from the hospital was taken mostly in silence until Olivia spoke. 'She does have a point about her house, honey. And be honest, if you and Harris get serious, you'll want to be with him, and he'll be on Skye.'

'I'm not leaving Inverness, Liv.'

A parcel sat on her doorstep when Bella returned to the apartment; it had the insignia of the online college on the front, so she guessed it was her course materials. She picked it up and unlocked the door.

She was still reeling from Isla's admission, and everything was beginning to weigh heavily on her mind. She clicked the kettle on, figuring she was British, and things could always seem better with a cup of tea. Well, surely they couldn't seem worse?

Bella sat and cried into her mug of tea at the kitchen table. She had lied to her granny by omission about Harris, when she knew Isla would have been so happy for her. The trouble was it would have fuelled her reasons for talking about old people's homes and the end of her life, which were things Bella wasn't prepared to hear.

She picked up her phone to check for messages from Harris but there were none.

Beau was still up in the castle with Brodie and Olivia's dogs, so she decided to open the course materials and have a look over them to keep her occupied. Eventually she fell asleep on the sofa with books about interior design strewn all over her and the floor.

* * *

Bella awoke to a scuffling sound and someone shouting. She was a little disorientated until she realised she was on the sofa where she had fallen asleep. She glanced at her watch to find it was 8 a.m. and was relieved she had slept; there was no doubt she needed it, but Harris hadn't turned up, which compounded her worry he had believed Aiden's cruel words. And now she was listening to something that sounded like a fight going on right outside her apartment. Her heart began to pound as she listened, frozen to the spot, wondering if she should call the police.

'Candace!' came a screeching male voice. 'Candace, you're being ridiculous! I told you it's a writing retreat!'

'Shit, that's Aiden,' Bella said to the empty room as she felt the colour rapidly drain from her face. Had his crazy ex found him and turned up?

'You're a liar, Aiden O'Dowd!' came another voice, this time female. 'You always lie and I've had enough!' This time, the woman was sobbing.

Bella held her breath in order to hear. She stared out of the peep hole on the front door, but her view was limited. She saw the back of a blonde woman, her arms waving aggressively when she shouted, 'I swore I wouldn't put up with it again. I had to come and see for myself and here you are with *her*! That's it! You're not welcome at home any more.'

'But this isn't what it looks like, Candace!' Aiden shouted and the woman stormed out of the foyer.

'You say that every time!'

As Aiden followed the woman, Ailsa from the gift shop exited his apartment, a bundle of clothes in one arm, her hair messy and pulling her shirt on with the other hand. *What the hell?*

Bella's phone pinged and she looked at the screen, doing her best to hold it steady.

Bella! The police are here! Are you okay?

The message was from Olivia. *They're already here? Thank goodness!* She hit reply immediately.

I'm okay but I think Aiden's psycho ex is here!

Olivia sent another message.

Look outside!

With no little trepidation, Bella opened the front door and stepped out as Aiden was holding the wrist of the blonde woman. 'Candace, please, let's talk and I'll explain. It was... it was all research!' A police car pulled into the entrance to the courtyard and she watched as Harris and Mel exited the vehicle.

The blonde woman turned profile on and it was then Bella spotted her huge baby bump. 'You had to research the naked body of yet *another* woman, did you, Aiden? And have you told *her* that your wife is heavily pregnant? And how about your agent's secretary, Susie? You didn't tell her either! Well, she knows now because I went to see her! Let go of me!'

Bella gawped in shock as *Aiden the lying hypocrite's* dirty deeds were aired for everyone to hear. *What a shithead!*

Harris and Mel approached Aiden. 'Come on, Aiden, release Candace now, you're going to hurt her. Think of the baby,' Harris said, hands held aloft.

'You keep out of this, PC Plod!' Aiden spat, his fist now clenched and held up.

'Come on now, you need to calm down,' Harris insisted. 'You're going to get yourself arrested.'

'Piss off!' Aiden said. 'Candace, I didn't sleep with Susie and I didn't sleep with Ailsa. They're lying.'

Ailsa took two steps forward from her position by the police car. 'I'm sorry but *I'm* not lying,' she said. She was now fully dressed. 'He... he told me he was Carrick Murphy, and his wife'd had an affair, and how he was hiding here to get away from her new boyfriend who'd made threats.'

Bella gasped. *So it's a line he's fed others! Slimeball! Bloody lucky escape!*

Aiden growled, and as Harris lurched to try to stop him, Aiden swung and his fist connected with Harris's cheek.

Candace dashed over to the police car and Mel joined Harris as he said, 'Aiden O'Dowd, I'm arresting you under section 89 of the Police Act 1996 for assaulting a police officer.' He went on to cuff him and read him his rights as Bella looked on in complete and utter bewilderment.

'You're being stupid, you know that?' Aiden hissed. 'I bet all this is because you think I have a thing for your girlfriend.' He glanced over at Bella and sneered. 'I don't. She was rubbish in bed. You can have her.'

Bella gasped, her eyes wide and a desire to slap the lying cheat rose within her.

'You just admitted to having another affair!' Candace shouted as she too glared at Bella.

'Watch your head, Aiden,' Harris said as he manhandled the disgraced author into the back of the police car.

At that moment, Harris glanced back and made eye contact with Bella, whose hand covered her mouth as she watched everything unfold. He leaned forward and muttered something to Mel to which she nodded and gestured for him to go.

Harris jogged over to Bella. 'Hey, sorry about all that, are you okay?' he asked, dipping his head to look in her eyes.

'I'm... I'm okay. But I... I swear I didn't sleep with him, Harris.'

Harris winced. 'It seems he's well versed in lying. Turns out his lover down in London found out he was still married and contacted his wife. But it's not the first time he's done this allegedly. Uses his *pseudonym reveal* to seduce women. Makes me sick, especially when his wife is seven months pregnant. If you ask me, he's a narcissist. Anyway, I'd better get going.'

Bella nodded and Harris turned to leave. 'Harris!'

He stopped and turned around. 'Yes?'

'He was wrong, you know. What he said when he saw you leaving. I wasn't disgusted by you, for what it's worth. And I know there was the incident where you thought I sounded horrified about spending time with you when you overheard me talking to Granny that time. But... I really don't feel that way. I wish... I wish you hadn't believed him when he said those awful things.'

He frowned and stepped closer. 'Believed him?'

She bit the side of her bottom lip. 'Yes. You walked away and looked so hurt. And then you didn't come to stay last night so I presumed things were over.'

He closed the gap between them and cupped her face in his hand. 'You read the whole thing wrong, Bella. The way he acted simply confirmed what I'd been thinking about him. And I'm sorry I didn't come over, but my shift ran late and I didn't want to disturb you. Then time got away with me today. That's all. But you and me... this is real. It's not over at all. It's only just begun, and I can't wait to see where it takes us.' He smiled. 'I'm crazy about you, Bella Douglas.'

Now Bella's heart was racing for a different reason. He was crazy about her. He'd said it aloud and she could see the sincerity in his eyes; he meant it. 'I'm crazy about you too,' she replied with a wide smile.

He beamed. 'Right, so there you go. Nothing is over. And if it's okay with you, I'll come over tonight.'

'That would be good.'

He glanced over his shoulder to where the patrol car was waiting and then back at Bella. In a loud, over-exaggerated voice, he said, 'Actually, I need to come in and ask you a few questions about what you've witnessed.'

She crumpled her brow. 'Oh, okay.' She walked back into the

house and no sooner was she inside than Harris pulled her into his arms and kissed her with a need and an urgency she felt right down to her core because it matched her own.

He released her and said, 'That was incredibly unprofessional of me but worth every second. See you tonight.' And with that, he dashed from the apartment and jogged back to the waiting patrol car, leaving Bella weak-limbed and swooning.

* * *

Later that night, after she had spoken to her granny and her parents, she waited for Harris. At around 11 p.m., there was a knock on the door and she rushed to check who it was. Harris stood there in his civilian clothes, holding a bottle of white wine and freshly showered, judging by his damp hair.

She opened the door and he smiled. 'Hey, how are you doing?' She didn't reply, instead she pulled him inside and closed the door. Before he could take off his jacket, she had him pressed up against the wall and kissed him. When she pulled away, he gazed down at her and exhaled. 'That was quite a welcome.'

She took the bottle of wine from him and placed it on the hall table. She then took his hand to lead him down the hallway. She paused outside her bedroom door and turned the handle. 'Can I take you to bed?'

Harris glanced back at the bottle of wine. 'Oh, I brought you some Sauvignon Blanc, I thought we might stay up a bit longer, I'm not that tired surprisingly.'

'Neither am I,' she informed him.

His eyes widened. 'Oh, you meant to *bed*...'

Bella nodded as she led him through the door.

He stopped her when they reached the bed. 'Are you sure?'

She nodded, pulled his face to hers and kissed him deeply,

passionately, releasing the feelings she had suppressed the night before.

She reached for the hem of her shirt and pulled it up and over her head.

He stood back and gazed down at her. 'Beautiful,' he whispered.

She couldn't remember a time when she had felt this way. Every nerve ending in her body awakened, and every sense sprang into high alert as he gently moved his fingertips down the sides of her body, following the shape of her curves, causing her to shiver.

She pulled the jacket from his body, followed by his T-shirt, and kissed the bare skin of his chest as he sighed, head back, eyes closed. She unfastened the belt of his jeans and knelt as she slipped them from his body. When she stood, he wrapped her in his arms and pulled her back onto the bed with him, ready to worship her for the very first of what she hoped would be many, many times...

* * *

Waking up in Harris's arms again was wonderful. It was something she could definitely get used to. As this thought crossed her mind, however, Bella was suddenly reminded it wouldn't be happening for much longer. Not regularly, anyway. Soon she would have to wait possibly weeks for it to happen again and that fact saddened her.

'Hey, penny for them,' Harris said, clearly noticing her change of expression as he lay beside her.

'Oh, it's nothing. I'm getting ahead of myself and thinking about when you leave.'

He pulled her on top of him and wrapped his arms around her.

'Don't think about that. Not yet. We have two months of this, and I intend to make the most of it.'

She rested her head on his chest and listened to his heart beating a steady, hypnotic rhythm. 'I'm going to miss you,' she said.

'And I'll miss you, but we agreed to make this work and we will.' He fell silent and she could almost hear the cogs whirring in his mind. Eventually he said, 'Are you free on Saturday?'

Bella lifted her head. 'I can be, why?'

He propped himself up on his elbows. 'Let me take you to Skye. That way you can see where I'm going to be and where you'll be coming to visit.'

'I'd like that,' she said with a wide smile. 'Very much.'

'I'll take you on the bike.'

She glared at him and pushed herself to sit straddling his torso. 'You certainly will not!'

Harris chuckled. 'You trust me, don't you?' She nodded. 'Don't you find it a thrill to travel so fast?' She pulled a face and he laughed. 'And it means I get your arms around me for the whole journey.'

She bent and kissed his chest, where a smattering of hair lightly covered his smooth skin. 'Well, when you put it like that…'

'That's settled then.' He pulled her down into his arms again and held her as he peppered her face and neck with kisses.

33

I've decided I'm definitely moving out of my house,' Isla announced out of the blue as Bella and her family sat around her hospital bed.

Bella's dad burst out laughing. 'Aye, all right, then. Where are you planning on going? The Maldives?'

Isla scowled at her son. 'I've not decided yet but I'm selling the house once it's liveable again. And I'm moving into sheltered housing. It's time.'

Bella's dad laughed again. 'Aye, whatever you say, Mum.'

Isla crossed her arms over her chest with clear indignation. 'I'm not kidding, son. I've made up my mind.'

Bella's dad's grin disappeared suddenly. 'You always said you'd disown us if we put you in a home.'

'Aye, but *you're* not putting me in a home, *I'm* doing it.'

Bella's mum tried to reason with her. 'Mum, you love your house. You'll hate it in sheltered housing. All those *old* people, remember?'

Isla folded her arms, annoyed and with pursed lips. 'How do you know? And they're not *old* people; they're folks my own age. I won't be on my own and you won't have to worry about me all the time.'

'But Bella lives with you, Granny, so we know you're safe already,' Callum added to the conversation.

'Arabella is a young woman who has her future ahead of her. She doesn't need me as an Albert Ross around her neck.'

'An albatross, Mum.'

'Aye, that's what a said.'

'Granny, you're not a burden to me, I love living with you,' Bella insisted.

Isla huffed. 'Can you all give me and Bella the room, please?' she said, like a character in a US cop show. Bella's parents sighed and left, closely followed by Callum. 'Is that the real saying? Albatross?' Isla asked with a crumpled expression when they had gone.

Bella tried not to smile. 'Aye, it is, Granny.'

'But why would you have a bird around your neck? That doesn't make any sense. I thought an Albert Ross was a kind of heavy gold chain like the rappers wear. They must get neck ache from those things. Gold is very heavy, you know. I presumed Albert Ross was the jeweller who designed them.'

Bella smiled. 'No, it's from a poem where a sailor shoots a seabird and has to wear the body around his neck as punishment.'

Isla scrunched her face. 'Eeeuw, that's not very nice.'

'Neither is shooting a poor bird.'

'Aye, no, fair point.'

'Anyway, why did you want to clear the room like that?' Bella asked, both concerned and intrigued.

Isla glanced at the door, making sure no one was listening. 'I know about you and the sergeant.'

Bella raised her eyebrows. 'Oh.'

'Aye, Maeve messaged me on the WhatsUp. She and I both think it's wonderful. He's a very kind man and he's right for you.'

Apart from that motorbike, but we'll let him off so long as you never go on it again.'

Bella was reminded of the conversation about her impending trip to Skye on the back of said bike. She chose not to mention it.

'Anyway, I've decided I'm going to sell my house and give something to you and Callum towards places of your own. That way you can live wherever you want to live. You don't have to hang around with me cramping your style.'

It was Bella's turn to be indignant. 'You don't cramp my style. I'm not leaving Inverness.'

'Aye, well, I might be.'

Bella scoffed. 'And where will you go exactly?'

'Skye with Maeve.'

'Granny, you're being silly. Skye is over two hours away and your family is here.'

'Not if you go to Skye too.'

'Whoa, you're way ahead of yourself. Me and Harris have only just got together. And I have my job at the castle. And anyway, what about Beau?'

'I can take him, I've checked. Well, Maeve has.'

'This is crazy, Granny. I'm not going to go running off to Skye with a man when I don't know what the future holds.'

Isla shook her head. 'Believe me, when you know, you know. Like me and your grandpa.'

Bella scowled. 'Well, Harris doesn't need me putting pressure on the relationship either. He's got enough going on; he's going to start a new job in a new location. I don't want to become his *Albert Ross*.'

'Funny,' Isla sneered. 'Now, I know you. And I think you need to have the freedom to be able to go if you choose to. Maybe not right now, but maybe in a few months, who knows. And I've decided I'd like to go with Maeve.'

'Again, your family is here,' Bella said, pointing to the floor as if to emphasise her point. 'And you're injured, you'll need us. What do you think Mum and Dad will say about it?'

'Arabella, children move abroad all the time and leave their parents behind while they go off to start new lives. Australia, Canada, you name it. What's stopping me from moving a few hours away? Your mum and dad both drive. So does Callum. And your dad was talking about moving away and doing something different when he retires. That happens next year.'

'But don't you think it's all a bit sudden; a bit knee-jerk, so to speak? I think you need to think it through some more. You would be leaving us all behind. And what if Harris and I don't work out? Then you'll be in Skye all by yourself.'

'I'll still have Maeve. Family means the world to me, Bella. *You* mean the world to me. But I refuse to be one of those gyratics who stops their family from living their own lives. My house is worth enough to help you and Callum and your mum and dad. My savings will pay for my place at the home in Skye. Once I'm up and about again, which I know might be a while, I'm going. My mind is made up.'

* * *

In the couple of days that followed, Isla refused to speak any more on the matter of her relocation. Her mind was definitely made up. Bella's mum and dad kept expecting Isla to eventually say it was a joke but when she didn't, they asked Bella to try to convince her that it was a bad idea.

Bella refused.

Friday was rainy and as Bella was leaving her apartment to go to the castle, she bumped into Aiden. He had a box in his arms and a bag over his shoulder.

'Oh, hi, are you okay?' she asked with sincerity.

He curled his lip. 'Like you care.'

She was in no mood to flog a dead horse so simply replied, 'Okay, bye.' Then turned to lock her door.

'I'm moving back to London, in case you actually do care. Although Candace won't take me back.'

Bella felt no pity. 'I'm sorry, Aiden, but there's no one to blame here but you.' She turned once more.

'Look, I'm sorry about saying you were rubbish in bed.'

She turned to face him. 'Luckily Harris trusts me and knows we didn't sleep together. Regardless of whether you like it or not, you're about to become a parent. I think you need to take a long hard look at yourself and your choices. Good luck, Aiden, I think you may need it.' And with that she left, knowing she would be unlikely to ever see him again. And she was fine with that.

Saturday arrived all too quickly for Bella. She stood there, by Harris's bike, all kitted out in leathers and a helmet borrowed from Mel, who, it turned out, didn't only ride horses. Her heart was trying to escape through her jacket and her stomach trying to escape through her boots.

'You look incredible,' Harris said. 'I'm so glad they fit you. And boy do they fit you.'

If she wasn't so nervous, she would have been happy with the compliment and the way he devoured her with his gaze.

'I'm dreading this,' she admitted as she stepped from foot to foot.

He put his arms around her waist and rested his crash helmet on hers. 'I'll keep you safe, Bella. You have no need to worry, hold on and enjoy the ride.'

He climbed onto the bike and held out his hand for her to mount the metal beast behind him. Once she was gripping on for dear life, he patted her arm and started the engine. She tucked her head in tight and closed her eyes. She felt a rumble of laughter through his back and would've happily slapped him if she wasn't clinging to him like a life raft.

After a while, Bella began settling into the tilts and motion of the bike and she lifted her face. Fir trees gave way to mountain views and eventually to a body of water. Harris pulled the bike to a halt in a layby car park and helped her off the bike. They removed their helmets and Bella breathed in the fresh air. Deep lungfuls of it. She was surprisingly warm considering the cool air blasting them as they'd cut through it at what she presumed was over 80 mph.

'This is Loch Cluanie viewpoint. Stunning, isn't it?' he said with an appreciative smile.

'It really is,' Bella replied as she took in the view.

The sun had made an appearance now and the cerulean blue of the sky was reflected in the still water of the loch, like a mirror. Rugged mountains skirted the loch on the opposite side of the water in deep purple and green hues and were crowned with fluffy white cumulus clouds. Large shingles formed a kind of beach at the water's edge and Bella watched as Harris took out his phone. He filmed the peace and quiet of the water gently lapping at the stones for a few moments before turning the camera on Bella.

'Come on, let's get a picture.' She happily tucked herself into his side as he snapped several shots of them against the stunning backdrop. One of the photos was of him kissing the side of her head. She especially liked that the sweet moment had been captured forever.

They climbed back onto the bike and set off towards Skye once again. Bella was beginning to enjoy the ride. It was a rush and a thrill, like Harris had said. Even though they were travelling at speed, Harris was so careful and courteous to other drivers on the road. And the views truly were spectacular.

After around another thirty minutes, they reached Eilean Donan Castle and stopped once more to take in the view. The castle sat on a little stony outcrop reached by a long footbridge linking the island to the mainland. It was somewhere Bella had visited as a child but seeing it again as an adult took her breath away. Harris snapped more photos of the two of them but also insisted on taking one of Bella with the castle in the background.

'My beautiful Bella,' he said as he showed her the photo on his phone. 'How did I get so lucky?' He kissed her and she revelled in the feeling of his lips on her, and his hands in her hair. She filed this kiss in her memory bank with all the others so she could revisit them when he had left for Skye.

'I've been asking myself the same question,' she replied with a smile as she stroked his face tenderly, feeling the scratch of the stubble under her fingertips.

'You really didn't like my beard then?' he asked as they left the water's edge and made their way back to the bike.

'Looking back, I actually think I did. I didn't want to admit I was attracted to you back then because I didn't want to admit my granny knows me better than I know myself.' She laughed. 'But clearly she does.'

'Well, I'm so glad you gave in to my charms,' he said with a wink. As he zipped up his jacket and went to pull on his helmet, she watched every movement, the look of concentration, the way his brow crumpled and the way the sun highlighted his nose and cheeks. She didn't think she could ever tire of watching him. He stopped. 'What?' he asked. 'Have I got something on my face? Why are you looking at me like that?' He laughed.

She shook her head. 'I'm admiring the view,' she replied. 'And making sure I remember every moment for when you leave. Saying the words caused a bubble of emotion to rise up from deep within her and she walked over to rest her head on his shoulder.

'Hey, I'm not going to the other side of the world. And I *will* see you. We *will* make this work, Bella. I'm in this for the long haul.' He paused and tilted her face up with his finger. 'You could always come with me.'

'But this is all so new. It's a huge step to take, for both of us. What if we don't work out?'

He frowned for a moment and then fixed her with a stern gaze. 'I don't care if it's new, Bella. I've never felt this way about anyone. And I'll do whatever it takes to make this work. And I'll wait for however long it takes for us to be together. And if you're never ready to leave Inverness, we will be that one couple who lasts at the long-distance thing.'

Once back on the road, they eventually crossed the Skye Bridge and Bella's stomach rolled with giddiness as they rose with the arc of the bridge and then descended the other side. They entered a picturesque village with a pub, a row of white-painted houses, a bakery, an outdoor shop and a village hall that sat on an expanse of green beside a church. It was picture-postcard perfect, like something from a movie. It really was beautiful.

Harris pulled to a halt by a fenced inlet and parked the bike again. He took off his crash helmet and said, 'Welcome to Glentorrin.'

'*This* is Glentorrin?' Bella asked, a little in disbelief as she removed her own helmet.

'It sure is. The station and house are up there.' He pointed to the road leading out of the village at the opposite side to where they had entered. 'But this is the heart of the place.'

A couple walked by with a fluffy Hungarian Vizsla, smiled and said hello. A boy came running after them. 'Mum! Dad! Can we go to Caitlin's for cake?' he shouted. 'Chewie wants cake, don't you, boy?' The dog barked and Bella giggled. Chewie was the perfect name for that dog, especially when the boy resembled a young Han Solo.

Bella looked across the other side of the water to see the bakery was called Caitlin's Bakes and her stomach growled. 'Shall we go and grab a cake?' she asked.

'Sounds like a plan. We could come and sit on the bench to eat it, enjoy the sunshine.'

They made their way across to the bakery and walked inside past the dog who sat, waiting patiently, with his tongue lolling out. Once the family had been served and had left, Bella walked up to the counter.

'Hi there, what can I get you?' a woman with fiery red hair asked.

Bella examined the variety of cakes, biscuits and scones shielded behind a glass cabinet. 'It all looks amazing. But can I have two pieces of Malteser traybake and two coffees, please.'

'Sure. Are you guys on holiday here?' the woman asked as she prepared Bella's order.

Harris stepped forward. 'I'm actually the new inspector. I'm taking over the newly converted bothy police station outside the village.'

'Oh, wow! You're the guy from Inverness? Welcome to Glentorrin. I wish I'd known who you were a few minutes earlier. The bothy used to belong to my friend Jules's grandparents. She was just in here. I'm Caitlin, by the way.'

'Ah, that's lovely. Nice to meet you. I'm Harris and this is Bella. I'm sure I'll get to meet everyone pretty soon.'

'So, are you the lucky wife who gets to enjoy our girls' nights?' the woman asked Bella. 'We often gather at each other's houses for wine and nibbles. It's great fun.'

'Oh... erm... I'm not actually his wife. We've only just started seeing each other,' Bella replied, her face warming as she hoped she'd said the right thing. She glanced over at Harris, who was watching her with a contented smile.

Caitlin looked over at Harris and then back at Bella. She gave a knowing smile. 'Oh, I think we'll definitely be seeing you at the girls' nights soon enough. I have a knack for foreseeing these kinds of things.'

Bella's stomach flipped with what felt like excitement. 'We'll see,' she said and laughed as she handed over cash and took her purchases. 'Thank you.'

'Mind how you go now. And if you need anything, pop back in,' Caitlin said.

'Thanks, see you soon,' Harris replied with his usual nod. 'Well, the people are friendly, that's for sure,' he said as they walked away from the bakery.

'They certainly seem to be.' They sat on the bench and watched a fisherman washing down the deck of his boat moored to the railings. 'This place is idyllic,' Bella said with a sigh.

'Aye, it is. Now you can see my attraction to the job,' Harris said.

She inhaled the fresh sea air. 'Absolutely. I think you'll be really happy here.'

'Aye, I think so too. It's just a shame I won't be waking up with you every day.'

She turned to see that a shadow of melancholy had washed over his features. His mouth was downturned slightly and a crease had formed between his brows.

'Isla wants to move to Skye,' she informed him.

Harris's eyebrows shot up. 'What? She's actually serious about that? Mum mentioned it but I must admit I laughed it off.'

Bella nodded. 'It's true. She wants to be with Maeve. She says once her hip is healed, she wants to move to the same sheltered housing. Maeve sent her a link for the place on the WhatsUp.' She giggled.

'Wow. I'm shocked.'

Bella shrugged. 'Not as shocked as my parents were. Although my dad has said he fancies moving away from the city when he retires. So, who knows, they may follow her.'

Harris turned on the bench to face her. 'That's it then. You have no reason to stay at Drumblair. You can move to Skye too.' The hope in his eyes was an improvement on the sadness of moments before.

Bella almost choked on her coffee. 'You're kidding, aren't you? I can't up sticks, and leave. I have my job, I've just started my course.'

'Bella, you can get another job here, you could even set up your business. Your course is online so can be done anywhere. And I have a feeling about us. I know it's fast but when you know, you know.'

Bella rolled her eyes. 'You sound like my granny.'

'Maybe she's right.'

She gazed into his eyes and knew the thought of being away from him was not one she wanted to entertain. But it was crazy to rush into something and have it all go horribly wrong.

'Can I think about it?' she asked, knowing he had no choice there.

'Of course you can. But look at this place. I don't think you'll take much convincing.'

Once their coffee and traybakes were finished, they climbed back onto the bike and set off for the very short ride to the bothy. It was a squat, whitewashed building that had once housed people who worked the land on the original Glentorrin estate. It had a parking area to the front and a noticeboard. There was no station sign up as yet but Harris informed Bella they wouldn't put that up until the place was up and running, so as not to cause confusion.

The house was a double-fronted cottage that had been built as an extension of the bothy. It matched the houses they had seen in the village, with a porch over the front door. The wooden windows had been painted sage green, along with the front door. It was quaint and picturesque.

'Come on. I'll show you inside.'

Bella loved viewing houses and butterflies set to fluttering inside her. Harris unlocked the front door, and they stepped inside. Off to the left was a dining room and to the right was a living room with a log burner already installed. Ideas for colour palettes raced around her head. Straight ahead were stairs that led to the bedrooms. Through the living room was the kitchen with beautiful real oak units, a small room that could be used as a study, a utility room and the door to the rear garden.

What I could do to bring this house to life.

Harris opened the back door and they stepped into a fenced garden. The edges were skirted with fir trees that formed a copse behind the property and birdsong filled the air.

'It's the perfect garden for birdwatching,' Harris said as he placed his arm round her shoulder. 'I think I'll put a bird table over there.' He pointed to the left rear corner of the garden. 'And I think maybe a patio here so we... so *I* can sit and enjoy the sun in the summer.'

She knew he had corrected himself so as not to put pressure on her and she appreciated it. But she did love the place. It felt homely and fresh, like a blank canvas. Ideas buzzed around her head, and she let herself get excited a little.

'Could I maybe be your first official client for your interior design business?' he asked with a kiss to her head.

'Of course. It's funny you should ask that because I've already envisaged what could be done here. It will make you a beautiful home.'

He nodded and turned to her. 'Look, I'm not going to pressure you, and I know you love Inverness and your job but just know, if you decided you might like to come here to be with me at any point, you'd be welcomed with open arms.'

She tiptoed to kiss him and once again hope sprang up from within her. *Could this be it?* She certainly hoped so.

Once they had looked around the rest of the house, they climbed back on the bike and headed north along the coast road to Broadford. The sea was to their right and sporadic houses were dotted along the road on the left with spectacular views over the Inner Sound. Bella could see why people were drawn to this small but beautiful island. They passed through a couple of pretty little hamlets and eventually Harris pulled into the car park of a smart looking stone building with a sign that read:

Pabay View Retirement Home

Once they were off the motorbike, Harris said, 'You see the isle off in the distance in the Sound?' Bella nodded. 'That's Pabay. It's an uninhabited wee place now so it's a bit of a nature reserve. There are all sorts of birds over there as well as otters, seals and rabbits. There are also the remains of a chapel from the thirteenth century over there.'

Bella glanced up at the building and then out across to the island. 'It's a lovely location.'

'Aye, they have all sorts going on too. Sing-along nights, quiz nights, movie clubs, there's a heated pool where they do gentle exercise classes. But they also go on bus trips across to the mainland and to the other islands. There's a couple of different types of accommodation too. The little self-contained units are good because they have a wee enclosed patch of garden and residents in those units are allowed one pet. My mum can't wait. She says it's like a holiday resort compared to Sunnyside.' He laughed.

'Wow, no wonder she's excited.'

'It's peaceful here too. None of the hustle and bustle of the city. Just views, nature and miles of open sky.'

'Sounds perfect,' Bella replied. She could definitely see the attraction for her granny and Maeve. But *she* had lots to think about. Could she realistically follow a man she had recently fallen for all the way to a Hebridean island to start a new life?

It was tempting.

34

Bella's dad had messaged while they were out to say 'the stubborn old boot' was coming home on Monday and was desperate to see her wee dog.

They agreed that Harris wouldn't stay the night when they returned from Skye. He said he had something important to do the following morning, so he'd be better staying at home, and Bella wanted to visit her granny, and of course, collect Beau. But she couldn't help regretting the arrangement a little. She had loved waking up with him.

'Thank you for coming with me today. And for trusting me to take you across on the bike.'

'I think it's I who should be thanking you. It was fun. And Glentorrin is such a lovely place.'

'I agree. And you heard what the baker said. She sees Glentorrin ladies' nights in your future.'

She reached up and kissed his neck, inhaling his scent. She smoothed her hands down his chest as she gazed deep into his eyes. 'Hmm, I heard that too.'

* * *

Bella made her way up to the castle to collect Beau. Mirren was finishing off some home baking for the shop.

'I hear you and that handsome sergeant are an item,' Mirren said as Bella sat drinking tea and sampling Mirren's work – of course, someone had to taste test it before it went on sale in the café.

'Aye, Harris is wonderful.'

'It's going to be difficult when he leaves.'

Bella gave a deep sigh. 'I know. We have less than two months together before he goes to Skye. And now my granny is saying she wants to go too to be with her best friend.'

'Oh, bless her.'

Brodie and Olivia arrived with Wilf, Marley and Beau. 'Here he is,' Brodie announced as they walked into the castle kitchen.

Beau gave excited yips as he skipped around and jumped up at Bella's legs, tail wagging frantically. 'Hey, beautiful boy, I've missed you,' Bella said as she crouched down to greet the dog. He jumped into her lap and licked at her face. 'Granny is coming home soon. I bet you can't wait.'

'How was Skye?' Olivia asked with a clasp of her hands that told of her excitement.

'Absolutely beautiful. I can see why Harris is keen to go.'

'And how about you? How do you feel about it?'

Bella shook her head. 'I'm not thinking about it. It's too soon. I'm making the most of having him close for now,' she lied. She had done nothing but think about it and that was even before she saw Skye for herself.

* * *

That evening, she headed to the hospital to visit her granny. Her parents had been earlier in the day, so it was just the two of them now.

'Dad messaged to tell me you're coming home on Monday. I'm so happy,' Bella said with a squeeze to her granny's hand.

'Aye, I *cannae* wait. Olivia sent me some photos of my Beau this morning. I thought I would give her a quick phone call so I've spoken to her and she's happy for us to stay at the apartment while I sell my house and go through my physio.'

'You're going ahead with it then?' Bella asked, a little shocked.

'If I can get one of the little units where I can keep wee Beau with me, then yes. I've told your mum and dad and they're not too happy about it at the moment, but before they left, your dad said, "I guess our retirement location is sorted then."' Isla mocked his deep voice and then laughed. 'So, I reckon he'll come around to it fine.'

'Get you, Granny, moving the whole family.'

Isla shrugged. 'It's where you're going to be.'

Bella narrowed her eyes. 'You seem very sure of that considering I've been with him a few days.'

'Aye, but I know you, love. And I know your heart.'

The following morning, Bella was woken by a honking sound. Beau jumped up from Bella's bed and started to bark; he ran from the bedroom and skipped off down the hallway to the front door.

Bella rubbed her eyes and glanced at her watch. 'Who the hell is making all that noise at 8 a.m. on a Sunday morning?' She climbed out of bed and slipped on her shoes as the honking continued, and she dashed for the door. She flung it open and stepped outside, ready to give both barrels to whoever the culprit was.

'Finally!' Harris said with a laugh. 'I thought you'd left without telling me.' He followed this with, 'Tadaaaa!'

Bella covered her mouth with both hands as her eyes welled with tears. 'Fifi!' She ran across the gravel to where Harris stood with her newly repaired car, looking shiny, polished and almost like new. 'But how? I haven't paid for the repairs yet!'

He slipped his arms around her. 'I know. This is my gift to you. I know moving to Skye with me is a step too far for you right now, so I figured you'd need your wheels if you're going to come and visit.'

'I can't believe you did that for me. I'll pay you back.'

He shook his head and ran his nose down hers. 'Seeing the smile on your face is all the payment I need, Bella.'

'Thank you so much.' She reached up and kissed him. He lifted her off the ground and carried her back into the apartment, with Beau following on.

They sat snuggled up on the sofa chatting, kissing and looking at the photos of themselves on Harris's phone. Then she told him all about her course and the ideas she'd had for his new house. 'You're not upset, are you, about me not coming to Skye right away?'

He traced her cheek with his fingertips. 'Not at all. Isla will be having physio for a few months, and she needs to sell her house. And you're able to stay here for now, which is better for Isla with it being single-storey.'

'She's spoken to the managers at Pabay View and they have a unit coming up in four months. One of the residents is moving down to England to be nearer to family so she's put her name down and is wiring a deposit this week when she's home. I can't quite believe she's going through with it.'

'Wow, there's no stopping her.'

Bella laughed. 'It's like you said, they get more stubborn with age.'

Harris winced. 'Aye, I have a lot to look forward to then, eh?'

Bella was confused. 'In what way?'

He leaned closer and kissed her once more before saying, 'Because you'll no doubt take after her and I intend to be in your future, Arabella Douglas. For a very, very long time. If you'll have me, of course.'

'Oh, I think that can be arranged.'

He pulled her onto his lap and kissed her tenderly. She knew then, as she had done since the first time he kissed her, it was only a matter of time before she followed him to Skye. Because she'd follow him anywhere if he asked her to.

EPILOGUE
FOUR MONTHS LATER

Bella's stomach did the loop-de-loop as she drove Fifi along the coastal road past Eilean Donan Castle. The late November sun was hanging low in the sky and heat was blowing from the vent inside the car. She was going to see Harris again soon and she could not wait. And what made this even better was it was his birthday.

'I hope this old heap doesn't collapse under the weight of all my belongings,' Isla said as she glanced over at the back seat which was crammed full of 'stuff' to one side and had Beau strapped into his seat at the other. The dog was gazing out the window at the passing scenery.

'Hey, she's not a heap any more. Neil worked wonders on her so she drives like a dream now, don't you, Fifi?' Isla rolled her eyes and Bella giggled. 'Don't worry anyway, Granny, you haven't actually brought that much. The van took the bulk of it yesterday and they were setting up your living room and bedroom, so you'll be all set by this time tomorrow.'

'Did you leave the bottle of fizzy plonk for Ben and Skye like asked?'

'I did. They were so excited when I saw them. They'll love having their own place at last.'

'It's funny, isn't it, Skye bought my house and I'm moving to Skye,' Isla said with a chuckle.

'It is. I don't think they could believe their luck when you accepted their offer. They've been looking for ages but have kept missing out on the houses they've loved. So yours is a dream come true for them.'

'I was happy to help them out. You know me; I'm a sucker for a love story.'

Bella switched her CD player on, safe in the knowledge that Neil had repaired it so the discs no longer shot across the vehicle when it went over a bump. No more risk of decapitation, yay! 'Dog Days Are Over' began to play and Harris immediately sprang to Bella's mind. This song reminded her of him so much these days. It lifted her spirits and reminded her of dancing around the garden at his new house as the song played in the background and laughter rang through the air as he chased her with handfuls of dried leaves. She hadn't seen him for three weeks and it had been agony waiting for Isla's moving day.

But she'd been kept busy with the goings on at Drumblair Castle. The apartments were now being let to holiday makers, not just the creative types that Olivia had intended. The drama Aiden brought had apparently put her off. Brodie's divorce had come through, so Bella was waiting with bated breath for an announcement and Olivia had assured her she'd be the first to know. And just before she had left for Skye, Kerr had turned up at the castle, looking like a tramp. He had sobbed and begged Olivia's forgiveness but of course she was understandably wary. In a strange turn of events, Innes had thrown off the mantle of confirmed bachelor and had taken Adaira Wallace out on several dates, so of course, Bella was waiting on news there too.

'Ooh, this is a nice song. Who is it?' Isla asked, pulling Bella from her thoughts.

'This, Granny dearest, is Florence and the Machine.'

'Ooh, what kind of machine?'

'Sorry?'

'What type of machine has she got?'

'Who?'

'Florence? Is it a music machine?'

'Oh, no, Granny, the Machine is Florence's song-writing partner.'

'Really? Wow, they can get machines to do anything these days. Is it one of the Andrex things?'

'Do you mean Android?'

'Aye, that's what I said.'

Bella snickered. 'No, Granny, she's a person, the machine is just her name.'

Isla snorted. 'Well, what were her parents thinking? Honestly, that's so wrong.'

'It's not her *actual* name, you *bampot*,' Bella said with a chuckle. 'It's Isabella Summers, I think.'

'Thank goodness for that.'

It had been a long four months for Isla, going through physio and all the discomfort that came with it and then her best friend moving away. Bella had found it amusing sitting on an evening in the apartment and listening to one side of the conversation between Isla and Maeve, who was happily ensconced in her new home on Skye. They were like a pair of teenagers gossiping. Bella was excited to see the two friends reunited again.

'Did you see that article in the newspaper yesterday about the murder writer? His wife did a full exposé on him!'

'I did. I felt so bad for her, but she has a beautiful new baby to care for now, she's well rid of him.' Seeing the article hadn't really surprised Bella. It had only been a matter of time.

'I'm going to drop you and Beau off with your things so you can get settled, then I'll come back later with Harris, okay?'

Isla feigned hurt. 'It's fine,' she sighed, 'go abandon your poor old granny so you can go and see your fancy man.'

'Yep, that about sums it up,' Bella said, laughing.

'Charming.'

As they passed through Glentorrin, Bella's heart skipped as she looked out of Isla's window to see if Harris was on walkabout. He wasn't but she did spot Evin, the young Han Solo, and his dog Chewie, whom she had met again the last time she'd visited. Harris had taken her to the Coxswain pub then, too, where a bearded man called Greg something or other had been playing guitar and singing. The locals had been so warm and welcoming. And she had been looking forward to visiting again and getting to know everyone a little better.

It had been hard to be away from Harris, but it had only made their bond stronger. She had fallen deeper in love with her police sergeant-turned-inspector each time she had seen him. And it was evident the feeling was mutual. Last time she had left, they had both been emotional and leaving him had been heart-wrenching. She had cried for a solid hour as she drove Fifi away and back to Inverness.

Harris still wanted her to come and live with him, but she hadn't wanted to let Olivia down, and her parents were still in Inverness. She was doing really well on her interior design course and had been overjoyed to get full marks on all but one assignment so far and had even begun to make preparations to set up her own business with the money her granny had insisted on giving her. Her website was ready to go and the business cards were printed. She would soon have her dream within her grasp. How things were changing.

Bella parked up outside Pabay View Retirement Home and walked around to help Isla out of the car. She was still walking with a stick but had come such a long way on her recovery journey.

The manager, Dorothy Lyndhurst, met them at the door. She was an English woman who had grown up in London and had relocated to Scotland when she had met her partner. It was amazing what Isla could wheedle out of people.

'Ah, Mrs Douglas, it's good to see you again. You're looking well. And you're lots more mobile since your last visit. And this little chap must be Beau. I can see where the name came from, he's very bonny. Come on, I've got the keys to your flat.'

They walked along a covered corridor past a courtyard garden and to a door at the corner of the L-shaped section. 'Here we go. This is the unit with the largest garden, so Beau should be happy. But of course there's the shingle beach across the road. And you can always walk along to the post office and have a cuppa at the café next door. It's dog friendly.'

'That's grand,' Isla replied. 'Can I go inside?' she asked Dorothy eagerly.

'Of course you can, it's your home now. I'll leave you to it. There's a buzzer by the door in case of emergencies or you can telephone reception by pressing one on the phone's keypad.'

'Thank you, bye for now,' Isla said.

She turned the key in the lock and opened the door, but before she could enter, a voice called from next door. 'Hello, neighbour! Welcome to Pabay.'

Bella and Isla turned to see a dapper elderly gentleman wearing smart grey trousers, a blue shirt and a navy-blue and white spotted dickie bow.

'Oh, hi there, I'm Bella and this is my granny, Isla Douglas.'

'Lovely to meet you, Mrs Douglas,' he said as he sauntered over to them. 'I'm Tam Guthrie.'

'Lovely to meet you, Mr Guthrie, but please call me Isla.'

He held out his hand. 'Then you must call me Tam,' he said with a bow of his head. Isla shook his hand.

Bella noticed her granny's cheeks turn a little pink and she smiled, she was going to have to keep an eye on this situation.

Once Isla's bags were unloaded, Isla patted Bella's arm. 'Go on, get to your Harris, I know you're desperate to see him. I'm going to drop a message to Maeve on the WhatsUp and invite her to my swanky new pad for a cuppa,' she said with a little giddy jiggle. It was so good to see her happy.

Bella left and climbed back into Fifi. She clicked her favourite song back to the start again and sang along with Florence at the top of her lungs right the way back to Glentorrin.

She stopped in the small car park in front of the police station and climbed out of the car. Birdsong was the only audible sound and she closed her eyes and tilted her face skyward for a moment, inhaling the clean, salty air.

She was nervous and excited in equal measure as she pushed through the police station doors. Harris was on the phone with his back to her when she walked in.

'Aye, that's no bother, Dex, I appreciate you sorting that out, pal. I'll collect the bike tomorrow then if that's okay. Cheers, buddy. Bye.' He hung up his call.

'I've come to hand myself in, inspector,' Bella said in as sultry a voice as she could muster when her heartrate was almost through the roof.

Harris turned and beamed at her. 'I knew you were here!' he said as he launched himself over the counter and scooped her up. 'I could smell your perfume. God, I've missed you,' he said as he kissed her cheeks, her forehead, her neck and then finally her lips. 'I think it's been the longest three weeks of my life.'

She reciprocated his kisses and clung to him. 'I know, it's been far too long. Happy birthday!'

'Thank you. I'm sure you get more beautiful every time I see you,' he said, his eyes filled with emotion. 'I've got another officer coming down in half an hour to do the evening shift, so I thought we could maybe go and check on Isla, call at the Chinese takeaway for some birthday food and then come back here and make up for lost time. I've got to make the most of every minute with you because you'll be leaving again before I know it.' His expression always filled with sadness when he talked about her going home.

'Hey, I've only just arrived; don't be talking about me leaving already. Anyway, I have news.'

Still holding her in his arms, he gazed down at her. 'What news?'

'I got another A.'

'That's amazing. I'm so proud of you.'

'I have a gift for you, do you want it now?'

'I'm still on duty, so maybe I can unwrap you later after dinner?'

Bella giggled. 'I'm not the gift, you *bampot.*'

'Aww, shame.'

'You can still unwrap me later, but this is a special gift.'

'Okay, should I close my eyes?'

'Yes, and hold out your hands.' He did as instructed and Bella reached into her handbag and pulled out a small box with a ribbon around it. 'Open it!'

Harris opened his eyes and looked down at the box. 'Ooh pretty, may I?'

She nodded enthusiastically and he untied the bow and removed the lid. He took out a piece of paper and read aloud, 'I got fired.' He lifted his chin and gave her a questioning glance. 'Seriously?'

Bella inhaled a deep, calming breath and nodded. 'Yes. I got fired. Olivia fired me.' Bella couldn't hide her smile, no matter how hard she tried. Of course there had been no malice in the firing; in fact, she had agreed to work remotely for the time being.

'Why do you look so happy about that? Do you want me to call Olivia? I don't understand.'

Bella shook her head slowly. 'Think about it, Harris, and lift the second piece of paper up and turn it over.'

He lifted the second piece of paper up and his eyes widened as he mouthed the words written on it:

Honey, I'm home.

'Wait... does this mean...?'

Her eyes began to sting with happy tears. 'It means I'm here forever if you'll have me,' she told him in a trembling voice.

He grabbed her and pulled her to him again. 'What, *now*? You're not going back? *Ever*?'

'Well, I may have to go and help my folks pack up when they're ready to move but no, I'm here and I'm all yours. Happy birthday, Harris. I love you.'

He picked her up and spun her around on the spot. 'I love you too, Bella, so, so, so much.' He peppered her with kisses once again. 'Best. Birthday. Ever.'

ACKNOWLEDGEMENTS

I'm going to try and keep this one short, I promise. Writing this book took place at such a difficult time in my life. One of my closest friends, whom I had known since I was around sixteen years old, was seriously ill, and on so many occasions I wanted to be back in Yorkshire with her rather than in Scotland writing. But Mel was always so supportive of me whether it was singing, writing or just in general. So I knuckled down, for her, and told a happy story while feeling, at times, anything but.

Mel believed in love, and married the love of her life. After she passed away her husband, Neil, had one request of me, that I name a character after her to keep her memory alive. So I have done just that. Although my real life Mel wasn't a police officer, she was a very talented keyboard player – she and I were in a band together for a very brief moment back in the late 1980s – a fab mum, an amazing wife and an incredible friend, and she loved horses. So Mel in the book has many elements of my real life Mel and a few added for the purpose of the story. But in my mind she is the Mel I knew and loved.

I want to thank every single person who has been involved in my writing career thus far: my wonderful agent Lorella and her team, the incredible people at Boldwood Books (Caroline, my fab editor, especially for putting up with me!). And whether you're someone who has read my books from the start or someone who is reading me for the first time; please know that I'm very grateful to you all.

I also want to say a massive thank you to Fiona and Sue who have been so fantastic in organising my online launch parties. You ladies are amazing! And of course Eilidh Beaton, the awesome audiobook narrator, thank you for your talent and many voices, and for being such a lovely person.

Thank you too, to the wonderful supportive authors at Boldwood for your reassurance, kind words and encouragement.

I want to give a shout out to Shirleyann Simpson who won the competition to name the beagle in the book. Beau fits the character perfectly, so thank you!

And as always thank you to my mum, dad, bookshop business partner/fab friend Claire, my daughter Gee, and my gorgeous muse/husband Rich. You really do mean the world to me.

This wasn't as short as I had hoped but I have so many people to be grateful for!

ABOUT THE AUTHOR

Lisa Hobman has written many brilliantly reviewed women's fiction titles - the first of which was shortlisted by the RNA for their debut novel award. In 2012 Lisa relocated her family from Yorkshire to a village in Scotland and this beautiful backdrop now inspires her uplifting and romantic stories.

Sign up to Lisa Hobman's mailing list for news, competitions and updates on future books.

Visit Lisa's website: http://www.lisajhobman.com

Follow Lisa on social media:

facebook.com/LisaJHobmanAuthor

instagram.com/lisahobmanauthor

x.com/lisajhobmanauth

ALSO BY LISA HOBMAN

Starting Over At Sunset Cottage

It Started with a Kiss

The Skye Collection Series

Dreaming Under An Island Skye

Under An Italian Sky

Wishing Under a Starlit Skye

Together Under A Snowy Skye

The Highlands Series

Coming Home to the Highlands

Chasing a Highland Dream

LOVE IN EVERY CHAPTER

WHERE ALL YOUR ROMANCE
DREAMS COME TRUE!

THE HOME OF BESTSELLING
ROMANCE AND WOMEN'S
FICTION

 WARNING:
MAY CONTAIN SPICE

SIGN UP TO OUR
NEWSLETTER

https://bit.ly/Lovenotesnews

Boldwood

Boldwood Books is an award-winning fiction publishing company seeking out the best stories from around the world.

Find out more at www.boldwoodbooks.com

Join our reader community for brilliant books, competitions and offers!

Follow us
@BoldwoodBooks
@TheBoldBookClub

Sign up to our weekly deals newsletter

https://bit.ly/BoldwoodBNewsletter

Printed in Great Britain
by Amazon